# The Vampire King's Mate
## Fate of Imperium
### Book 2

By C.A. Worley

PUBLISHED BY:
C.A. Worley

The Vampire King's Mate
Fate of Imperium Book 2
Copyright © 2018 by C.A. Worley

This book contains mature content and is intended for adult readers.

This book is a work of fiction and any resemblance to persons, living or dead, or places, events or locales is purely coincidental. The characters are productions of the author's imagination and used fictitiously.

## ACKNOWLEDGEMENTS

I would like to take a moment to thank Katherine Lowry Logan for her advice and encouragement to pursue this series under my real name. It's been a bit terrifying, putting myself out there. While, yes, I have published other books, they were all under a different moniker. I can hide behind that pen name. "Real" me has to own this.

So, thank you, Kathy. Thank you for the suggestion, for the inspiration to continue pursuing this path, and for being the catalyst to get me to put on my big girl panties and own the words I put on paper.

Map of Imperium

Northland
Kingdom of Burghard

Sanctus Femina

Eastland
Kingdom of Prajna

Westland
Kingdom of Gwydion

Southland
Kingdom of Sundari

*"No Gwydion, no demon, no Northland beast.*
*When you search your truth, look to the East."*
~Nora to her sister, Eden

# Prologue

*Westland, Kingdom of Gwydion*

The Wolf King's lips, soft and warm, pressed to the back of Eden's hand. His firm grip held her in place, leaving no question he was the one in charge.

The male's eyes sparkled. They were a fetching shade of pastel blue, so dazzling they seemed to glow. For a second, she was sure she had seen those eyes somewhere before.

They were his best feature, not that the rest of him wasn't attractive. His skin was a light shade of olive, substantially darker than her own porcelain flesh. The contrast made his cerulean irises stand out.

Both his skin and eyes distinctly marked him as wolf. The Burghards all had similar coloring, or so she had been told. Eden and her sisters lacked much experience with beings outside of Gwydion.

Atop Kellan's head grew wavy, light brown hair, almost reaching his shoulders. A light stubble covered his masculine face. She'd expected a full beard to shroud his rugged jaw, thinking the Burghards would be as hairy as the animals inside them. Eden liked that he did not appear beastly, aside from his size.

He was large, even for a wolf. He stood almost a head taller than the male accompanying him, and that male, Foley, easily dwarfed Eden. He was the King's second in command and travelled with him often.

The visitors made quite an imposing duo. Not only were they tall, their frames were thick and sturdy-looking, reminding Eden of the giant sequoias growing along Gwydion's northern border.

They wore similar grey tunics and fitted black trousers designed for horseback riding. Tunics weren't usually so snug, but Kellan's muscled body was impossible to hide under his clothing.

His steely eyes missed nothing. They took in every inch of the small meeting room and the people in it. Kellan had long known the girls' father, King Edward, as well as their grandfather, Flynn. He didn't have to spend as much time studying them—trust between the males had already been established.

The bulk of his consideration was on Eden and her sister, Evelyn. They were the only beings in the room needing an introduction and, thus, earned a thorough examination.

When Kellan was introduced to Evelyn, Eden took the opportunity to observe him intently. He had the look of a male who would run to meet danger head-on—and win. He was so obviously built for battle she thought he might have been created in the forge and not birthed.

His rugged appearance was appealing. She could see how so many females found him fetching.

Eden had hoped she would be attracted to her betrothed, that she would feel some sort of a carnal response when they finally met. It would make this whole situation easier to stomach. She reasoned with herself that a physical foundation was better than no foundation. At least it would be a starting point.

Unfortunately, despite his nice-looking exterior, Eden felt nothing. No butterflies. No hint of womanly desire. Just a simple appreciation for his warrior-like physique.

It was the same with every male she'd ever met. Countless men had caught the eyes of her friends in town. Some of the girls had pursued the males relentlessly. Eden lacked any sort of inclination.

Granted, she'd been betrothed since shortly after her birth, so it could be that her mind wouldn't allow her to consider any other possibility.

Eden knew Kellan was a good man. She tried to focus on that instead of the more superficial things. She did not want to be small-minded, but one of her greatest apprehensions, where this arranged marriage was concerned, was her ability to perform her "wifely" duties.

She'd overheard many young females profess their longing for a husband capable of satisfying their *needs*—whatever those were. Eden could see the need to procreate, but apart from bearing children, what was the allure?

She understood the mechanics and had been taught her body would soften and allow for the intrusion. Even so, the appeal of being a willing participant was lost on her.

Eden had never felt, much less understood, the drive to couple. When Mara, her governess, warned her of the sexual proclivities of wolves, Eden was beside herself.

She had prayed lust would take root, so the rest of what was expected would occur without difficulty. Judging by this first meeting, her prayers were not going to be answered.

It was just as well. Her fate was never of her own design. It had been decided by her parents before she'd left the cradle. It was foolish to think she'd be lucky enough to have what she wanted.

Kellan stared at Eden, as though he was looking for something. It made her nervous, which troubled her. Eden wasn't one to get nervous, especially from someone's stare. She was the daughter of royalty, raised to control her emotions and calmly influence those around her. She was by far the most level-headed of King Edward's children.

She was also the most studious. Eden loved learning and had taken it upon herself to learn all she could of Imperium. If she was to rule in the North, she needed to be armed with knowledge. She'd assumed if she was well-educated on the people of Burghard, she'd be better equipped to handle their king.

Finally being in his presence, she understood nothing she had done could have prepared her. He was not a creature to be handled.

Eden supposed some of her unease could be attributed to the fact the sizeable male in front of her could shift into an animal. The wolves of Burghard were warriors. Their shapes huge. Their senses sharp. Their teeth even sharper.

Eden was a Princess of Gwydion, an elemental. She had magic within her, but aside from setting him on fire, she was no physical match for Kellan's strength or speed up close. If he could reach her, he could easily kill her before she even knew she was being attacked.

Elementals were considered the weakest of the beings of Imperium. The wolves were the strongest. They were quick and natural-born hunters, easily taking down creatures three or four times their size. She-wolves were smaller, but just as deadly.

By marrying Eden, Kellan was giving up any chance of finding a she-wolf of his own, of finding his mate. Eden found herself feeling a little sad for Kellan.

The only reason a king from another faction would consider a marriage with an elemental would be for political gain. In Kellan's case, he believed binding himself to someone with an affinity to nature could help with Burghard's dying forest.

She supposed if she had to be married off into one of the other factions in Imperium, the Wolf King was a good option. Wolves were known for being very considerate with their wives, so Eden should not fear a lack of care. Neither should she fear his strength. He'd never harm her.

The demons of the Sundari Kingdom, in the Southland, were also physically stronger than the elementals. Eden had learned they could mentally control others, but they were predisposed to fits of madness. This made them very dangerous.

As for the Prajna—the vampires—in the Eastland, they were the most mysterious. Eden's father had warned his children the Prajna were not to be trifled with. They were known for being cold and calculating. Nearly as strong as wolves, and allegedly much faster.

Eden had never met a vampire. They rarely travelled, and it had been years since Edward had seen one. His accounts were meant to caution his daughters, yet Eden found her father's stories fascinating, as opposed to frightening.

She understood the need to be logical and make decisions without emotion. Sometimes she envied the Prajna, in that regard.

She was also painfully curious about what was inside their mouths. Burghards used their teeth for hunting and fighting. The Prajna's fangs were for feeding. Allegedly, they could only feed from other vampires of the opposite sex. It seemed an awfully personal activity to perform at the dining table.

Her attention lingered on Kellan's canines, wondering how often they'd been used in his many years. He was more than 200 years old. Wolves aged slowly in comparison to elementals. By now, he would have torn into many a hide with them.

It was odd to think about the differences between the races, especially in terms of lifespans. Though, if he imprinted upon her, her life force would be tied to his and she would age at the rate of a wolf.

His thumb swept across her knuckles, distracting her from her musings.

"It is a pleasure to finally meet you, Eden," he said.

"Likewise, my lord," she replied, forcing her eyes away from his teeth and planting a demure smile on her lips.

Eden, who prided herself on her ability to control her reactions, slowed her respiration to ensure her heartbeat remained steady. With his animal's near-perfect hearing, he would know if the pace altered and she refused to tempt his beast.

Kellan seemed about to say something else when the door opened, and Nora, Eden's youngest sister, stood in the doorway. Eden tilted her head, taking in her sister's condition. She constantly worried about Nora and her health.

When their mother, Elora, gave birth to Nora, something terrible happened. Elora died and the force of the magic leaving her body was so strong it ripped a hole open in Nora's soul. Nora had to continuously replenish her energies, drawing off the power of nature.

Nora looked well-enough, much better than she had earlier. Her eyes were bright and curious, one green and one pale blue. Eden frowned.

Studying Nora's right eye and then both of Kellan's, Eden suddenly realized why the color had looked so familiar. His were the exact same shade as Nora's one cerulean iris.

Kellan's grip on Eden's hand tightened, but he didn't seem to be aware of it. As he straightened to his full height, the birthmark on Eden's palm began to pulse, painfully.

The crescent-shaped mark, which never had any feeling in it before, had become itchy lately. It reminded

13

Eden of the sensation in her fingers when she was about to call forth fire.

The longer he held onto her, the more the mark burned. She extracted her hand from his grasp and the pain immediately receded.

Eden and Kellan locked eyes. His chest was still, as though he wasn't breathing. When he slowly began to turn away from her, he inhaled deeply.

Eden looked at Evelyn, whose mouth was open in confusion. They stared at one another, then at their sister.

Kellan took in another pull of air and took a stride closer to Nora. Evelyn made to step forward, but Eden grabbed her arm and shook her head.

Kellan was a wolf. He'd caught a scent that had forced him to move away from Eden, towards a female he had never met. A female who had one pastel blue eye, the same as his. He drew deep breaths like a compulsion, like he would die without more.

Eden was smart enough to know the King of Burghard would only turn his back on his affianced for one reason. He would only behave in such a way, risking the arrangement he'd made almost two decades ago, for one reason.

The Wolf King had scented his mate.

Eden should have been alarmed. She should have responded in some manner as Kellan crept closer to her youngest sibling.

Eden was the first-born daughter of the most powerful elemental to ever live, had more power inside her than anyone, other than her family, knew. She should be reacting.

As the atmosphere in the room tensed, everyone remained still, watching for what Kellan would do.

Nora held the wolf's gaze. She wasn't frightened in the least. *This was good*, Eden thought. If they were fated, Nora would be a good match.

Unfortunately, Nora was only a child. Someone should intervene and tell Kellan to back off. Eden was tempted, yet she did nothing. She was too busy concentrating on not visibly reacting to the knowledge there was no possible way she would be the one to marry the wolf.

She would never be Queen of the North. Her heart rejoiced as she forced the oxygen in her blood to decelerate, never giving any outward sign of her thoughts.

Her fate was now her own—she was free of the wolf. She was free to choose her own path.

* * *

*Eastland, Kingdom of Prajna*

Viktor roughly maneuvered the female to turn away from him. This time, as he pistoned in and out, he preferred to not look upon her face.

He lifted her hair from her neck, laying it across her opposite shoulder. With his left hand, he held her jaw. The second he touched her skin, he felt an ache on his palm. He ignored it, driven by his hunger.

His fangs extended right before he struck. His bedmate moaned in ecstasy. Two long pulls on her blood and the ache had grown into a painful burn. He released her jaw and rotated his hand to get a look at the cicatrice on his palm.

It was glowing. The mark he'd had since birth, the one he'd thought would lie dormant for eternity, had just woken. He glared at the crescent shape, resenting the faint silver light emanating from within.

It reminded him of a sinister smile, mocking him with its ill-timed appearance. Viktor closed his eyes in total disregard for what it meant. He knew, ultimately, Fate would have her way.

For now, he would do as he damn well pleased.

# Chapter 1

*Westland, Kingdom of Gwydion*
*Five years later ...*

Eden couldn't sleep. Her thoughts were a tangled mess and she was wasting energy attempting to sort through them. Logic was not working this night.

Tomorrow, the Wolf King would come for Nora. Eden wasn't sure her baby sister was ready. She wasn't sure her family was ready, either.

It would not be easy for any of them to watch Nora marry and move away, all in the same day. Eden accepted this was a normal part of life, for a female to leave her childhood home once old enough for marriage. It would still hurt to let her go.

Added to the disquiet over the wedding was the fact Nora was uprooting her life to go live among the wolves. The Burghards were formidable creatures who lived life as if it was a game of dominance. Only the strongest could ascend to and maintain hold on the throne.

Nora was not a formidable creature, yet she was about to be placed upon the highest seat of power, second only to the King. The tiny nugget of guilt Eden had long ago buried over the relief at not being the Burghard Queen reemerged.

Eden could handle herself far better than Nora in a difficult environment. In terms of magic, so could any child of Gwydion. Nora simply had no ability to call upon the elements. The only hint of magic she possessed was the occasional vision, too scrambled to be of any use. It was a useless power.

The night Kellan departed, Edward sat with his daughters to have a long and frank conversation about what would need to be done to ensure Nora's safety.

Their father had never allowed them to feel vulnerable. He'd taught Eden and Evelyn how to use their magics in the most efficient ways, to preserve energy, but strike fiercely.

They'd learned not only defensive strategies, but how and when to go on the offense. Thankfully, there had never been an occasion where such skills had been necessary.

As for Nora, because she had no magic to call, she'd learned to fight hand-to-hand. Since the day she'd met Kellan, Nora's training had increased tenfold. She was now more than proficient with a sword and a bow.

Lying there, Eden's worried mind continuously ticked through the possibilities, sorting and cataloguing what she knew of Kellan and of wolves in general.

The wolf would not tolerate anyone harming his mate. It did not mean he could ensure Nora's wellbeing. It was possible no wolf would dare cross Kellan by physically challenging Nora, but if she was perceived as weak, she would not be respected.

There could be dire consequences if the wolves found out Nora's lifeforce was in a state of constant drain and no one had warned the king. Lies of omission were, after all, still lies.

Edward had ordered his children to keep Nora's condition quiet, fearing blowback from the Burghards. Eden did not agree, but she kept her opinion to herself. She never went against her father in front of her sisters. She adored the man, and he was often very open to her ideas.

However, at the time, Nora was only fourteen and her state of deterioration could be exacerbated by family discord—or so they believed. Emotional upheaval could be physically taxing, especially to an elemental.

Eden and Evelyn agreed long ago to never lay unnecessary burdens at Nora's feet. Her uphill battle to live was burden enough.

Edward alleged if the wolves knew the truth, Nora could be challenged or, at the very least, undermined. She would be viewed as frail and wolves were not keen on following a queen who was sickly.

Eden also kept her mouth shut because she believed the point to be moot. Being Kellan's true mate, Nora's lifeforce would be tied to his. Theoretically, this would solve the problem of her constant drain of energy. Kellan was going to unknowingly save Nora.

Eden had been confident in her assertion. For over five years Eden did not doubt; she knew Kellan was the answer to Nora's problem.

Except, as the wedding date neared, so did the reality that there was no way to know for certain. Only after Nora and Kellan were mated would they get their answer.

Eden debated approaching her father again and asking if he would change his mind. He may have ordered them to keep their mouths shut, but Nora was now twenty and would be a married woman tomorrow. She may not find following her father's orders quite so easy as when she was young. It was certainly the case for Eden.

More and more Eden found herself questioning everything, especially her father. He would often laugh when she pushed back on something, telling her she was acting like her mother.

Eden didn't know what to make of his comments, to know if he was being complementary or not. She barely remembered her mother; Elora had died when Eden was only four.

It was while she was trying to picture her mother's face that Eden heard Nora cry out from her room next door.

Nora often had vivid dreams and would talk in her sleep. This sound was different. Nora's cry was one of distress.

Though she hid it, Eden could tell her sister's anxiety over the coming nuptials had gradually increased over the past year. It would all come to a head in the morning.

Eden jumped out of bed, forgoing her robe in her haste. She was in her nightgown but there were no guards near their rooms, so it wasn't likely she would be seen.

She ran to the small door separating their quarters. As she reached for the handle, she felt a sharp pain in her palm. She turned her hand over, checking for injury.

The crescent on her palm was giving off an odd silver glow, flickering like a flame from a lit candle. Eden closed her fist, not trusting her eyes. Before she opened her hand to look once more, Nora whimpered.

Ignoring her birthmark, Eden flung open the door and dashed into the room, coming to an abrupt stop when she saw Nora sitting up in the bed. She must have woken.

"Nora?" Eden whispered, moving slowly towards her sister, not wanting to startle her.

Nora's eyes opened, and Eden gasped. They were shining with silver. Nora did not have silver eyes.

Eden's palm throbbed. She looked down and the silver glow was still there. She was about to shout for her father when Nora spoke in a voice so deep and low Eden could have sworn a demon was in the room.

"*No Gwydion, no demon, no Northland beast. When you search your truth, look to the East.*"

Eden balked, nearly not believing what she'd just witnessed. She stayed still, waiting for Nora to say or do something more. Instead, Nora closed her eyes and fell back onto her pillow.

"Nora?"

Nora did not respond. Her breathing was slow and even. She was asleep. Eden debated waking her, but decided Nora needed to rest before tomorrow's travels to the Northland.

Eden couldn't reason Nora was dreaming, not with the silver light emanating from Nora's eyes, her altered voice, and the odd glow of the crescent on Eden's palm. She didn't understand the connection to the mark on her hand, but she knew exactly what her sister had just done.

Nora had given Eden a portent.

Her father told each of his daughters how their mother had done the same, time and again. He taught them to trust the magics as they manifested, to accept and have faith in them. They were their mother's daughters, and powers they could not fathom ran in their blood.

Had he not prepared her for magic's possibilities, Eden would be scared out of her mind. Nora had never prophesied, had never spoken in a riddle as their mother had done.

She pushed her sense of logic front and center, fixating on reason. A portent was a gift, one given only when needed.

Eden knew better than to question or be surprised by Nora's revelation, not that she knew what it meant. The question now, was what to do with it.

Presages rarely came in any form other than a riddle. Their mother had predicted many things in her short life, but none of the messages were clearly interpreted.

Edward told Eden it was the counterbalance of being blessed with sight. Eden wasn't convinced such power was a blessing. It was usually only after an event took place that the words were truly understood. *How very useless.*

Eden tucked the blanket back around Nora's body and kissed her cheek before returning to her own room. The pain in her palm had diminished, but it was not entirely gone.

She tossed and turned most of the night, unable to stop the ideas running rampant through her head. She debated the merits of telling her family what occurred in Nora's room.

Eden decided to keep it to herself. Tomorrow was Nora's wedding day. Her father and younger sister had enough to deal with as it was. They could discuss it after life went back to normal. Besides, years could pass before she ever knew what Nora's words meant.

She had no way of knowing Fate would reveal the meaning in a matter of days.

\* \* \*

*Eastland, Kingdom of Prajna*

Viktor stood on the stone balcony outside his chambers, staring out at the ocean below. He loved the reflection of the waves as they undulated in the moonlight. They were his one constant companion in this lonely existence.

He often stood in this spot when he wanted to be alone with the ocean. He gave much consideration to his people while listening to the water crash against the rocks.

Tonight, however, it wasn't only his subjects on his mind. Tonight, The King of Prajna was in need of counsel—something he would never admit aloud.

Viktor was rarely indecisive. In fact, he typically made decisions swiftly, without a hint of emotion. His apparent aloofness in front of his fellow Prajna had earned him his nickname.

The Heartless King, they called him. To other factions within Imperium, this would be an insult. To vampires? It held a hint of admiration, though it was rarely spoken in his presence.

It wasn't that vampires were unfeeling. They, in fact, could feel deeply. It just wasn't a trait they wanted in their leader.

Most were old enough to remember the unrest in the Eastland before Viktor's rule, and could describe in detail King Nikolai's inability to control his impulses.

Viktor's rise to power was a bloody one. Taking the throne from his father had been difficult. Killing him, nearly impossible. But the son refused to allow the sins of the father to further taint the kingdom.

Unfortunately, the darkness had already taken root. There hadn't been a true-mating since the day Viktor removed his father's head over a century ago, and not one live birth in the last twenty.

The vampires were similar to the wolves in that they were able to mate with another who was not a sieva—a true mate. Fortunately, though, Prajna did not need to imprint in order to produce young.

Bonding to one's destined other half was, of course, the preference, but not everyone was fortunate in their search.

It only took a blood exchange to mate. It was a blessing to those unlucky souls who never found their sievas.

Vampires had extremely long lives, so they often waited many centuries in hopes of finding their fated mates. It was simply a matter of waiting for the mate to be born. Without any live births, however, the odds of finding one's mate were virtually obliterated.

No one had been able to figure out the reason behind the vampires' misfortune. Luka, Viktor's younger brother, suspected their father had cursed them all with his deeds.

Viktor did not dispute Luka's inference, though he couldn't discount himself as a contributor to cursing the Prajna. Taking a life when not in self-defense went against their strict laws. Taking the life of one's father, the king, no less, surely warranted nature's rebuke.

Viktor raised the tumbler in his hand to his mouth, the spirits within a sore substitute for the blood he craved. Perhaps he should call for Bianca again. Her blood would never satisfy his growing hunger, but her body could provide a distraction. She was most agreeable when tied down.

The mark on his left hand flared at the mental image of Bianca chained to the wall in his feeding room. It had been making itself known for the past five years, acting out, much like a youngling throwing a tantrum, each time he touched any female who was not his mate.

It was only getting worse.

Viktor had gone half a millennium without so much as a twitch from his cicatrice. Why now, when he was finally ready to come to terms with his obligations, did it come to life?

It was a complication he did not need. Unfortunately, it was also one he could not ignore. Once a cicatrice had awoken, only the blood of his true-mate would quell the desire to feed.

As he swallowed the last of the liquor, he decided a visit to the temple was in order.

# Chapter 2

*Westland, Kingdom of Gwydion*

Five nights later, Eden awoke in a panic. She'd had another nightmare. She couldn't remember anything, but she felt nauseous. She'd been doing this every night since Nora left with her new husband.

Evelyn had joked Eden was having an allergic reaction to Nora's absence. Eden felt she may be right.

She knew there was no use trying to sleep, so she put on her robe and went down the stairs to see if her father was still awake. Judging from the light coming from his study, he was up working.

He had been acting differently since Nora left, especially the past two days. He was distracted.

When Eden approached him about it, he waived off her concern. But Eden knew something was weighing on him. His refusal to share his burden hurt her, but she forced herself to be patient.

Once she was close enough, she could see the door was cracked. She heard voices coming from inside. It was the middle of the night and a visitor in his study could only spell trouble.

Before she could knock, she heard a male say, "Sir, we are no longer alone."

"What?" her father responded.

"There is someone in the hall, my lord."

Eden wondered how the man could possibly know she was there. She hadn't made a sound.

The door opened, and she was surprised to see one of the Burghards standing there. They were always easy to spot with their beautiful blue eyes.

"My lady," he greeted and stepped aside.

Eden entered and walked to her father's desk. He sat on the other side, rubbing his temples as though they pained him. There were several parchments on his desk. The wolf must be a courier.

"What is the matter?" she asked her father.

"Sit," Edward pointed to the chair beside his desk. He would have to share the news with her sooner or later. He may as well do it now.

"This arrived yesterday," he said, sliding one sheet in her direction. Eden picked it up and read.

The letter had come from King Kellan himself. During a banquet meant to welcome Nora to the kingdom, someone had tried to kill her by putting hellebore in her drink. Hellebore was a plant poison fatal to elementals. Somehow, Nora had survived it.

It was Edward's worse fear come to life. He'd been on edge since Nora's departure, but he'd chalked it up to a father's angst over having a child move so far away.

He'd always known Burghards were keen on contesting weak leaders, but he'd never anticipated such underhandedness. The whole thing reeked of a hauntingly familiar travesty he'd experienced twenty years ago.

Edward watched as Eden processed the news of Nora's having been poisoned. As usual, she did not react as he anticipated. The only show of emotional strain was her left hand rubbing the skin along her collarbone.

When she finished, she put the paper back on the desk.

"Now this one," he said, handing her another letter, "which arrived an hour ago."

Eden read the second letter. This one was from Nora. Her sister tried to be assuring, but Eden knew she must be terrified. The letter was succinct, almost matter-of-fact about the involvement of not only a wolf, but also a demon and a vampire.

Three factions had banded together to end Nora's life. Eden's pupils changed size.

Edward knew the moment the implication registered with Eden. He had never kept anything surrounding her mother's death a secret from her.

She and Evelyn both knew of the dangerous group known as Sephtis Kenelm and their misguided attempt to balance power in Imperium. The brotherhood had been active for over a thousand years.

It was always a group of four working together: one elemental, one wolf, one vampire, and one demon. It had started with good intentions, to topple the corrupt and put the power in reliable hands. Somewhere along the way, the brotherhood's purpose became twisted.

Years ago, Edward found proof the group of assassins had poisoned his wife, Elora, when she was pregnant, almost killing baby Nora in the process. The group had also killed Kellan's father, which was why the Wolf King helped Edward hunt them down and kill them.

Sadly, though Elora had prophesied her own death, her puzzled words gave no indication of when or how. Edward took it especially hard, believing he'd failed to protect his wife.

He openly shared what happened with two of his children. Only Eden had ever questioned his decision to keep it from Nora. Though she had concerns, Eden did not defy him by revealing the truth to her youngest sister.

Edward's only excuse was, deep down, he wanted to keep the ugliness of the world away from Nora.

Sephtis Kenelm was responsible for the hole torn in her soul. He did not want to give them imaginary power over Nora by making her fear those who had wanted to harm her mother and injured Nora in the process.

Now, members of three of the four factions of Imperium had attempted to murder the elemental sitting on the throne of Burghard. He didn't have proof, but the information in Nora's letter was too coincidental. He hoped he was wrong, but his gut was telling him the group was still active—and very much a threat to his children.

Eden slowly lowered the letter back to the desk.

"What do we do?" she asked.

"That is the question, isn't it?" he sighed, leaning back in his chair. "As first in line, Eden, what would you suggest?"

Eden's palm prickled as Nora's words from last week came back to her. She kept her fisted hand in her lap, instinct telling her to keep it hidden.

"I think we need to go East," she answered.

"To the Temple of Sanctus Femina?"

Eden nodded. The temple was close, due East from their main residence. It was the best place to ask for help or insight.

Beyond the sacred ground was the Kingdom of Prajna. It could be that the vampire member of the brotherhood was hiding in the Eastland and Nora was hinting at it.

Eden doubted Nora's words would lead her to track down any of the Sephtis Kenelm on her own. Though, it was suspect the portent mentioned three of the four factions, the one left out being the one to the East.

The temple was also the safest place for them to go. Her birthmark lessened its irritation. Yes, that was where they should start.

"I agree, Eden. Theron will need to be informed and I'd prefer to do that in person."

Theron had been the temple priest for ages. He had his finger on the pulse of every kingdom, and the ear of every king.

He was also keeper of the scrolls, most of which contained prophecies Elora had given throughout her life. Since she had predicted her own death, she may have made other predictions that would be imperative to know, especially now.

"Also," Edward continued, "you and Evelyn will be safer there. Every being in Imperium knows better than to court the wrath of the Goddess."

He was right. It was rumored to spill blood on the sacred ground of Sanctus Femina was akin to starting the end of the world. No one had ever dared.

Eden stood. "I'll leave you to reply to Kellan and Nora. I'll inform Evelyn in the morning and we'll pack at first light."

She turned on her heel and exited the study.

Edward stared at Eden's retreating back. No quiver had beset her voice, no wrinkles marred her brow. Not one tear was shed over her sister's attempted murder.

Eden remained, as always, composed, while Edward couldn't help but mourn the loss of the carefree child she'd once been.

\* \* \*

*Eastland, Kingdom of Prajna*

Viktor awoke hours before dawn, looking to the empty space beside him, half-expecting to find someone there. He'd been dreaming. He rubbed his face, trying to recall the details.

Green eyes. One, a dark green iris, like the tall grass in the dunes down by the beach. The other was a bright emerald. It reminded him of the lagoons near the southern coast. It was how his mother described his eyes when he was a young.

A sudden, sharp stinging in his palm had him turning his hand up. The cicatrice was giving off a soft silver light. Viktor closed his eyes and returned his head to his pillow.

He was cursed, indeed.

# Chapter 3

*Temple of Sanctus Femina*

"Gibberish. It's all gibberish. How are we to know what we're looking for? And if we've found it?" Evelyn complained.

Eden and her sister had spent several fruitless days in the temple's massive library. Edward instructed them to start reading each scroll, looking for anything that might be linked to Nora or Sephtis Kenelm.

At least it was a beautiful room, with a great deal of natural light coming in from the enormous windows. The blue tiled floor reminded her of the sky. Greenery garnished every corner in enormous pots.

It was as close to being outdoors as she could get. Elementals preferred to be in nature. If she had to be inside for most of the day, Eden was thankful it was in this library.

Only one wall contained bound books. Small shelves scattered throughout the interior were packed with various correspondence, journals, and diaries.

Yesterday, Evelyn had found a decorative box of love letters sitting on top of one of the shelves. They had been written before Imperium's borders had been drawn, before the kingdoms had been created.

Eden detested the idea of reading someone's personal contemplations. It was too invasive, especially for someone who was constantly fighting her instincts and holding back her emotions.

She'd had to pry the box from Evelyn's greedy fingers. Her younger sister took no issue with sticking her nose in someone else's affairs.

"They're long dead, Eden, I doubt they care," she had retorted. Thankfully, Evelyn didn't fight too hard and relinquished the box.

When Eden asked Theron why such things were kept here, out in the open, he'd said, "My dear girl, writing down one's thought is the only way to prove the thought ever existed once the soul has moved beyond the veil."

"That doesn't exactly answer my question," she'd replied.

"No, it does not. Next time ask what you actually need to know."

Eden had been miffed by his response. Theron did not orate prophecies like her mother had, but he did speak in riddles. She let it go as he explained how they should go about searching.

The rest of the shelving around the edges of the room held the scrolls. Most of them had come from Elora. Other factions had Seers, but they were extremely rare. Theron wasn't sure how many were still alive. The kings of Imperium were very similar in their desire to keep secrets.

He had suggested they start with Elora's first, then move through the others chronologically. Eden read and reread so many scrolls, she'd lost count. Her father and Theron helped, staying each night to work long after Eden and Evelyn had gone off to bed.

It was time-consuming work. If one person found something, they would bring it to the group. Discussion followed, and Theron took notes. That was it. No great revelation or discovery occurred, no moment of clarity blessed them.

Several of Kellan's men arrived yesterday, including Foley, his Second, to assist in their search. Foley voiced the Wolf Council's concern that this was bigger than a lone assassination attempt on Nora.

Taking into account the dying forest in Burghard, the rumors of demons gaining powers, and the reemergence of the Sephtis Kenelm, something was brewing in Imperium. In this, they all agreed.

None of the men had shown up this morning. Eden assumed they were still resting after a late night. Everyone was desperate to find something of value, some sign of the way to proceed forward. Edward had allowed himself little time for resting.

"Did you hear me?" Evelyn whined.

"Yes, and I heard you the last time, as well," Eden replied coolly.

Evelyn, as good natured as always, laughed. "I apologize. I don't like feeling ignored."

Eden pressed her lips together to stop the smile that wanted to break free. Evelyn was special. Often annoyingly spirited, but special in that she never held a grudge, never held tight to her negative emotions.

She also rarely complained. Evelyn should take a break. It would do them both good to walk away for a short time.

"You are forgiven, child," Eden announced in her most regal voice and Evelyn laughed again.

"Why sister, I do believe you made a joke. The world may be ending, after all."

Eden's face fell. "I wish you would not say such things, Evie. And do not let Father hear you. His mind is bothered, and you should not add to it. I know this is tiresome. Maybe you should go clear your head?"

Evelyn put her hands on her hips, biting the inside of her cheek. A second later she sighed.

"Fine. Yes, I could use a moment of fresh air. You could use the same." She stood and walked out the door, mumbling under her breath.

Eden pressed her fingertips to her brow. Evelyn was right. Eden needed to get out of the library. Checking on her father was as good a reason as any. She rolled up the scroll she'd been reading and put it back in its metal container.

Once she returned it to the shelf, her birthmark began to itch, as it had every day for the past week. The edges had grown more defined and the coloring had changed. It had lightened to almost white.

It looked like a near-perfect crescent moon had been branded into her skin. She still hadn't told her father or Evelyn. Whenever she deliberated saying something, it seemed some calamity or pressing news fell into their laps. It never seemed like the right time to bring it up, especially with the looming danger Nora was now facing.

No, she would hang on to this information a little longer. There were bigger problems in Imperium than what was happening to Eden's right hand.

She tidied up the rest of the table and went in search of her father and the others. As she got closer to Theron's study, she could hear her father's voice rising.

Instead of knocking, she listened.

"As I stated before, it's no longer a problem, Foley," Edward said.

"Edward, we cannot be sure of that," Theron interjected.

"I'm not asking for information or accusing you of anything, Edward," Foley stated in a calm voice. "I'm merely telling you what Kellan and I know. We could barely pick up the scent of magic. Each time we've visited Gwydion, it's become more noticeable. When we arrived for the binding ceremony, the odor was virtually nonexistent."

"Yes, well, Nora's in the Northland now, so she'll no longer be pulling magic from Gwydion," Edward insisted.

Eden covered her mouth to keep from making a noise. Nora had always had to replenish the magic she was losing from the injury to her soul. Was she unknowingly taking from the elementals in the kingdom?

Theron cleared his throat. "Perhaps. But we cannot discount everything else happening concurrently. The sickness in the forests in the North, the reports of the Sundari Demons gaining powers in questionable manners, and the Eastland ..." he paused.

Eden stepped closer, wanting to know what was happening in the East. There was rarely news from Prajna. The vampires typically kept to themselves. She tilted her head, so her ear was close to the door.

Eden scowled as she felt a sudden, cooling sensation on her birthmark.

"You know, eavesdropping is impolite, *mala vestica*."

Eden whirled around, towards the deep voice behind her, nearly screaming. Thankfully, she'd still had her hand on her mouth and was able to muffle the sound.

A vampire stood not three feet away, looking down on her with his arms crossed. He did not look pleased.

# Chapter 4

Viktor ported himself to a small clearing near the Temple of Sanctus Femina. Theron did not like to be surprised, so Viktor never ported directly to the priest. He also had no way of knowing if Theron was alone and was averse to the idea of revealing his power to a stranger, especially one who may be armed.

The vampires were not fond of others knowing they had the ability to teleport from one place to another. It wasn't a secret, per se, but they did not flaunt it and rarely, if ever, did it in front of those who were not Prajna.

His long legs glided fluidly towards the temple. Vampires moved smoothly and soundlessly—so much so they were often accused of being able to float or levitate. It was a strategy of war to keep one's enemies guessing.

Viktor remained alert, listening for signs of others in the building. Once he reached the stairs, he heard Theron's voice, along with several others.

Vampires had impeccable hearing, maybe even better than the wolves. He didn't have to be in the building to make out what they were saying. He didn't even need to be in the same room to hear their heartbeats.

He recognized King Edward's vocal sounds immediately. He was one of the few elementals Viktor had ever met. Edward was well-liked and appeared to be a respectable ruler. Their interactions during meetings at the temple had been pleasant enough.

The gravelly tones of the third voice were distinctly wolf—Kellan's Second, if memory served correct. *Well, then*. It seemed the wolves and the witches had also come to pay a visit. Viktor did not believe in coincidences.

The males were discussing the state of Imperium. Viktor did not want Theron disclosing things the Prajna did not want known. He trusted the old man, but only to a point. Viktor did not get to his current position by being naïve.

Rather than waiting for the meeting to finish, Viktor decided to join it, curious to know how much the foreigners would share with a vampire present. He moved silently up the stairs and turned right towards Theron's study.

His steps slowed when he saw a small female standing outside the door. From her size, he knew she must be an elemental. Female wolves and vampires were much taller, their bodies broader, designed to take impact in battle, and to withstand the lust-filled aggressions of their males.

She was obviously listening to the exchange inside the study, and his mouth flattened at her impudence. Viktor could easily hear the exchange, as well, but it was because his hearing was enhanced, not because he was skulking about, eavesdropping. She should be taken over someone's knee, grown or not.

He visualized it being his hand reminding her of her manners. Viktor's palm tingled as he pictured it coming down on her round bottom. It stung as if he'd actually performed the act.

His muscles flexed and bunched as he fought the urge to pounce. It made him uneasy. Viktor never had to fight with himself. He was cold. Calculating. His actions were never unplanned.

Inch by inch Viktor closed the distance. He reigned in his unbridled lust by slamming down his ironclad shields over his emotions. Centuries of practice living under his father had made it second nature.

Once he was fully in control again, he paused to study the female.

Her long hair swayed as she tilted her head. The light coming in from the skylights above reflected strands of gold and copper among the mass of light brunette waves.

It was the most unique head of hair he'd ever seen. He briefly wondered what it would feel like in his hands.

It was at this moment his cicatrice forced his palm up, towards the female. It sent reassuring waves of encouragement through his body, that he should continue his path. Touch her. Caress her. Teleport her to his rooms and claim her.

Viktor froze. The reality of what was before him hit with the force of a thousand ocean waves. Only his strength due to his age kept him off his knees—the eldest of the Prajna were the strongest.

Viktor was seeing his sieva for the first time. She was close enough to touch. *Well, that certainly explains the need to spank her*, he mused.

He forced his arm down, knowing he should not touch her. Not yet.

If his cicatrice touched hers, the soul-bonding would begin. They would both be powerless to stop it. Here, outside Theron's study, was not the place to perform such rituals.

Somewhere in the recess of his mind, he remembered this was the complication he had wanted to avoid. Finding her now, after all these years, put him in an awkward position. His shields buckled.

The cicatrice pulsed again, this time with a soothing balm, wiping away his troubled thoughts. No, finding her was right. Finding her was a blessing. He would handle whatever came as a result.

Desire like he'd never known shook his body, pushed him to move towards the small creature. He worried he would break her in half once he had her alone. She was so petite compared to him.

He also knew he would probably frighten her. Most of Imperium feared the Prajna, especially the elementals. He did not want her to fear him. It would interfere with his plans for her in his bed.

Viktor fought the need to grab his little mate and port her away to the privacy of his chambers. No, if she was here at the temple, it meant Edward brought her. Viktor would not invite trouble from the King of Gwydion.

Still, this female belonged to Viktor. When he left the temple, she would be leaving with him. Freely, and with the Good King's blessing. He presumed Edward would relent once he knew Viktor and the female were mates.

He wanted to see her face. He also wanted to see how she would react to the nature of his personality. Not many sought his company for the sake of his company. His gruff persona ensured others let him be.

Viktor widened his stance and crossed his arms, trying to strike a pose that would prevent him from reaching for her lithe form. He kept his voice quiet so those in the study would not interrupt.

"You know, eavesdropping is impolite, *mala vestica.*" Little witch, he'd called her.

She turned so fast he had to school his features to hide his shock. Elementals weren't known for their speed of movement. This was no ordinary witch.

The hand over her mouth stifled her reaction. Her eyes were wide, but only for a second. As she lowered her hand, she masked her fright.

Viktor's breath caught. She was beautiful, more beautiful than any image he could have conjured in his mind. He'd always considered Bianca to be stunning with her white hair and dark brows; she was nothing compared to Viktor's mate.

Her flawless skin made her look almost doll-like, giving the impression she was more fragile than was probably true. Her irises did not match, but it only made her more attractive, more exceptional. They were the same hypnotic hues from his dreams.

The right eye was undeniably the trademark emerald of his own, much like all Prajna. Nature had given the vampires eyes that were hard to look away from. It made catching and hypnotizing prey much easier.

He quirked an eyebrow as she looked him up and down, then boldly met his eyes. It was a far cry from the frightened reaction she had when he'd startled her. She was a delightful mixture of contradictions and she hadn't even opened her sinful mouth.

Eden's perusal of the enormous Prajna revealed she was not so immune to the male gender, after all. His hair was dark and cut short. The sharp angles of his chiseled face gave him a stately appearance.

He was tall. So very tall. His face had to be a foot and half above hers. His build matched his height, making him an imposing figure. He was by far the largest person she had ever seen, bigger than King Kellan.

As opposed to a sturdy sequoia, this male was built like the coastal redwood. Just as strong, but towering to the point all that muscle was lengthened, giving a false impression of lankiness.

He was dressed impeccably well, donning a dark suit of a fashion that seemed a bit antiquated for their time. The darkness of his clothing accentuated the arresting color of his eyes. Emerald green, so radiant they shined.

Her entire body flushed with warmth. At first, she assumed it was anger heating her skin. The dampness between her legs told her otherwise. For the first time in her life, Eden was attracted to another. No, not just attracted. Enthralled. She'd never felt anything like it.

Instinct told her to close the distance between them, to touch him. Her mind insisted she stay put. Eden's hand practically moved of its own volition and she had to force it to remain at her side. Her mind would always win over her instincts. She'd spent most of her life practicing, ensuring it would.

Once she felt she could constrain her reactions to the Prajna, she finally responded.

"And, as I am sure you know, calling an elemental a witch is *most* insulting."

The corner of his mouth twitched. Eden wondered what it would take to get both corners to stretch across his face.

"You know the Old Language?" he asked, wondering how old she was. The Gwydions did not live nearly as long as the other factions of Imperium. He assumed few of them spoke or even knew the native tongue of the early peoples. The demons were the only ones who used it habitually.

"More or less. A lot less than you, I'm sure."

"Indeed."

He leaned forward a few inches. Not enough to invade her personal space, but enough to be sure he held her full attention. He inhaled, needing to know her scent, wanting to taste it upon his tongue. She smelled like a summer rain falling upon the ocean. It was his favorite aroma in all the world.

He heard her heartrate increase, then, slowly decrease. It sounded as though her heart was pumping hard, but her blood refused to move. It was ... unnatural, almost as if it was forced.

He noticed a faint trace of magic in the air. Did she compel her blood to slow with magic? He'd never heard of such a thing. Viktor worried she would damage herself internally.

He was about to command her to stop whatever it was she was doing to her blood when the door swung open and Theron stepped through. Two other men stood behind him.

Viktor straightened his spine. He didn't like his mate being between him and the three males, but the female didn't so much as flinch when the door opened. It was obvious she did not view the interlopers as dangerous.

Theron's multi-colored eyes met Viktor's. They moved to the female, then back to Viktor, who remained still, allowing Theron to assess the situation and speak first. It was the only diplomatic tactic his father had ever taught him.

The priest's long white hair was as unkempt as ever. Viktor knew the Theron's appearance was a façade. There was great power under his disheveled guise.

No one knew from which faction he had come. The colors of the irises usually gave it away. But Theron's were like a kaleidoscope, constantly moving and mixing colors. It had taken years for Viktor to get used to it.

Scent was the other way to identify which race Theron was, but he never smelled the same. The last time Viktor was here, the old man smelled of cinnamon. No being in Imperium smelled of cinnamon.

47

Today, he smelled of earth. It was faint, but definitely earth.

"Viktor," Theron greeted him. "Welcome."

"Theron," Viktor replied. He peered over the priest's shoulder to the men behind him. "It seems I am late to the festivities."

Theron smiled, his eyes twinkling in delight as he looked at Viktor's mate, who hadn't moved an inch since the door was opened.

"On the contrary, I'd wager you've arrived at the exact moment you were meant to."

# Chapter 5

Viktor's jaw ticked, but he held himself in check. Theron knew. He had to know. It was the only plausible explanation for why he seemed pleased to see Viktor with the female.

"Yes, so it would it seem," Viktor responded.

Edward cleared his throat and drew Viktor's attention.

"Viktor. It is good to see you again."

Viktor inclined his head towards the gentleman. "Likewise, Edward."

Edward gestured towards the third man. "You remember Foley."

"Of course."

Edward stepped forward and put his hand on the delicate shoulder of the female. Viktor caught the growl in his chest before it was able to escape.

He'd never been possessive of anyone, but he found he did not like the Witch King touching what belonged to

49

Viktor. If she was Edward's second wife, he would be forced to kill the man.

Edward's power over air sent warning signals across the space. He eyed the vampire, sensing an undercurrent of hostility from the male. Viktor was never jovial, but he never gave off such antagonistic vibes.

"Aren't you going to introduce us?" Viktor inquired, attempting a tone of politeness. It came out ominous instead.

Edward cleared his throat. "Viktor, this is my oldest daughter, Eden. Eden, meet the King of Prajna."

Daughter. Not wife. *How very interesting—and lucky for Edward*, he thought.

Viktor loved her name. He looked forward to whispering it in her ear.

Eden curtsied and put her right hand out for him, as was customary in her kingdom. Viktor ignored it and bowed low.

He was sure she thought him rude, but touching the skin on that hand was not an option at the moment. He could explain it later.

As Viktor raised from his bow, he found striking green eyes narrowed on him. He cocked his head, challenging her to say something of his behavior.

Eden's face reddened at Viktor's rebuff. The King of Prajna had silently refused her offered hand. It was an insult to do such a thing to a lady, especially one born into a royal family.

Her birthmark pulsed and soothed like a steady heartbeat. Soon she was able to reassess and shift her frame of mind.

Maybe vampires did not touch strangers. She would need to ask her father before she rushed to judgement again. She stole a glance at her palm, thankful for whatever it was doing to her.

Eden looked back up at the huge male and saw him staring intently at her hand. She clenched her fist and turned to her father. She didn't know why, but catching Viktor regarding her hand so keenly affected her deeply.

"Yes, well, are you ready?" Theron asked.

Viktor eyed the old man. "Ready for what?"

"To discuss whatever you came to discuss, of course."

"I am. Though, I am more than happy to wait here until you've finished with your other guests, if you prefer," he offered, wanting to stay close to Eden.

"Nonsense. Come in, everyone," Theron motioned for them to follow him back into the study.

Edward and Foley returned to the room and Viktor was left standing alone with Eden. He didn't want to leave her, but it was unlikely she had plans to go anywhere without her father.

He would deal with matters of state first. It would give him time to come up with a plan where Edward's daughter was concerned. A smooth departure was his preference. Though, if Edward put up a fight, Viktor would take her anyway.

"If you'll excuse me, Eden," he dipped his head and strode into the room after the others.

Eden bit her lip as a pang struck her chest at the sound of her name upon his lips. She almost trailed after him through the doorway.

Her arm started to reach towards the male. She put her left hand over her right, holding it down. Eden's palm was acting like a magnet, attracted to whichever direction he went.

She was going to have to ask Theron about the birthmark. She'd never heard of a body part behaving as if it was its own entity.

Her offending skin prickled and the same soothing sensation crept through her body. She wanted to go to him, to be near him. Eden thought it might be quite nice to feel his fingers clasp her own.

Staring longingly after him, she sighed, and her logic took over. What was wrong with her? He was a vampire—the Vampire King of Prajna. They called him the Heartless King for a reason.

Eden had no business panting over someone like Viktor. She should put him out of her mind and go find Evelyn to continue their search.

Eden took a step towards the library when she heard Theron call her name.

"Well, child? Are you coming in or not?"

Without a hint of protest from her reasonable mind, she entered the study.

* * *

"I think the time for secrets has passed, don't you?" Theron pressed.

A vein throbbed near Viktor's forehead. He did not appreciate being cornered.

Since Theron had closed the door, the priest had disclosed the current conditions in the West and the North, including the resurrection of the Sephtis Kenelm and an assassination attempt on Edward's youngest daughter.

Viktor tensed, but not because he was upset over Eden's sister. He cared little for strangers, especially those who were not vampire.

His only concern was for Eden and what the group's resurrection meant for her. She was the sieva to the King of Prajna, just as Nora was the mate to the King of Burghard.

*An upset of the balance, indeed.*

The group, as far as he knew, had never operated in the Eastland. It was true there had been Prajna involved historically, but never had they brought their cause as far East as his castle. Considering he had no intention of putting Eden on the throne, it might not matter.

He could tell Edward was hesitant to openly discuss it, but Theron had argued if their assumptions were correct, and something was amiss across Imperium, the entire continent could be in peril. Each kingdom was facing its own plight.

Well, aside from Gwydion. Technically, their power drain ended the day Nora headed to the Northland. Edward's people may be on the mend, but he now had a vested interest in the kingdom to the North. He'd soon know he also had equitable interest in the East.

Theron ended his speech, allowing the enormity of his words to settle. Then, the wily greybeard asked Viktor to disclose the curse plaguing the vampires. He asked, knowing Viktor had taken care to hide this misfortune.

"Says the one who knows them all," Viktor replied tersely.

Theron remained unruffled. Nothing ever rattled the male.

"I hold the trust of each ruler, I guard your secrets and advise as best I can. It's time the four kings start trusting one another so we may work together. I'll be calling on Marrok by week's end."

Marrok was the ruler in the Southland, a powerful Sundari—a demon. Viktor knew the demons were having their own troubles, much more serious than his if the rumors were true.

Viktor weighed his options, calculating what was in the best interest of the Prajna. Though he had no proof, all evidence pointed to Theron's theory of some grave influence sweeping across the continent.

If his people's sufferings were related to the other factions' difficulties, he would want to be in on whatever they discovered, be it through tracking down the Sephtis Kenelm or finding clues in the scrolls. He had a duty to help the vampire kingdom.

The King continued to deliberate silently, assessing the costs compared to the benefits of throwing in his support to the other rulers. Having allies might prove useful.

In the end, his decision to cooperate wasn't altogether magnanimous. Staring hard at Eden, he took a gamble.

"Very well. I shall cooperate. I'll even help you root out the last of the Sephtis Kenelm."

Edward and Foley visibly relaxed.

"On one condition," Viktor added, surveying his sieva. She had not relaxed at his promise to assist. Beautiful and intelligent, too, it seemed.

Eden was seated to her father's left. Viktor's gaze shifted to Edward. He doubted the female would go against Edward's wishes, so he would need to first clear his path.

"And what condition would that be?" Edward queried suspiciously.

"Eden returns to Castra Nocte with me. Willingly."

Foley growled at the same time Edward spat, "Absolutely not!"

Eden sat, stunned at Viktor's stipulation, as her father hurled a string of insults at the Vampire King. Foley threw in a few choice words, as well. Viktor simply sat there, not so much as blinking. He almost looked as if he was enjoying their denunciations.

She looked at Theron, wanting him to do something to quiet the men. Wasn't that his job?

Theron's prismatic eyes were already locked on hers, ignoring the rising tensions surrounding them. He nodded towards her lap, where her hands were tightly clasped together.

"Eden, do be a dear and show your father your palm."

Eden inhaled sharply. *How could he possibly know?*

She sat still, immobilized by his request. Edward started to rise from his chair. Things were about to get out of hand.

"I suggest," Theron continued, this time speaking loudly, "you do so immediately and put a stop to this nonsense."

The mark pulsed, and silver light emitted from her hand casting a faint glow on her leg. She turned her palm face up.

"Father?"

The tremor in Eden's voice caught Edward's attention. He looked down and she extended her arm in front of him. Her crescent birthmark was producing a soft, silvery light.

"What. Is. That?" Edward gritted.

"I do believe," Viktor interposed, "*that* is the perfect match to *this*. Wouldn't you agree, Eden?"

He raised his hand to show his cicatrice, which was the same size and shape, and releasing the same silver light as Eden's. If his marking had awoken five years earlier, hers would have, as well. It seemed his little witch was keeping secrets from her father.

*Deviant female*, he almost complemented. Eden was a puzzle he was looking forward to solving.

"Oh, dear Goddess above," Foley sighed.

"What?" Eden asked her father, who had sunk back into his chair, both hands in his hair. He looked utterly and completely defeated.

"What does this mean?" she demanded.

Viktor stood, towering over Eden and her father. His heated stare felt like flames licking at her skin, like when she used her powers to warm herself in winter, only this was more intense.

"It means, *mala vestica*, you are mine."

"Your what, exactly?" she bristled at being called 'little witch' again.

"My sieva. My mate. That crescent you don is what my people call a cicatrice. Each one has a match, and only one match, to the one person who can bond with his or her soul. You're mine."

Eden heard the truth in his declaration. Their identical markings could not be mere happenstance. Her body's reaction to his went beyond ordinary attraction.

Nora's words came to her mind. *When you search your truth, look to the East*. This was what she meant. All Eden's logic and powers of deduction agreed. For once, so did her instincts.

The riddle finally made sense. The East wasn't a location. It was a person. Viktor was where she would find her truth.

Eden had a choice to make. She could deny her fate, possibly drawing the ire of the Goddess, or, worse, forsaking her own wants and desires. Or she could meet her destiny head-on.

One look at Viktor's severe countenance and her choice was made. She would go with him. Not solely because of the mark, and certainly not because he dared to mandate she do so in exchange for his assistance.

It was mostly because, underneath his harsh expression, Eden saw Viktor's vulnerability. Some part of him was afraid she would refuse. The cool pulse of her marking told her she was making the right decision.

# Chapter 6

"I agree to your terms," Eden announced. "Now tell us what we want to know.

Viktor blinked. His tiny mate had easily agreed to leaving with him, then subsequently made a demand of him, all in one breath. No one demanded anything of King Viktor.

He wanted to laugh at the absurdity of it. It was refreshing to be challenged by a female, but it would not become a habit of hers. Taking his hand to her bottom may happen sooner rather than later.

"Eden, you do not have to do this," Edward told his daughter.

Viktor wanted to argue, but he remained silent, allowing Eden to make her own case. She must be feeling the lure of her own cicatrice. Why else would she choose to leave with a stranger?

"I know. But do you think it would end here if I refused? We both know it wouldn't. There is no possibility these marks are coincidence. So, let's accept it and move past it."

The edges of Edward's mouth turned down. He reached up to tuck a strand of hair behind her ear, like he'd done a thousand times before.

"Always so logical," he told her. She'd been this way since shortly after her mother passed.

Edward gestured to Viktor. "It seems the floor is yours."

Viktor returned to his seat, ignoring the fact he did not like how his sieva had arrived at her decision. Irrationally, he wanted her to feel something, to argue she felt compelled to go with him. Which, for someone who had rarely allowed his own emotions to dictate his decisions, was entirely hypocritical.

Resigned to cooperate, Viktor started talking. He confessed the misfortunes of the Prajna, hoping he was doing the right thing.

Having just found his own mate, he had a newfound appreciation for his people's frustrations. He and Eden were the first true-mates to find one another in a hundred years. He prayed they weren't the last.

When he finished, the room was quiet.

"In ancient times," Theron broke the silence, "many of the Prajna could not conceive until their clan's leader found his own mate and bore young. It's possible this is your problem."

Eden's face flushed, fully understanding the implication. She'd never been so much as kissed before, had never wanted to be. Until today.

"Yes, I know," Viktor replied. "However, I'm not convinced that is the issue. We have experienced a number of cases of conception. Unfortunately, none of the young have been brought to term. Not in decades."

"Which is extremely regrettable, Viktor. Truly, it is a travesty your people face. I still believe there is hope it will be rectified once the leader has his house in order."

Theron's words dug into Viktor, sharp and biting. The insinuation was he needed to impregnate his sieva.

He purposefully kept quiet that this subject was one of the reasons he had come here. His intention had been to discuss Bianca and the plan to attempt getting her with child, despite the awakening of his cicatrice.

There was no need to further enrage Edward or to make Eden uncomfortable. He would have to broker the conversation eventually, but, for now, he would not rock the boat. Eden was his and he intended to keep her, no matter what.

Theron arose from his chair. "I think we should conclude here. Viktor, I will send word once I've spoken to Marrok. Hopefully, we'll come across something in the scrolls that may be of use. I'll summon my courier now."

Viktor and the others stood, as Theron left the study. He motioned to his mate, whose eyes had scarcely left him.

"Eden. Now would be the time to tell your family goodbye. I will wait for you outside the temple. I advise you to hurry."

Her eyes glinted with displeasure. "I need to pack my things," her level voice countered.

"Find your sister. Tell her to pack your belongings and I will have someone bring them along shortly."

"Oh. You travelled here with another?"

"No."

"I don't understand."

"You don't need to. You have ten minutes."

Eden held her tongue, not wanting to cause a scene, and took off in search of Evelyn. She shoved her fists into the pockets of her long skirt, thinking singeing the King might be unwise.

Viktor turned to Edward. "I know I don't have to tell you the way of things between sievas. However, I feel compelled to assure you she will be safe with me. I would never harm my mate or allow any threat to come near her."

The tightness in Edward's jaw eased a small amount, knowing Viktor was making an attempt on his behalf. He felt like he'd been tense since the day Kellan had come to meet Eden, half a decade ago.

His wife had warned him, once their children chose their path, to let them go. If he interfered, it would have drastic consequences for Imperium. It was hell obeying her wishes.

"I know," he told the vampire. "I like you, Viktor. I'm probably the only Gwydion who does. So, I feel obligated to tell you it's not Eden's physical safety that is most concerning to me. She is powerful and could likely handle whatever the Prajna throw at her."

Viktor believed Edward, judging from her abnormal speed and the way she controlled her heart rate earlier.

"Then what is your concern?"

"Eden guards her heart. She does things to herself to control her emotions. It isn't healthy, and I've never been able to break her of it. So, as her father, I am telling you to take care of her heart. Do nothing to damage it."

Viktor was nonplussed. Of all the warnings he'd expected to hear from his mate's father, he hadn't expected this.

Part of Viktor wanted to tell Edward the bond between he and his sieva was none of Edward's business. Maybe the elemental was brighter than Viktor knew. Viktor wasn't known for taking care with others in word or deed.

Regardless, he would not depart with Edward feeling like Viktor would be careless with Eden's emotions. He could be distant and cold, but he had no intention of hurting or mistreating Eden.

His cicatrice burned at the lie. Admittedly, there was one predicament in his life that would cause her grief, but they would work around it. There was no other option. No vampire would ever willingly let go of his mate once he found her.

"I will do my best. You have my word." Viktor bowed and swiftly exited.

Edward watched the King of Prajna walk out the front entrance of the temple to wait for Eden. Foley put a hand on Edward's shoulder.

"You do realize you just asked The Heartless King of Prajna to take care with your daughter's heart?"

"I assure you, Foley, the irony is not lost on me."

\* \* \*

Eden exited the temple and came down the stairs, feeling much lighter after having a few moments with her family and enduring Evelyn's overzealous excitement.

Her sister was a hopeless romantic, spouting off nonsense about not fighting Fate and cherishing an enduring love. Evelyn would have jumped right into the vampire's arms in front of everyone if she'd been the one with the matching birthmark.

If their father had not been present, Eden would have assured Evelyn what she was feeling had nothing to do with love or romance and everything to do with the natural laws of attraction. Mates were meant to procreate. It was why nature saddled them with outrageously incessant physical cravings.

It didn't stop the tiny seed of hope from planting itself firmly inside her. She cursed herself for it, but then her mark lit up and she could once again think rationally.

Eden reached the bottom of the staircase and moved towards the awaiting male. She stopped when she saw the severe sloping of Viktor's eyebrows.

"What are you wearing?" he scolded more than asked.

She looked down at her riding breeches and tall black boots, then she inspected her shirt and cloak. Nothing seemed out of place. She took in his old-fashioned suit and wondered if he'd ever seen a woman in trousers.

"This is what I typically wear when I go riding."

Eden looked around, expecting to see horses, but there weren't any.

"Is your horse in the stable?" she asked.

"No. I do not travel by horse."

He seemed on edge. More so than before. Mayhap he was afraid she could not handle hiking the terrain on foot?

"Is this the fashion of females in Gwydion?" he asked.

"For some. Do you ... do you not like it?"

Viktor's green eyes flashed brightly.

"The problem, *mala vestica*, is that I like it very much."

Eden's body thrummed in awareness that his gaze was travelling all over her figure, and he openly enjoyed what he saw. She was suddenly very hot under her heavy cloak.

Her hand drifted towards his and lightning-fast he grabbed her wrist, judiciously avoiding the end of her limb.

"Careful. This is not the time or the place to start such a thing."

"I only meant to touch your hand."

"Come. Once we are in Castra Nocte, I will explain things to you."

"How far away is it?" she asked. No one, other than the vampires, knew exactly where the King of Prajna resided.

"It is on the far coast, well hidden from anyone wishing to do you harm."

The far coast would take days on horseback. Weeks, if they had to walk.

"But how will we—"

Before she could ask about their mode of travel, Viktor had his arm around her waist. Suddenly, she was being compressed so hard she couldn't breathe. A second later she felt a cool breeze on her skin.

"What—what was that?"

"That was how I travel. Porting is much more efficient than riding on horses, don't you think?"

Eden looked around. They were no longer outside the temple. They were standing on a stone balcony. A single chair and small table sat nearby.

They'd ported to his castle on the eastern coast of Imperium, hundreds of miles from the temple. A snap of a finger and she was in a far-off land.

This was why Prajna had a reputation for being abnormally fast. They could cross a great distance in the span of a heartbeat. It would take some getting used to.

Seagulls cried in the distance. Eden turned her head towards the sound, but she couldn't see past the thick mist rolling off the ocean below.

"A storm is coming. Let's get you inside," he said.

Viktor, still with his arm around her waist, led her through the arched doors and straight into his bedroom.

# Chapter 7

Once they crossed the threshold, Viktor released his hold. Eden wanted it back, having relished the feel of his possessively firm grip. But she wasn't sure she was ready for what would follow if she invited him to touch her.

It was dim inside the chamber, the overcast from the storm made it feel like it was dusk. There was just enough light to see.

She was curious how the King of Prajna lived, what his quarters were like. Did he find comfort here? Her eyes flicked to the bed, knowing she would not be the first to *comfort* the king in this space.

The bitter flavor of jealousy was as unfamiliar as it was unexpected. They'd only met today, yet it didn't stop Eden from feeling possessive of him.

She slowly explored with her eyes, then moved about, seeking information. Her bedroom was surrounded with things that made her happy and reminded her of those she loved. She wondered which of his possessions held any sentimental value to Viktor.

The King watched as Eden walked around his chamber—*their* chamber—touching his things, taking in her new surroundings, her new home. He'd never imagined having a female share this room with him.

Even with Bianca, he'd intended for her to live in the Queen's quarters, having no desire to spend time with her outside of feedings or bedding her. It would be the same arrangement they'd had for decades, only she would hold a title.

Viktor's cicatrice burned and brought his attention back to his sieva. So easily the mark seared away reflections of another. The powers within would not tolerate any deviation from the path towards joining with his mate's soul.

He had removed his arm from Eden the second he saw the bed, afraid he would not be able to hold back if he was touching her in any way. He'd never felt as though he wasn't in control of his actions. The longer he was around her, the more unmanageable his compulsions became.

It was the influence of the cicatrice. It was how the Prajna knew they had found their sieva. It possessed prevailing magic to push mates into coupling, into bonding. The sooner they shared blood and completed the soul-bond, the sooner he would feel more like himself.

His fangs ached, thinking of taking Eden's blood, and of her taking his. If not for the cicatrice on her palm, he would worry what ingesting his blood would do to an elemental. Destiny would not bring them together if they were not a match in every capacity.

The image of feeding from his mate was interrupted when Eden raised her hands and simultaneously lit all the candles in the room, then ignited the large fireplace behind him. He wondered if she knew vampires were drawn to fire.

With the illumination from the candles around the chamber, Eden could better see her surroundings. The room fit what little she knew of Viktor.

The decor was dark. Red and black tapestries hung on the walls. A black and gold quilt covered the bed. Smatterings of dark wood peaked out from the cushions covering various pieces of furniture. It was very masculine, as well as a little morbid.

What it lacked in femininity, it more than made up for in opulence. Virtually every piece of furniture was oversized and gilded in some manner.

The bed was huge, the top of each of the four posts crowned with the head of a hawk. Her elemental senses told her they were pure gold. The eyes were made of emeralds.

Numerous items secured precious jewels as decoration. Several chairs were adorned with rubies. One of the tapestries was an image of what had to be Viktor's family crest, the outline of which looked to be lustrous, precious gems. Even the letter opener on the desk was jeweled.

Viktor was certainly living like a king. Her family's royal dwelling was quaint in comparison. Even their castle near the Gwydion coast drew short in its simplicity.

Eden preferred simplicity.

As she circled back to where he was standing, she noticed a piece of furniture incongruous compared to the rest of his chamber. His hand was resting on the back of the large, plush chair. It was sky blue with a pattern of minute white roses. The ottoman in front of it matched. She couldn't picture him sitting in it.

Simple and worn. It was her favorite item in the room.

Eden pointed to the chair. "This seems a little out of place. A little feminine for your tastes."

He squeezed the soft material under his fingers, thinking back to when the previous owner used to sit in it. Eden was right, it stood out from the others.

"It was my mother's."

Eden swallowed. The Heartless King had a soft spot for his mother.

"She didn't want it anymore?"

"It was of no use to her in death."

Eden made to raise her hand to his in comfort, then thought better of it. He had warned her about touching him.

"I am sorry, Viktor."

"No need. It was long ago."

He ran one finger across the arm. "I'm not even sure why I dragged it in here."

Eden understood why. It was the same reason she wore her mother's necklace and rarely took it off.

They stood for a moment, staring at one another. His eyes made her feel unguarded, like he could see so far inside her she no longer had any secrets.

71

She'd spent her life ensuring the world around her only saw her exterior. Things would be different when it came to Viktor.

"Do you have any other family?" she inquired, wanting a way out from under his inspection.

"My brother, Luka. But he's … I would prefer it if you kept your distance from him. He can be difficult, and that is putting it mildly."

Eden wasn't positive, but she perceived a trace of regret in his tone. She couldn't imagine life without her doting father and loving sisters or what it would be like to be at odds with them, unable to trust a loved one.

In her peripheral, she noticed a door next to the fireplace with an odd metal lock. The paneling was made of oak, but bars of iron were evenly spaced up, down, and across, making small squares atop the natural grain of the wood. It looked like the doors in Gwydion's jail.

She knew it wasn't the main door to exit the room. That door was large and arched, similar to the one leading to the balcony.

"Where does that lead?" she asked, hoping to give him a reprieve from his mother's memory.

"Nowhere," Viktor replied, not bothering to look where she had indicated. He knew very well to what she was referring.

Eden's mouth had gone dry under the intensity of his scrutiny. Her birthmark pulsed with an erotic heat. Its power circulated throughout her system, warming her from the inside.

It would be so easy to step into Viktor, to touch him and lose herself to his magnetic lure; but his answer bothered her.

"You don't want me to know," she stated.

Viktor ran his tongue across his upper teeth, debating. He wasn't hiding anything, he simply had other things in mind to do with their time.

Eden would need to acclimate, and quickly. He wasn't a gentleman. He rarely had consideration for his partners aside from making sure they climaxed. It made females more malleable to his sexual impulses if he allowed them to come.

With Eden, he needed to tread carefully. She was untouched—or, at least, very inexperienced—and would not know what he expected until he taught her. He hardened at the thought.

Viktor had never taken anyone's innocence. He required experienced females to slake this thirst. For blood. For sex. For complete and total domination of their bodies.

He was confident they would be more than compatible in his bed. It was only a matter of training her. He'd also need to acclimate her to being bitten on a regular basis.

Male and female Prajna fed from one another often because they could not live without blood. They could eat the same foods as other factions, but blood was what provided the nourishment they needed to live.

Eden did not consume blood, but he wanted her to enjoy that part of their experience, to crave his as he craved hers. The exchange was an intimate experience between mates.

He'd never let a female feed from him. Sharing blood during intercourse would start the blood-bonding between those who were not true mates. He greedily drank from his partners during their interludes, but they were never allowed to take from him.

As long as it was one-sided, there was no risk of an unintentional mating. It was why he never went near Bianca's teeth. She was ambitious, and he knew better than to allow her to 'accidentally' graze him.

Viktor glanced at the door.

Behind it was his feeding room. It was where he took blood almost daily. The stronger of the species required more feedings. Most Prajna could go a week or so without it. Not Viktor, especially once his cicatrice had awoken. His hunger had grown to an almost insatiable level, pushing him to find his sieva and subdue his need.

The room was also where he copulated with a plethora of Prajna females. They were never allowed in his bed. He trusted no one to be in his personal domain, especially when he was sleeping. Eden would be the first. She would also be the last.

Viktor walked to the door and scrolled through the lock's symbols until the combination released the pin. He swung the door open with one arm and held it. It was an open invitation for Eden to enter.

As she stepped in front of him, her arm grazed his stomach. Viktor bent, putting his mouth to her ear.

"Careful what you ask for, Sieva, especially when I am inclined to give it to you."

# Chapter 8

Eden shuddered at his breath tickling her ear and the reminder she was his mate. She pressed her tongue to the back of her teeth to prevent any sound from escaping her lips. She focused on the dark room before her.

This room had no windows, and, thus, was much darker than the bedroom. She could make out the candelabras inside and used her magic to light them.

The flames flickered brightly. There had to be well over a hundred candles lining the walls. Once she realized what was inside the room, she considered snuffing them out.

In the middle was a bed, covered in only a dark sheet. No pillows, no blankets, just the sheet.

To the left was a wooden chair. Or, she thought it was a chair. The seat was awfully small. It had rope attached to the arms and legs and was tilted so that whomever sat in it was reclined. It was also high off the ground. She would have to be lifted to sit in it.

To the right of the bed was a couch, of sorts. It was narrow and oddly shaped, looking like the back of a serpent, or a rolling wave. It would provide a comfortable position in which to lounge and read, but she knew this item of furniture was not meant for reading.

There were chains and cuffs attached to the walls in various spots, anchored to the grooves within the stone. Shelving stood near another door, which she presumed exited into the hall. It held a dozen or so towels. She'd never seen black towels before.

Eden may not have known much in the ways of sex, but she was intelligent and had a perfectly good imagination, one that was now giving her quite a show inside her head.

She should be frightened, not intrigued. She imagined his teeth penetrating her skin, how it would feel. Would he cuff her to the wall, so she could not flee? What else would he do to her?

Eden pictured countless Prajna coming and going from this room to service their king. She knew they offered more than their veins. How many of them had he allowed into his bed of gold?

"Why do you have this room? Why—why is it important enough to be attached to your bed chamber?"

Viktor tried to see it through her virginal eyes. It was fairly obvious what occurred in here. Sex often followed a feeding, and he almost always partook of what was so freely offered.

Eden, of course, would have to become accustomed to his bite, as well as to whatever preceded and followed. He was guessing she lacked knowledge of what a Prajna's bite was like, that it could be highly pleasurable.

"This is my feeding room," he told her.

"Your feeding room."

"Yes."

"This is where you ... drink from others?"

"Yes."

"Why?"

"Why do I feed from others or why do I do it here?"

"I know why you feed. You need blood to live. Why here?"

Viktor shrugged. "I do not care to have anyone in my personal quarters."

Eden tensed, thinking he did not intend to have her share his room. "Is this where I am to sleep, then? In your feeding room?"

He frowned. "Of course not."

"Will I have a separate room?"

"No," his voice boomed, causing her to flinch. He immediately reigned in his displeasure, softening his speech.

"No, Eden. My sieva is welcome in my room. The others are not."

Unable to stop herself, she smiled, beyond pleased with this information. It was almost sweet that his bed was only for her.

Viktor swore his heart stopped at the sight of her beaming up at him. He dug his fingernails into his palms, needing to find a way to avoid slicing through her clothing and taking her against the stone wall.

He pictured cuffing her, commanding her actions as he commanded her pleasure. *How long would it take her to submit?* She was nowhere near ready for what he wanted her to give him.

Eden cleared her throat and pointed to the unconventional furniture. "This room is not solely used for feeding, is it?"

The hulking male's eyebrows drew down and together, not liking where his mate's questions were headed. It was easily discernible what occurred when he utilized the equipment in this place. Eden was going to make him say it aloud.

Being bluntly honest, which he'd told himself he'd be, was more difficult than expected. It didn't help that his resistance to her was waning.

"No. It is not solely used for feeding."

She nodded, processing his answer. Her left hand rubbed absently along her collar bone, deep in thought.

Viktor felt like a piece of her had withdrawn. He disliked it, but for now he would allow it. They had time for Eden to learn how to answer his demands—and he would demand she give him everything.

He stared as she stroked the delicate skin below her neck. He zeroed in on the artery pulsating above her finger tips. He was close to losing it. The cicatrice would not stop him. It wanted him to push inside her, to lap up her lifeblood, and bond his soul to hers.

"You need to leave," he announced.

Eden's mouth dropped open.

"Now, Eden."

Before she could reply, he had her by the elbow, dragging her back into his bedchamber. Eden jerked her arm away, upset at being manhandled, and her mark quickly sent out its calming vibes.

"Do not be upset," he ordered, locking the door behind him. "It is very distracting having you in that room. It's easier for me to talk to you in here."

"You didn't like me asking questions."

"Your questions do not bother me. Having you in the room I use for feeding and for ... sating many appetites, well, let's just say I doubt your ability to handle the answer to that question. If I were you, I would give up this topic of conversation."

Eden wasn't some immature child. She wanted truth. She could handle his truth. If she was his destined mate, that was how it would have to be. She resented him a little for treating her as though she was less capable than the females he'd had in his feeding room.

At the contemplation of those who had come before her, her palm tingled, transferring its peaceful magic again. This time, she didn't want it to alter her mental state. She worried it would prevent her from having an honest dialog with Viktor.

She would leave it be, as he suggested. For now. But only because she had a more compulsory line of questioning.

She held her palm up in front of his face. "Why is it, every time I am riled, this birthmark lights up and calms me down? And why am I so quick to anger in the first place? I am never emotional. The longer I am in your presence the more I feel this back-and-forth pull."

*Clever little witch*, he thought. Instead of trusting her emotions, she catalogued and analyzed the change in them. They were very well-suited.

"Lower you hand, Eden."

"Why?"

"Because," he replied, holding up his left hand, which was still emitting the soft light from earlier. "I want to grab it with my own. If I do so, your question will go unanswered until much later, if at all. We'll be so caught up in one another, I doubt you'll even remember what you wanted to know."

Eden lowered her arm, comprehending his meaning. Then she remembered she was in her riding clothes and reached into the pocket of her cloak.

Viktor watched as Eden extracted a leather glove from within her cloak. She waved it in front of him, her lips shaping into a self-satisfied smirk. Then she slid her fingers into the opening.

It would cover the cicatrice completely. She really was sharp as a tack. It made her all the more attractive.

Her small hand pulled at the leather, sliding it down to her wrist until it was securely in place. It would help, but only for so long. Sooner or later, the cicatrice would ensure the soul-bond took place, whether they wanted it or not.

Eden removed her cloak and put it on the bench next to the door. Then she dropped into the chair on the opposite side of the fireplace from the blue wingback and indicated he should also sit. Viktor remained standing.

"Please?" she requested.

Viktor liked hearing 'please' come from her mouth, so he lowered himself into the chair. She would be saying the word again. Soon.

"Will you help me understand what's happening to me?"

"Very well."

"Thank you," she exhaled. *Finally, some answers!*

"As I told you in the temple, the marking is what the Prajna call a cicatrice. We are all born with one. Our sievas, our true mates, are born with the identical mark. When we touch them together and exchange blood, we will be bonded. It is important, Eden, for you to understand Fate chose you as mine from the time of your birth."

"Which would mean you were mine, as well, yes?"

Viktor smirked.

"Yes. Though, it is extremely rare for a sieva to not be a vampire. A handful of demon mates have been found, but I have not heard of anyone from Gwydion bearing the mark."

"Yes, well, we are the only faction to be born without a pre-ordained mate."

Viktor's smirked vanished. "I would think, with your sister being a true mate to a wolf, and you being my sieva, that statement is not entirely accurate."

Evelyn's face popped into Eden's mind. If anyone would be open to such a notion as fated mates, it would be Evelyn. She'd acted all starry-eyed over Nora's experience and almost envious of Eden's.

If the powers of the universe created a mate for her sweet Evie, her sister would run into his arms and ask questions later. Eden wasn't quite so fanciful in her concept of love.

"The cicatrice?" she prodded.

"Yes, well, it is first and foremost how one knows he or she has found their intended," he paused, wanting to choose his next words carefully. He would not risk Eden misinterpreting its effects on her disposition.

"What else is it, other than a means to make me question my sanity?"

Viktor chuckled, and Eden thought it the most wonderful sound she had ever heard. She had a feeling it did not happen often.

"Trust me, I understand your frustration. It makes you question if you ever felt what you knew you had been feeling. But that is the magic of the cicatrice. Its power will placate its bearer, wanting to ensure there is no animosity between mates."

"Why? It sounds almost like trickery."

Viktor narrowed his eyes. "It is not trickery. It is insurance that the soul-bonding will occur in a timely fashion. Once it does, the power it has over your emotions will fade."

It was temporary. *Thank the Goddess.*

"So, my . . . annoyance will also be more manageable?"

Viktor chuckled again. "Doubtful. The cicatrice mollifies you, erasing your vexations. It would not push you into feeling such negative emotions. That, my dear Eden, is all you."

# Chapter 9

"More like it's a result of being near *you*," she muttered in response.

Eden gulped as the huge male was suddenly in front of her, one hand on each thigh, holding them apart, as he knelt between the V of her legs. He had moved so fast, he must have ported. Her heart pounded, and she used her magic to force the oxygen in her bloodstream to slow its speed.

"Do not do that," Viktor snarled and tightened his grip on her thighs.

"Do what?" she whispered, adrenaline flooding her system. Her skin felt tight as her hormones surged.

"Whatever you are doing to your heart. It's contracting, and you are denying it its natural response. You could harm yourself. I will not allow it to continue."

"You think I am hurting myself?"

"Of course, you are. And I. Do. *Not*. Like. It," he gritted through his teeth.

Despite his domineering attitude, his command was endearing. In his own way, he was trying to protect her. Her palm buzzed, then pushed itself to the side of his face.

Viktor held still, feeling the cool leather of her glove touch his cheek. He could feel the cicatrice's pull as it beckoned to his own. He wanted to feel her skin slide along his, to join their hands as he emptied himself inside her.

Eden released the hold on the oxygen in her veins, allowing her heart to thump wildly while her blood flowed through it. Her breathing accelerated.

Viktor's eyes moved to the artery on her neck and his fangs elongated as his cock became fully erect. He would need to feed soon. First, he would sample her flesh.

He mimicked her touch and ran his thumb along her bottom lip.

"Tell me, *mala vestica*, has anyone tasted these before?"

"No," she panted, reveling in the feel of his skin upon her face.

"Good. I'd hate to have to kill anyone who had dared."

He barely got the words out before his lips were on hers. She groaned when she felt his tongue enter and explore her mouth. Eden tentatively pressed her tongue to his, and a purring sound came from his throat.

She'd been wrong about his laugh. *This* was the most wonderful sound to ever reach her ears. Her undergarments flooded with her juices and she inched forward, pressing as hard as she could into his stomach.

Viktor's hands moved to her backside, lifting her slightly off the chair and rubbing her up and down his abdominal muscles. The scent of her sweet honey filled the air and he couldn't wait to lap it up.

Eden twisted and pulled at his hair as she wrapped her legs around his waist in a feeble attempt to get better purchase, to feel more pressure between her legs. She could sob from the want.

Viktor broke the kiss, needing to see the yearning in her eyes, wanting her to feel as uncontrolled as he felt.

Eden's lips were swollen from his sensual assault. Her hooded eyes implored him for more. She squeezed her legs tight around him and his fingers dug into her flesh.

When she whined and stretched to kiss him again, his heart thudded heavily. Her fingers nimbly unbuttoned his jacket and slid it down his arms. He let it drop absently to the floor, in a hurry to get her body back in his hands.

Viktor slowed the kiss and his lips drifted across her cheek to her ear.

"Do you have any idea what I'm going to do you?"

Eden whimpered and nipped at the skin on his neck. It nearly made him spill inside his pants. He had never allowed anyone near his neck. If he could, he'd keep her mouth there forever.

His control was slipping. The feel of her in his arms, the scent of her sweet arousal, it was all overloading his senses. The chaotic sensory overload was almost more than he could bear.

His cicatrice was quiet, it's power unnecessary. His predatory nature had taken over, a driving force demanding to join with its mate.

Viktor grabbed the front of Eden's shirt and tore it open. Buttons flew in all directions, bouncing off the floor and rolling around in circles.

Eden was still kissing and licking his neck, unconcerned with his aggression. She did not feel in control of her body and it did not bother her. It was exhilarating, untamed, and life-affirming all at once.

Viktor placed both hands on her shoulders and pushed until her back hit the chair. He wanted to look at what was now his, what would always be his.

Unlike female Prajna, Eden wore another layer under her blouse. It compressed her breasts in and up. He couldn't decide if he loved it or hated it.

"Are you fond of this garment?" he asked, running his fingertips down the valley of her chest.

"I—"

Before she could respond, he'd ripped it down the middle, her breasts now on full display for him. Impatient to touch them, he dove forward, laving and sucking at her erect nipples.

Eden cried out at the sensation of Viktor's hot mouth on her chest. With each suckle, her core pulsed and throbbed. He was making her crazy.

The heat from her birthmark had stoked a fire within her as it spread through every inch of her being. No thought or reason fought against his claiming. Everything inside Eden was welcoming Viktor to do as he pleased.

All these years, Eden had believed herself incapable of ever wanting a male, of thinking her friends ridiculous to seek them out. As Viktor's tongue slid across her sensitive skin in a loving caress, she knew why those females agreed to meet males in the woods at night. Finally, she understood.

Viktor's respiration was increasing. She could feel it against her breasts. His hot breath added to the eroticism of what he was doing. Eden held on to his hair, unsure if she was pushing or pulling. She needed more.

As if reading her mind, Viktor cupped her between her legs, pressing and rubbing over her pants. Eden gasped, rejoicing in the pleasure mounting from the base of her spine to the skin of her core.

"Viktor," she begged, "please."

For what she was asking, she wasn't sure. All she knew was only he could give it to her.

Viktor smiled against her chest as he heard her plea. He could make her come like this, but he wanted to see her bared—all of her—before he allowed it.

He lifted from her supple body, grabbing the front of her trousers to unbutton them. Slowly, he lowered the zipper. Eden closed her eyes, too embarrassed to watch.

"Open your eyes, Sieva. You will watch as I bring you pleasure. If you close them, I will stop."

Eden's eyes popped open.

Viktor reached for the fabric on her hips and pulled. Eden lifted her lower half to assist him. The riding breeches were tight-fitting and did not easily slide down her legs.

He eyed her boots, which were still on. They would hinder his progress with her trousers. With his patience shot, he grabbed the offending fabric and tore it down the seam. The material hung loosely to the sides of her legs, but he paid it no mind. His focus was zeroed in on what lie at the apex of her thighs.

Lace. Eden's nakedness was covered in white lace, a stark reminder of her innocence. He leaned forward and put his mouth to the top of her mound, kissing it reverently.

Eden's heart softened as she watched Viktor kiss the lace of her undergarments. His gaze met hers, so full of heat and determination she had trouble keeping her eyes open.

Without looking away, he fisted the delicate fabric, tearing it from her body. Air hit her pinkened skin and she exhaled in anticipation.

Viktor ran his nose along her folds, committing her scent to memory. Nothing had ever smelled sweeter.

He shoved her legs further apart and licked up the seam of her center. He should have taken his time, teased her, but all he could concentrate on was swallowing her essence.

"Ah!" she squeaked, her body trembling.

Eden's reaction set his body aflame. Viktor growled as he lapped furiously at her, unable to get enough. He used his thumb to press against the pinnacle of her cleft, as his tongue dipped inside as far as it could go.

With that single touch, Eden flew apart, screaming so loud she was sure someone would think he was killing her. In a way, he was. Her body spasmed and euphoria flooded her system.

Her heartrate was out of control, but she left it alone, thinking it would slow on its own. It didn't.

Viktor gave no reprieve, continuously licking and sucking until she felt like she was going to peak again. He slid a long finger into her channel and sucked hard on her nub.

Eden fisted his hair, pulling his face forward as she rocked her hips against it. He added a second finger and another climax rushed to the surface.

She was too overwhelmed to keep her eyes open. She shouted his name and he roared, porting away abruptly.

Eden suddenly felt bereft at the loss of his touch. She opened her eyes. He was across the room, looking unsteady on his feet. His chest was heaving, his eyes wild.

Viktor lifted his hand, and she was shocked to see how much it was shaking. The tip of one finger was covered in blood. Her blood. He must have breached her maidenhead and she'd been so enraptured she had felt nothing but pleasure.

He deliberately placed his finger in his mouth and groaned. The drugging effect of her taste combined with her blood awoke something inside him.

If he didn't leave her now, Viktor would feast upon her virgin blood and he didn't know if he would be able to stop drinking. He wanted to tear into her, to swallow her lifeblood and mix it with his own, to take so much she would live inside him forever.

His damned cicatrice only encouraged him to do just that. Viktor was too dangerous to be anywhere near Eden right now. Once his fangs punctured her ivory skin, he would rut her like an animal. He feared he might drain her dry in his excitement.

Not once in his life had he been unable to control the bloodlust. Not until this moment.

Viktor had foolishly believed he could go slow with her. With Eden there was no such thing. He needed to leave and calm the beast inside.

Unfortunately, only one thing would curb his appetite. He took one last look at his mate and ported out of the room.

# Chapter 10

Viktor teleported directly into the center of the Komora, landing behind one of the pillars lining the courtyard. The large pavilion housed hundreds of female Prajna, most of which served him directly.

Some worked in the castle or at various trades around the town outside of Castra Nocte. Others were here solely to feed the king. It was a practice existing since well before Viktor had ever been born.

Their families sent them to Viktor, gifting the females as if they were chattel to be traded. He knew their hope was he would choose one and blood-bond with her. Or, at the very least, they hoped to gain favor with their liege.

He was always clear with his intentions, plainly communicating that bonding to any of the ladies of the Komora would never happen, but the families sent them anyway. He pitied the ones who were timid, who weren't shrewd enough to know they were expected to fulfill his every desire, not just give their blood.

Those were the ones he made sure learned some sort of trade immediately. They needed some way to find a purpose outside of his feeding room. He did not want to feel as if he was taking advantage.

As the years passed, however, and the females became accustomed to their newfound freedom, many of them grew bold. Some became aggressive, vying for his attention. Those were the ones he called for most often. The King greatly enjoyed a willing body, and enjoyed it often.

He never let himself dwell on the concept of the Komora for long. He'd always believed he had done as best he could for those living within its walls. By his standards, their arrangement was mutually beneficial.

Viktor gave the females a comfortable place to stay and encouraged them to pursue whatever was of interest, including other males. His soldiers and guards fed them, and, if the females were willing, they fed his men. Over the decades, several had even mated. All with his blessing.

If any of them moved out of the Komora, they were quickly replaced. A constant blood supply was imperative to Viktor and his army. He'd always believed the Komora would be here at the ready, no matter to whom he was wed.

He assumed his men would continue their arrangement and Viktor would, as well. He'd never contemplated marrying for love, much less finding his sieva.

Now, standing here in the small courtyard, he questioned his egotistical assumption. Seeking out these females did not feel right.

Viktor didn't really want to be here. It had been years since he'd even stepped foot into their living space, but he needed blood—a great deal of it—fast. His hands hadn't stopped shaking since he'd touched his mate's most intimate of places.

He needed to take care of his needs immediately, preferably in one of the private feeding rooms where few could witness his maniacal state. The females slept communally but preferred to feed and be fed in private. Sex almost always followed and, while free with their bodies, orgies weren't what they desired.

Burying his rampant thoughts, Viktor stepped out from the column. The few Prajna near him halted. The King had never ported here unannounced.

Viktor grabbed one of the closest females, pulling her close. She pressed against his quaking body, batting her eyelashes.

"You will meet me in the feeding room across from the bathing chamber," he commanded.

"Shall I come with you now, my liege?" she asked in a sultry tone, her hand rubbing over the rigid flesh barely contained in his trousers. "I am at your service."

"No. Go gather others. Today I'll need more than one."

Viktor released her and strode towards the room to prepare it for his multiple guests.

"Others?" she asked. "How many do you require?"

"Ten. No, a dozen."

Her eyes grew big. Occasionally he took two at a time. Once, long ago, he'd fed from three. He'd been wounded and needed to heal.

"Now!" he snapped. He was King. He would not explain himself.

* * *

For a second, Eden didn't move. She couldn't fathom what had gone wrong. How could he give her such physical delight, then simply vanish?

Something had spooked him, and it had something to do with her blood. She was under the impression he was supposed to want her blood, not run away from it.

*Was the blood down there ... different?* Had it displeased him? It wasn't like she could control it. Eden was untouched. Viktor should have expected blood at some point.

During her lessons on "wifely duties," she learned bleeding was customary the first time. Surely, he would have been taught the same, even if he had never been with a virgin. Though, technically, what he had done to her wasn't exactly sex.

Eden worried her body's response had turned him off, that she'd reacted too wantonly. It had all felt natural, but she was his virgin mate, maybe she should act like one.

She'd gone from one extreme to another. First, not once in her life had she ever had any inclination whatsoever to seek out a male. Then, after meeting a tall, dark, and dangerous vampire, she was having a fit to get the male inside her. Her face colored in shame.

Eden was offended by his desertion, but mostly she was disappointed. She finally experienced something wonderful, only to have it ripped away.

The constriction in her chest was one she hadn't felt in years. She felt inadequate. Her feminine wiles, what little she possessed, had not been enough to keep the male who claimed she was his fated mate.

The cicatrice answered with its reassuring power, telling her she was incorrect. He had ardently participated, done things to her to ensure she was satisfied. The problem must be something else.

Picturing his tortured face took away some of the sting. She considered going to look for him, but with his ability to teleport, he could be anywhere.

Moreover, her clothing was destroyed. Leaving the room naked was not an option. At least her favorite boots were still intact.

Eden leaned forward to remove them and winced. She was a little sore. Ignoring the slight irritation from his brief penetration, she unzipped her boots and put them next to the fireplace.

She gathered what was left of her clothing and threw it into the flames. Eden used her magic to make sure the fire burned hot enough to turn the rags into ash. She left on the glove, no longer trusting a soul-bond was in her immediate future.

Several drops of blood, mixed with her own fluids, trickled down the inside of her thigh. She watched as it slowly inched down her leg, reflecting the glint of light from the flames.

Mesmerized, she watched until it reached the floor. It reminded her of the room's ornamentation. Dark. Morose. Fitting of a being known as Heartless.

Eden found it perplexing how an act which had wrenched nothing but pleasure from her body had also caused minor damage. She had been in such ecstasy, she'd felt nothing else. Not until he'd ported away from her.

With nothing else to do, Eden went into the bathing chamber. It was old-fashioned. Fortunately, it did have a system of running water and stones for heating. Though, elementals who could control fire had no need of heated stones.

She filled the bathing pool, which was too large to be called a tub. It was square, with stone steps on all four sides leading down to deeper water. If Viktor was standing in the center, the water would be up to his chest.

Around the edges were various soaps and sponges sitting in expensive-looking dishes. There were far too many for one person. Just like his bedroom, his bath was opulent.

Once the water level was high enough, she removed the glove, put both hands into the water, and pushed heat down into the pool. She continued until steam rose off the surface. Then she lowered her body into the delicious warmth.

As she washed, she imagined Viktor returning and joining her. She wanted his hands on her again, despite his earlier behavior. She hated herself a little for it.

It would have been easier for Eden if he'd spoken, communicating whatever had spooked him. Instead, he said nothing and she was left to make sense of it on her own.

She felt a headache coming on. They always came when she was close to losing herself to her emotions. Her father believed it was due to the tension that resulted from never allowing herself to feel what she should.

With the evidence of their activities washed away, Eden drained the pool and pulled air currents to dry her hair. She had control over more than fire, though, her father had advised her to never disclose all that she could do.

Eden put the glove back on, feeling exposed without any other clothing. She entered Viktor's dressing room and took one of his shirts. It swallowed her, but it covered down to her knees, so it would do.

Rolling up the sleeves, she walked back to the fire, hoping to find a book on the mantel or something to keep her occupied. She stepped in something cold and wet. It was the remnants from earlier.

Eden looked at the chair, but the fabric was too dark to tell if it, too, was wet. She ran her hand over the fabric and felt a miniscule amount of dampness. Her fingers itched, as if they wanted to burn it away.

She returned to the bathing chamber and brought out a damp cloth with a bit of soap on it. She scrubbed the rug until the stain was no longer visible, then she cleaned the chair.

The white cloth now had a slight discoloration. Soiled, but not ruined. *How fitting*.

Not wanting any trace of whatever had upset Viktor lying around, she threw it in the fire and watched it burn.

# Chapter 11

"More," Viktor snapped, reaching for the next in line.

Sasha. This one he'd fed from often. He'd taken the vein of six already, but still his hunger rode him hard.

This female was the smallest of the lot, with a mane of light brunette. It reminded him of Eden's. Her hair was up, so he wouldn't have to hold it aside. This was good. He should have told the others to pin up their locks.

He also should have warned them they'd be denied climax. He was guilty enough for seeking them out in the first place. He would not add to the betrayal by bestowing the same pleasure reserved for his sieva.

One by one, he brought them to the brink. He fed until they were close and pushed them aside. Viktor sensed their frustration, but it was nothing compared to his own.

His cicatrice scorched painfully, as if screaming at him to stop. *Where was the tenacious mark's soothing balm now?* his inner voice mocked.

Viktor would not cease until he'd dampened his need. He'd feed from a thousand, if he had to. He would not return to Eden until he had some semblance of control.

He wiped his mouth, clearing away what was left from the last feeding. As his fingers drifted past his nostrils, the tangy aroma of his sieva shocked his senses.

His eyes gleamed. His shaft swelled painfully under the constricting fabric of his clothing. For once, he was refusing sex while feeding. He hadn't even considered it with these poor substitutes for what he truly wanted.

Now that a trace of sweet Eden was in his lungs he felt crazed, his body demanding release after that first taste of his mate. He bent Sasha over the bed and viciously bit into her neck.

She cried out and he closed his eyes, picturing Eden beneath him. Viktor ground his erection into Sasha's backside as he fed from her artery.

Sasha moaned and held onto his hips, encouraging his movements. A handful of shallow thrusts and he knew something was not right. His palm fired electric bolts of lightning up his arm towards his heart. The pain jarred his senses, bringing him back to reality.

He swallowed what was in his mouth, grimacing. The taste was wrong. The taste was not that of his sweet Eden. Viktor withdrew his fangs, backing away in a stupor.

It wasn't working. He'd imprudently believed he could be satisfied by the blood others. Sasha pushed off the bed until she was upright, smoothing down her dress. Viktor pointed towards the remaining females.

"Out," he commanded.

Sasha's lips quivered before she bowed her head and ran towards the group. They fled the room, leaving him alone in his misery. He sat on the cushioned bench near the bed, with his head in his hands. He was losing his damned mind.

Not long after, the door opened and Yuri, his lone advisor, entered.

"Viktor?" he said in his abnormally low voice, the one Viktor trusted above all others.

When Viktor and Yuri were young, someone had teased Yuri for his demon-like tone. Viktor knocked the aggressor unconscious and the pair's alliance was forged.

Viktor didn't acknowledge his friend.

"Are you alright?" Yuri tried again.

The King raised his head and Yuri knitted his brow. Viktor's eyes were unusually bright, his hair in complete disarray. His shirt was untucked, and blood was smeared across his face.

Yuri reached into his pocket and pulled out a handkerchief. He held it in front of Viktor, who, begrudgingly, snatched it and wiped his mouth and face.

Viktor never looked anything other than totally put-together. He'd never been reckless or driven by impulse. He was most often cold towards others, almost incapable of bringing himself to care for anything or anyone. Yuri knew otherwise, but the kingdom did not.

He also never came to the Komora. He sent for his females to be brought to his feeding room. Always.

"What's going on?" Yuri tried again.

103

Viktor gave a humorless laugh and held up his left palm, the silver glow brighter than ever.

"Well, that certainly explains things," Yuri mumbled.

He shut the door behind him and then sat on the bench next to Viktor.

"Where is she? Your sieva?"

"How do you know I've actually found her?"

"Because your cicatrice is practically burning a hole in your hand. You know once you've touched her you can't stop it."

Viktor scrubbed his face with both palms.

"I didn't. I mean, I touched her, but I did not touch her mark."

"Did you feed from her?"

"Not exactly."

Yuri shook his head. "Care to explain what that means?"

"A drop was all, just enough for a taste. It wasn't intentional." Viktor had no intention of sharing the actual intimate details with anyone, not even Yuri.

Yuri leaned forward, putting his elbows on his knees. He noticed Viktor's body was shaking, his hands clenched. His friend was wound so tight he was about to detonate from the pressure.

"You need to finish the soul-bond, Viktor."

"I don't think I can."

"If this is about Bianca—"

"No. It has nothing to do with her, Yuri. You are not to bring her up again, especially not in front of Eden."

"Eden? Your sieva's name is Eden?"

Viktor nodded.

"I don't believe I've met any female by that name."

"You wouldn't have. She is King Edward's oldest daughter."

Yuri covered his eyes, as if the information gave him a headache. He understood the complexity of Viktor's situation. Unfortunately, the King was in the midst of something that could be neither stopped nor postponed. There was only one way forward.

"Where is she?"

"In our bed chamber."

"Go back to her, Viktor. Finish what you've started. This," he pointed to Viktor's shivering body, "will only get worse. The longer you let it go, the more likely you are to do real damage to her."

"That's why I am here. I lost control and thought if I fed until sated I would be able to go back to her and ease her into it."

Yuri chortled at his King's foolhardy plan. As a mated male himself, he knew more of what to expect. It had been a hundred years since the last sieva pair had found one another. It seemed King Viktor had forgotten the pitfalls of the cicatrice's will.

"You know the cicatrice will burn, will push you to feed, until you have gorged on your sieva's blood."

"Yes. I know. I only meant to take the edge off. She is an elemental. Tiny. I'm liable to kill her!"

Yuri laughed again. "Impossible. Eden is yours, Viktor. She is the only thing, the only being, in this world created just for you. You could never get that far gone, not where she is concerned. Your fated mate would not be one who was incapable of handling you, or your ... requirements."

Viktor knew this, had even acknowledged it earlier to himself. But he wasn't thinking rationally, not since he'd swallowed that first drop.

"You have too much faith in me, Yuri."

"No, I trust Fate. The Goddess has blessed you, Viktor. You'd best embrace it. The cicatrice will not steer you wrong."

"Hasn't it? It's supposed to calm me, to help me control my emotions during this frenzy. Yet all I'm getting from it are burns and a drive to feed."

"Exactly. That is what happens once you have consumed your sieva's blood. The cicatrice becomes relentless, pushing you to madness until the bond is complete. Another's blood will do nothing for you now. Has it really been so long that you have forgotten what every vampire has been taught?"

Viktor dropped his head.

"It would seem so," he lamented, regretting his rash deeds.

"Go back to your room, Viktor. Don't come out until tomorrow. Or the next day. I'll sent food and sundries up later."

Viktor stood, and Yuri followed.

"Could you send someone to the temple to gather Eden's things? She was visiting with her father. That is how I found her."

"I will do it immediately."

Viktor took one step, then looked over his shoulder.

"How did you know I was in here?"

"One of the females came to my office after you pushed her out the door. You scared the hell out of her and she asked me to come immediately. You're never out of control, so I knew something was off."

"Hmm," he hummed, holding up his unsteady hand. "Yes, I dare say something was off. Thank you, Yuri," he bowed to his advisor.

"Of course, Sire, 'twas nothing," Yuri sputtered, unused to Viktor's gratitude.

Viktor made to open the door when Yuri put his arm on his shoulder.

"Might I suggest you port from this room instead of walking through the Komora?"

That was probably wise. He'd left seven females aching for more. It wasn't vanity speaking, it was simply what happened during a feeding.

"Agreed. You should invite some of the soldiers to tend the females. I will find you when I am finished with Eden."

With that, Viktor ported away, leaving Yuri to carry out his instructions. For the first time in a century, Yuri was concerned for his King.

# Chapter 12

Not wanting to startle his mate, Viktor ported to the balcony where he could see through the glass paneling. Eden was kneeling in front of the dark chair across from his own, her head bent towards the floor.

Instead of entering, he watched as she scrubbed at the rug with stiff arms, concentration and determination upon her face. The scratch of the rag sliding across the wool nettled him. Acutely.

She was erasing the resulting evidence of his touch, scouring it away and leaving no trace behind. His gut clenched when she stood and threw the cloth into the fire. It sizzled and hissed, an acerbic resonance to match his mood.

It was drizzling outside, but Viktor barely felt it. He was angry. Angry with fate for her atrocious timing. Angry with himself. Angry with Eden. The longer he stared at her, the more aggravated he became.

Though he was in the wrong, he was especially upset with his sieva. She was wiping away what he'd done to her, as if she'd meant to forget. As if she could not bear any hint of their activities.

Their passion would not be so easily forgotten. Aside from his actions in that final moment, it had been perfect. She had been perfect. She had been his, fully giving herself to him.

Eden had not shied away from him, had not acted as an innocent might. She'd accepted him. She'd wanted him—and, Goddess help him, how he wanted her in return.

Viktor opened the door and stepped inside, pausing before quietly closing it behind him. He approached her slowly, cautiously, unsure what her reaction would be when she saw him. Eden's attention remained on the flames currently consuming the cloth.

He waited, but still she did not acknowledge his presence. Viktor did not like her lack of notice. He wanted to be the center of her attention, even if it was undeserved.

Normally, he would say as much, but he was distracted by the fact she was wearing one of his shirts. No being in existence could possibly be lovelier than his sieva, or more desirable.

The silence stretched as they waited out one another. Viktor knew, if he touched her skin to skin, she would not resist. The cicatrice would compel her to respond to him.

He didn't want her to have to be compelled. He wanted Eden to *want* to touch him, to *choose* to touch him.

He would hold off as long as he could, but he needed to be close to her. In a single stride, his chest was against her shoulder. He strained to keep his arms at this sides.

"Where were you?" Her voice was almost inaudible.

"I had to leave. I was not myself, Eden."

She turned her face, glaring at him with such intensity he nearly stepped back.

"That was not what I asked."

"You do not want me to answer. Trust me," he said, bending to nuzzle her hair.

Eden turned her body and pushed with both hands to back him away. Viktor did not budge, but the message was clear enough.

"You mean to deny me?" he asked, disbelief and anxiety gnawing at him. He had never been denied.

"I can smell another's perfume on you."

Guilt, dark and ugly, ate away his other emotions. It was a dangerous thing for one such as he to allow. The last time he'd felt it, he'd behaved recklessly.

It had been a mistake fleeing to the Komora, but he did it for her. If he explained, would she understand? He wasn't used to explaining anything to anyone.

"Eden—"

"What was her name? Did you enjoy it? Did she?" she asked rapidly.

Viktor ran his hand through his hair.

"Did my ... taste make you stop? Was it so abhorrent you would seek another to replace it?"

Viktor was appalled Eden could think such a thing. What made it worse was there was no anger in her voice. She was hurt. He had hurt her by leaving. He had known it would, but seeing what he'd left in the wake of his departure tugged at the place where his heart should have been.

"No, don't be ridiculous."

"Then why did you leave?"

"I told you."

"Not being yourself tells me nothing. I do not know you. You are a stranger to me. But I wanted to know you. I felt something the first time I saw you, Viktor. When you declared I was yours, I knew it to be true. I did not question it. I came here willingly. I let you ..."

Eden couldn't bring herself to describe what he'd done, so she motioned towards the chair.

"I thought being your sieva meant—well, that it meant something far different than it does."

Viktor stepped towards Eden and she backed away. He growled at her retreat.

"I am the King of Prajna. I am in control of myself at all times. I do not *feel*. I do not act on emotions. I do not behave in this manner. Not ever, Eden. The cicatrice is driving me to tear open your neck and feast upon your lifeblood. The second your essence hit my mouth I wasn't sure I would be able to stop myself. I would sooner take my own life than harm my mate. Do not penalize me for protecting you."

"Protecting me? You ran to someone else for my own protection? If this is how you shield me, then I do not want to be protected."

His glimmering irises grew brighter. She did not want his protection? She'd have it whether she wanted it or not. He reached for her again and she sidestepped him. He could easily get to her, but they needed to resolve this before he did.

"Why are you resisting me?" he demanded.

"Is that a serious question?"

"Of course, it is."

"I. Can. Smell. Her. On. You," she seethed, her temper building with each word.

Viktor lowered his eyes, as if to hide his shame. Eden hadn't expected any sort of submission or acknowledgement of guilt. She didn't think hardened men capable of it.

His reaction was short-lived. Viktor raised his face, now turned stony, effectively erasing his indignity.

Whatever he'd done, he felt bad about it. But his pride would not allow him to admit his mistake. Eden would not let it go.

"Where were you, Viktor?" she asked again.

Viktor threw his hands in the air. His little witch was beyond infuriating. If she wanted truth, she would get it. He would test her resolve to be his sooner than he would have liked.

"I went to the Komora."

"The Komora," she repeated, contemplating his meaning.

"Do you know what a Komora is?"

"No."

"It's a pavilion, home to hundreds of Prajna. All female. My father built it for all his mistresses, his favorite ones that would do anything he asked. After his death, I dismissed his harem."

Some sense of relief entered her chest. It was instantly annihilated with his next words.

"Then I replaced his with my own. When I'm hungry, I send for them. When I want sex, I send for them. Every single one of them has been in my feeding room to service me. Most of them to give me both blood and sex. I take at least one every day. That's why there are so many in the Komora. My appetites are large, and it takes that many to keep me satiated."

Eden's eyes bulged, her hand flew to her clavicle. Hundreds? She could never take the place of so many. Had Fate thought she would voluntarily be one of hundreds? The cicatrice eased her and she silently cursed it.

"The second I knew I might harm you, I went there to feed. I thought if I consumed enough, it would take the edge off, so I could be what you needed. I only went there for blood, Eden."

He moved towards her, until their bodies were an inch apart.

"Normally, one feeding would suffice. I was so unhinged, I fed from seven. I assure you I had no interest in bedding any of them. Not when you'd been so perfect. *Are* so perfect."

Eden's hurt lessened the more he spoke. She could easily hear the truth in his declaration. Worry laced his words, evidence of his torment.

Viktor hadn't gone to his harem to couple. He'd fed. She didn't like it, but she understood it wasn't done to upset her or to betray her. He was a male losing control, desperate to regain it.

They would need to revisit the Komora issue later. For now, she was willing to let it go.

Her cicatrice pulled so hard she stumbled into him. Viktor caught her easily and his face softened. He lifted Eden until she was eye level. Her lust had her wrapping her legs around him.

"You didn't resist its pull this time, *mala vestica*."

"No, I didn't. Perhaps now you'll know to answer me honestly."

Viktor chuffed. "We will not be ourselves until we finish this."

Eden could feel small tremors moving through his body as he labored to restrain himself. He held himself back, doing so for her benefit.

"Promise me you won't leave again," she said.

He looked indecisive and she knew he was warring with himself. Eden wanted to allay his fears. She was not as breakable as he believed.

"I am not powerless, Viktor. If at any time I sense danger, or if you harm me in any way, I will set you on fire."

Viktor let out a hearty laugh and her stomach fluttered. His hands tightened around her.

"Yes, well, that would certainly get my attention."

Eden nodded towards the bed, but Viktor shook his head.

"No, little witch. Not yet. There is something else I want to do first."

# Chapter 13

Viktor carried his mate into the bathing chamber. He sat her on the vanity and went to the stones to make sure they were heating in the open flames of the pit next to the bath. He had no issue with immersing in cold water, but he wanted this to be an enjoyable experience for Eden.

He opened the large spout and water rushed into the pool. It would fill fast and he would be able to wash away the perfume Eden had detected on his clothing. The lingering scent made him uneasy and he wanted it gone.

As the bath filled, Viktor stood in front of his mate. He watched her as she watched him slide off his shoes, then his stockings.

Eden wet her lips when Viktor removed his shirt and threw it aside. He was a work of art, a giant marble sculpture come to life.

Every part of his physique was incredible—and large. His pale skin stretched tight across sinewy muscles shaped to perfection. The dips and curves were a landscape Eden wanted to explore with her touch.

Viktor's broad shoulders dwarfed everything around him. They held the weight of arms that could easily crush her.

His chiseled chest gave way to defined abdominals. A smattering of dark hair trailed below his navel and disappeared behind his trousers. The large bulge in front had her coughing nervously.

Viktor grinned at the panicky look on Eden's face. She would soon learn not to fear what was so uncomfortably hard for her. His throbbing flesh would give her nothing but gratification, especially when his fangs were piercing her supple flesh.

He dropped his pants and Eden looked away.

"Give me your eyes, my sieva."

Little by little, she did as he ordered. They drifted from his feet, up his powerful legs, which he was steadily widening.

Viktor grabbed his erection and stroked it leisurely. It was the most erotic thing Eden had ever witnessed, had ever fantasized. She wanted to know what it felt like in her own hand.

Abruptly, he ceased his motion and Eden made a small squeak. She wanted to watch.

"Soon," he promised. It would have to be soon. His hold over himself wouldn't last much longer.

Viktor went to check the stones again, dying to get them both in the water, to get his hands on her once more.

"I can heat the water. If you would like," she offered, hopping down from the vanity.

"By all means, warm our bath, Sieva."

"I already washed."

"I know. Next time, I'll be the one to clean you. You're not to wash it away again. Understood?"

"Of course, my lord," she replied in a saccharine-sweet tone. "Unless you disappear on me. Then, who knows what I'll be inclined to do."

He ignored her little barb, curious how she would heat the pool. Eden knelt and placed her hands in the water, shooting her energies down into the pool. The water bubbled and fizzed.

The shirt she was wearing shifted and Viktor caught a glimpse of what was underneath. He tore his eyes away and focused on the water, lest he mount her from behind.

Eden didn't shoot actual flames underwater, but the magic that produced fire still pushed out the same amount of energy. It was more than enough to boil the liquid, if she chose. If the vampire continued with his overlord attitude, she just might cook him alive.

Viktor found her use of magic just as stimulating as the sight of her bared under his shirt. When she withdrew her hands, the water was steaming.

Viktor took her elbow, helping her stand. "Raise your arms."

Eden put both hands in the air and Viktor pulled the shirt over her head, dropping it beside her feet. He picked her up and waded down into the deepest part of the pool, pleased she didn't shy away from him. He moved her body so they were face to face.

119

Eden automatically spread her legs to straddle his waist, like it was the most natural thing in the world. She slid her arms up his chest, over his shoulders, and encircled his neck.

Her nudity hadn't made her uncomfortable. His nudity hadn't made her anything other than aroused. She felt a sense of belonging—of rightness—wrapped around the Vampire King.

It could be the result of the cicatrice, but it mattered not. She'd felt Viktor's pull the second she'd laid eyes on him, the first male to ever spark her desire.

If her attraction to him hadn't been a sign, then she had to consider their marks. She didn't believe in coincidences. The cicatrices were perfect matches, created by forces beyond her knowledge or comprehension.

Even if she mistrusted her new libido, all her logic pointed to the evidence that she was Viktor's sieva. Eden would not borrow trouble by fighting it, and she would never question the Goddess above.

Viktor kissed Eden chastely, a reward for her boldness, then whispered, "Hold your breath."

Her nose crinkled in confusion, so adorable he almost changed his mind. Almost.

Eden was suddenly pulled under the surface. Just as fast, they shot out of the water. She wiped at the water streaming down her face, giggling.

"What was that for?" she accused, trying to sound indignant.

"That was for how you spoke to me. I didn't like it."

Eden snorted, causing Viktor to grin at her impish and unladylike manner. People did not speak to him in such a way. And no one questioned him. Ever.

He didn't know why he liked it now—or why he was smiling. Viktor was being truthful about Eden's words from earlier. He did not appreciate her attitude, and he certainly did not like the reminder he had disappeared on her.

"Yes, well, I didn't like how you spoke to me, either, Viktor."

She was still smiling, and it did things to him he could not put into words. Needing to occupy them both before he divested her of her virginity in the bathing pool, he moved to the edge and grabbed one of the soaps.

"Wash it away, Eden."

Eden's smile waned, recalling what "it" was. She made no move to take the bar from his hand.

Viktor waited her out.

She bit her lip, drawing his eyes to her mouth. A thrill danced along her spine, feeling sexually powerful when she'd been anything but all these years. Determined, she took the soap, meaning to lather it between her hands, but her glove was still on.

Viktor could tell she wasn't sure what to do, was likely afraid to expose her cicatrice after he'd all but ordered her to keep it away from him.

"Remove the glove," he told her.

"Are—are you sure?" Washing him, she believed she could handle. Soul-bonding in the bath was far more intimidating.

Viktor nodded, feeling the gravity of what they were going to do. It was more than blood and sex. Today he would bind his soul to his sieva. To Eden.

He'd never thought he would want it, had previously believed it an inconvenience, a curse. It interfered with his long-standing obligation to his dearly departed friend, Dmitri. Now that Eden was in his arms, Viktor could not deny it was what he wanted.

He would have his mate, be bound to her, and still fulfill his end of the contract he'd agreed to so long ago. He believed Dmitri would have understood, having been bound to his own sieva for hundreds of years. Though, he did not look forward to explaining it to his mate.

Eden slipped her hand out of the glove, expecting it to force itself upon his skin. She observed it closely, but the cicatrice only hummed slightly. She pitched the glove across the room and rubbed the soap between her hands.

Viktor groaned when Eden began working the soap into a lather against his skin with her fingers. She started at his head and massaged down his neck, tenderly. Suds dripped down his face and she wiped them away from his eyes.

"You should go under to rinse before it stings."

He ignored her words and brought her mouth to his. He couldn't be so close to her and not kiss her. As his lips worshipped hers, he slowly lowered them below the surface.

Under the water, they continued their kiss. Eden rubbed his hair, getting rid of the lather. When they resurfaced, she clung to him, undulating against his front.

The crown of his erection was poking her bottom. She arched her hips away until there was enough space for it lay in between them. Once it was where she wanted it, she ground against it, shamelessly.

Viktor's fangs extended, and he grazed her throat with one. She mewled and rocked frantically, daring him to do what he wanted.

She needed him inside her. Brazenly, she reached for his shaft and he flexed at the feel of her small fist around him. She positioned the head where she wanted it most and tried to lower herself.

They were both panting. Eden licked at the water trickling down his skin and nipped at his shoulder, feeling as though she should bite it, being encouraged by the cicatrice to draw his blood. So, she did.

Eden broke the skin and Viktor's fingers dug into her ribs. He was probably bruising her. He'd never been bitten before and struggled with his response to it. He remained taut, trying to stop himself from climaxing before he'd even fully entered her body.

The small amount of blood she ingested affected her greatly. His little mate keened and cried, working her hips to get more of him inside her as she licked at his shoulder, which was already healing. He didn't know how he was able to deny the urge to yank her down hard onto his cock.

"Lift your hand, Eden."

She disregarded his command, continuing her quest for more of him. She really was perfect. Viktor loved how needy she was, but he required her attention. He would not force their hands to touch. It had to be her choice.

His iron grip stilled her hips.

"Please don't stop," Eden pouted.

"Eden. Lift your hand."

Once his words registered she opened her eyes. Viktor's left hand was lifted out of the water, his palm facing her. There was no reluctance in her movement, as she reached up to join her cicatrice to his.

The power of their hands finally coming together rocked through both their bodies. Unimaginable bliss filled their souls. It was as pure as it was magnificent.

Unable to hold back any longer, Viktor ported them to the bed and drove his cock inside the rest of the way. Eden shrieked, coming so hard around him she drew out his seed.

Viktor forcefully turned her head and struck hard, suckling on the divine lifeforce of his mate. His chest rumbled with possessiveness as he thrust into her heat, launching her into another orgasm.

He drank until he'd emptied the last drop of himself deep inside her tight channel. He licked the puncture marks, using his saliva's healing power to close them. Prajna healed quickly, so he'd never had to perform the act on another. He would gladly lick Eden's wounds daily, and then some.

Viktor put his forehead to hers, listening to her erratic breathing, feeling for the bond. It was like a thread tethering her to him. It wasn't visible, but he could feel it. Strong and true, it would tie them together for eternity. Only death could sever it.

"How do you feel, *moj vestica*?" My witch, because now she was truly his.

"I—I don't know if I have a word for it."

He smiled against her skin, in total agreement. There was no word for it.

"Are you sore?" he asked, lifting his head enough so he could gage her emotions.

"Surprisingly, no. I feel good. Wonderful, actually. At least, in the physical sense."

Eden had always presumed sex would be painful, more an obligatory experience to be endured than the fevered whirlwind she'd just experienced.

Viktor kissed her throat and licked the shell of her ear, making her squirm. His cock flexed in response. He wanted to ask her about the bond, to know exactly what she felt, but he was still cocooned inside her slick heat—his new favorite place to be.

"We have things to discuss, but I cannot concentrate in this position," he admitted, nestling his face into the crook of her neck.

She couldn't see it, but she could feel her soul touching his. She wondered if they weren't physically touching, if it would still feel the same. She did not ever want to lose the sense they were connected so completely.

Stranger or not, she was his and he was hers. Their joining had been centuries in the making. If the rest of their lives together was a fraction as wonderful as their coupling, Eden would thank the Goddess every day for such a blessing.

Eden was quite comfortable where she was, delighting in the feel of his weight on top of her. But Viktor was right, they did need to talk. Despite being bonded, they knew hardly anything about one another.

Plus, Eden had questions. About the bond. About her role in Prajna. Would he be willing to do a binding ceremony, as Nora and Kellan had? They were soul-bonded together for eternity, so he may feel a ceremony was unnecessary. The Prajna might not even perform marriage rites.

Despite wanting to stay exactly as they were, she offered a more practical option.

"Do you want to get up? We can go over by the fire again."

"No, Eden," he murmured, nipping her shoulder. "I do not want to go over by the fire."

"Then what do you want?"

Viktor rolled his hips, effectively ending the conversation. He fully intended to keep her in their bed until morning.

# Chapter 14

The ocean breeze brushed gently across Eden's skin, moving stray hairs that tickled her face. Viktor had opened the large doors to cool the room shortly before they fell asleep.

She struggled to open her eyes, fighting fatigue. Viktor made love to her long into the night, insatiable in his lust. She had been just as hungry for him, matching his appetite until she could no longer move.

After sating themselves during their initial frenzy, they lost some of the tumultuous rush they'd experienced prior to completing the soul-bond. Eden had been just as turned on, but she had a handle on her mind. She was able to appreciate every kiss, every touch, every murmur of affection.

Sometimes Viktor was demanding. Other times he was gentle, treating her how she imagined a female would be treated by her beloved. She enjoyed both sides of him and wanted to relive every moment.

Eden snuggled closer into Viktor's side, inhaling and sighing contentedly. His spicy scent was an aphrodisiac to her. She couldn't help but slip one leg over his, rubbing it up and down his long limb.

"My sieva awakes in the most wonderful of ways," he said, his voice grumbly, still edged with sleepiness.

Eden kissed his chest and finally pried open her eyes. His were glowing brightly, watching her fixedly.

"Yes, well, you've given me incentive to awake favorably, haven't you?"

His mouth quirked. "Indeed. Come closer, Sieva."

Eden laughed. "I'm not sure I can get any closer."

"I disagree," he argued, pulling her up his body so he could kiss her mouth.

Eden shifted, covering his body with her own. Her legs bent to plant her knees on the bed. She could feel his hard length as she pressed her hips into his.

He groaned, pushing his tongue into her mouth and wrapping his arms around her back. She was slick, gliding her wetness along his manhood. His hunger for her hadn't diminished in the slightest.

While the soul-bonding had taken away some of his mental instabilities, it failed miserably in lessening the need to be inside her. From the feel of her, Eden was just as far gone.

He flipped them so she was on her back, pinned beneath his weight. She wiggled under him.

"Patience, Eden."

Viktor traced his tongue down the column of her throat and across her chest. He swirled it around her nipple before pulling it into his mouth. Eden arched her back and he bit her without breaking the skin.

His right hand slid up the inside of her thigh, towards her center. Viktor grazed his knuckles over her soft vulnerable flesh. Today he was going to spend time tasting her, as he should have done last night.

The bonding had been too frenzied and he'd not allowed his mouth near her mound as he had when he'd broken through her virginal wall in the chair. He didn't want to remind either of them of his lapse in judgement when he'd ported away.

Viktor was willing to ease her into his more aggressive preferences, but, having experienced her ability to endure his uncompromising desires, he would now put his mouth wherever he pleased.

He continued his path lower, growing more and more impatient by the second. He could smell her sweet nectar. It demanded his full attention.

Viktor lowered his mouth over her cleft and blew hot air across her skin. Eden whimpered and he did it again. He watched her nipples pinch even tighter as goosebumps broke out along her flesh.

He used his thumbs to open her. The sight had him grinding his hips into the bed as he licked long wet swipes up and down the length of her.

Over and over, he slowly drove her mad. Eden reached down to his head, pulling on his hair.

"More," she panted.

Viktor rarely allowed a female to dictate when she came, but he wanted her drenched before he entered her channel. He obliged and sucked on her bud.

"More!" she shouted, her climax just out of reach.

"As you wish," he said, sinking his fangs into the fleshy part of her mound and rapidly flicking his tongue.

Eden screamed, as waves of rapture radiated out through every cell in her body. Her limbs seized, frozen in ecstasy, a tidal wave of decadent palpitations destroying all sense of reality. All she knew was the exploding white light of pleasure.

She was so deep in her haze, she failed to notice Viktor's movements as he moved slowly up her body. She opened her eyes when she felt his blunt head nudge her opening.

He plunged deep, then held himself still, waiting for her to adjust.

"Kiss me," she purred.

Viktor growled and crashed his mouth to hers, taking her with abandon. He'd always prided himself on holding out for hours. With Eden, he had to fight it back, as he had when he was first introduced to sex.

Her nails dug into his back as she tightened around him. Unable to hold back, he exploded deep inside his mate, shouting into the pillow next to her head. He continued his thrusts until he'd come to completion.

They remained entwined, panting from exertion. Once he felt her heart return to a normal cadence, he rolled them to the side.

Viktor could smell her exhaustion when he burrowed his face into the back of her neck.

"Sleep, *moj vestica*," he said, releasing a little of his power of hypnosis. He would never be able to alter her mind because she was his mate, but he could nudge it a bit.

Her hand squeezed his and she allowed herself to succumb to her fatigue.

\* \* \*

Viktor lifted the tray of food sitting outside the door. Someone had left it a few minutes ago and he was slow to retrieve it. He hadn't wanted to leave the comfort of their bed, but Eden would be famished when she awoke.

The need to care for her, to see to her wellbeing, was surprising. Viktor had never been the nurturing type. Inexplicably, he wanted her to rely upon him, to count on him for things.

As quietly as he could, he set the tray on the small dining table to the side of the fireplace. His mate was still in a deep sleep and he wanted her to rest peacefully. Judging from the stirrings within his body just from looking at her, she'd need her strength again later.

He was debating the merits of tying Eden to the bed when the fragrance of lilacs wafted into the room. Viktor straightened, irate the female would dare port to his balcony.

"If you'd like to keep your head attached to your shoulders, I suggest you not step one foot inside."

He turned to see a very irritated Bianca paused in mid step, just beyond the balcony doors. No one was allowed in his private quarters. She knew better than to even consider entering without an invitation.

The female vampire's eyes flicked to the bed and he stepped into her line of sight, blocking her view of Eden's sleeping form.

Bianca clucked her tongue. "My word, Viktor, you've been busy while I was away."

He stalked towards the intruder and she quickly retreated to the railing. Though Bianca stood defiant, he could smell her fear. She should fear him. This was a trespass he would not soon forgive.

Viktor looked once more to his sieva to make sure she was still asleep, then gently closed the balcony doors behind him.

"You are very lucky you are Dmitri's daughter, Bianca. If you were anyone else you'd be dead."

She smiled seductively, angling her hip in subtle invitation. "Then I suppose it's a good thing I am so important to you."

His jaw clenched. She had always been such a spoiled child. She was now over a century old and not much had changed.

"*Dmitri* was important to me. *You* are nothing more than an obligation."

She barely contained the flinch. If he thought her capable of it, he would have interpreted the motion as pain. Recovering fast, her lips pursed and her eyes hardened.

Bianca was not as special as she led herself to believe. Viktor never hid the fact that he fed from and bedded others, that she would never be enough to satiate him. She may have been a highly desirable Prajna, but he'd never intended to treat her as he would a sieva.

He hadn't bothered to hide his intention to keep the Komora fully stocked after he was wed, not even when Dmitri made his request. Until Eden, he'd never considered himself capable of wanting and keeping only one female.

Viktor was always frank with Bianca, but rarely were his words purposefully cruel. Unfortunately, it seemed she needed to hear them.

If he thought she didn't know what Eden was to him, he wouldn't be so hard on her. But Bianca was cunning, and even more vindictive. There was only one reason she would dare to port to his balcony, something he had forbidden the entire kingdom from doing.

Shortly after he'd taken the throne, he had made an oath there would be radical penalties should anyone enter his private quarters who was not welcome. He had been in desperate need of distance from others for quite a long time. Eventually, his solitude became habit.

Content to be alone, he'd never made it known who was welcome, aside from Yuri and the maids. Bianca knew she should not be here. In fact, he'd told her more than

133

once the feeding room was the only place he would tend her.

"What, pray tell, did you hope to accomplish by defying my decree and sneaking into my chamber?"

"I haven't seen you in weeks. I—I missed you."

"Right," he scoffed. "You really thought I would welcome you? Now?"

"I didn't think I'd be quite so *un*welcome."

She was dancing around the wording of his vow. *How clever—and asinine*, he mused.

Bianca leaned against the stone railing and shrugged. Her crossed arms amplified her bosom, but, for once, he wasn't tempted.

She'd always been his favorite plaything, always willing to submit and do anything he asked. He'd thoroughly enjoyed her curves whenever it struck his fancy. One of her best qualities was she never said no, even when he wanted more than one female at once.

Countless times he'd fed from her vein while inside her body—or another's. He'd been enticed by her white hair, a rarity in the Eastland. She was considered a great beauty among his people.

Standing here, he couldn't remember why he'd ever believed such a thing, not when perfection was lying under the duvet on his bed.

"Last chance, Bianca. I suggest you be nothing less than honest."

"Fine," she huffed. "You sent me off on that ridiculous errand to visit those drab villages. I mean, really, Viktor? They were so ... sad. Their inability to reproduce is not my problem. What did you expect me to do? Provide comfort to them? Offer hope of some sort?"

He took a menacing step closer, fisting his hands to keep from encircling her neck and squeezing.

"I expected you to do your duty to the crown. You want to be a queen so badly? Act like one."

"I did!" she hissed. "I can play pretend with the best of them. I did what you asked to the best of my ability."

Viktor knew that ability was inadequate. He'd meant to teach her a lesson in compassion. Where he came across as hard and unforgiving, he'd wanted a queen who was the opposite. It seemed Bianca learned nothing other than how to pretend like she gave a damn.

"Imagine my surprise when I returned and heard the news you'd locked yourself in your quarters with a female, especially when no one, not even *I*, had ever been allowed inside."

"Let's not dance around this, Bianca. You know what she is to me."

"Yes, I do. And you know I have no intention of being set aside. I want to know what you intend to do with her."

"What I do or don't do with my sieva is none of your concern."

Bianca glowered, her eyes brightening with emotion.

"You can't possibly think the witch will want to stay with you after—"

Her voice cut off as she struggled to remain as still as possible. Surprise and fright drifted out of every pore.

Viktor's claws were shallowly embedded in her throat. Her blood beaded slowly, the sweet scent, the one he used to find so alluring, was now turning his stomach.

"Listen carefully, Bianca, for I will only say this once. You shall never speak ill of her, in or out of my presence."

A look of shock froze on her face. The brutality she understood. The regard for another's reputation, she did not. Viktor was The Heartless King of Prajna. He was negligent with others' emotions, especially those from whom he fed. *How could he possibly care for the witch?*

He leaned closer, keeping his voice low.

"You will not seek her out. You will not speak to her directly unless she allows it. If she enters a room, you will vacate it immediately if you are incapable of showing her anything other than respect. You will say absolutely nothing that would upset her in any way. This means you are forbidden from ever speaking of that cursed contract in front of her. Understood?"

She nodded slightly, her movement restricted by his merciless hold. Viktor retracted his claws and took one step backwards. He shook his hands to the sides in disgust, splattering small amounts of blood on the stone.

"Heed my warning, Bianca. If you do not, I swear upon my name I will make you regret it."

The magic of the oath snapped into place. He was now bound to follow through or face crippling consequences. All vampiric contracts, when sworn as such, were mystically enforced, linked to their hypnotic powers.

If Bianca did not obey him, he would be compelled to act in a way which would make her feel regret. Viktor supposed only the threat of death could elicit remorse from the female.

Bianca's shoulders hunched and water gathered in her eyes. Viktor couldn't be sure, but he swore he detected an ounce of sadness under all her fury. She shook with rage. She was smart enough not to act on it.

If Bianca thought he would have welcomed the sight of her after he'd found and bonded with his sieva, then she knew nothing of vampire mating.

Granted, the last fated pair of Prajna had met before Bianca was born, but that was no excuse. It was drilled into children to be cautious and patient because nothing was as strong, as compelling, as a soul-bond.

One could live for centuries before his or her sieva was known. Once they met, there was no stopping the cicatrice from binding the pair together for all time.

An invisible tug pulled at his back. *Damn it.*

"Leave before I do something rash, Bianca."

She glanced at the glass doors behind him. The corner of her mouth lifted just before she ported away.

Viktor ignored the urge to go after her and turned to face his mate.

# Chapter 15

Viktor beat Eden to the glass doors, quickly opening them and stepping inside before she could see the crimson drops on the balcony. He'd felt her approach—he just wasn't sure how much she had seen or heard.

"Who was that?" she asked.

"No one," he murmured, pressing his lips to her cheek as he slid by on his way to the table where he'd left their meal. It was incredibly difficult not to put his hands on her when she was in one of his shirts.

"Try again," she said, her voice loud and clear. Eden refused to be evaded.

Viktor lifted the lids off the plates and placed them on the mantle. He meticulously arranged her place setting as he'd seen the servants do and poured them both a glass of wine.

"Please," he said, indicating the chair in front of the meal.

Eden sat stiffly, her appetite all but gone.

"Eat, *mala vestica*. You've not had sustenance in over a day."

Eden took a sip of wine and reluctantly lifted the fork. She was relieved the food looked and smelled palatable. She wasn't sure what sorts of things the Prajna consumed, aside from the obvious.

Viktor drained his goblet then refilled it. He took the seat opposite Eden and waited for her to put her fork to use.

"You eat, I'll talk."

Eden lifted what looked to be potatoes to her mouth. Though no longer hot, they were seasoned to perfection. It appeared she wouldn't be starved in Prajna.

"I apologize for the unannounced visitor. No one is allowed in these chambers, including on the balcony. It won't happen again."

She continued chewing in the silence that followed. She took two more bites, but Viktor remained mute. Swallowing, she put down her utensil.

"Eden—"

"You talk, I eat," she threw back at him.

Viktor's eyes shimmered with mirth, enjoying the way she refused to yield. She was the only being whose challenge he actually looked forward to meeting.

"Saucy female."

He said it like he'd meant it as a compliment. Despite herself, Eden flushed under the unconventional praise.

She picked up the fork and held it aloft over the plate, challenging him to continue.

Viktor bellowed a full, hearty laugh. He hadn't enjoyed time with a female like this in, well, ever. Everyone feared him and he used that fear against them. He couldn't recall the last time he'd found himself in a standoff with someone who refused to yield.

Eden grinned, loving the sound he made. It was deep and masculine. It had a rasp to it, making it sound as though it was rusty from lack of use.

"You should do that more often," she told him.

"What? Laugh?"

She nodded. "I've liked it when you've managed it. All two times."

He laughed again, the sound and feeling becoming less and less foreign. He wondered when he'd last done it. Eden was bringing out things—feelings—in him he'd long believed were dead and gone.

"Yes, well, I haven't had much in my life to laugh about," he divulged.

Eden's face fell and he waved off her concern. "Tales for another time, *moj vestica*. Let's explore one thing at a time, shall we?"

"Okay."

"Okay," he parroted, the modern term feeling alien on his tongue.

He gulped down the rest of his wine and sat the goblet on the table. He needed to pay attention to Eden's body language during his disclosure.

"The female's name is Bianca. She's the daughter of one of the few men I've ever been lucky enough to consider a friend. She, ah, lives here at Castra Nocte."

Eden dabbed her mouth with her napkin, thinking.

"With her father?" she asked.

"No."

"As a servant?"

"No."

She wet her lips. "In the Komora?"

"No."

Eden's stomach churned as she threw out suggestions and Viktor shot them down. *Use your head, Eden*, she chastised herself.

Bianca was not Viktor's mate. Vampire's only got one sieva ever and his was Eden. The knot in her gut loosened.

From the brief glimpse Eden had caught of the white-haired beauty, she could tell she'd been upset. If no one was allowed near these quarters, aside from the feeding room, what would drive her to break his rule?

The question was easy enough to answer. It was the same reason Eden had stopped short when she saw Viktor outside with another female.

Jealousy.

"She was your lover?"

"Of sorts."

"Care to explain what you mean?"

"Not really, but I will. I have been ... intimate with Bianca and I have fed from her. But she was never someone I would consider a lover. The term implies feelings, a connection of some kind. I've never experienced either with her, or any Prajna female for that matter."

Eden's heart thumped. Was Viktor implying he felt those things for someone who was not Prajna? Possibly for her?

"Of course, I feel a connection to you, Eden. We are soul-bonded. We are two halves of a whole."

Eden choked on the meat she was chewing, swiftly washing it down with her drink.

"Are you a mind reader?"

"Hardly. Your pulse altered and I could smell your adrenaline. I doubt you were getting excited over my talk of bedding Bianca."

Eden gave him a withering look.

"Yes, continue speaking of your activities with her. I so enjoy it. All females adore hearing of their male's previous conquests. By all means, go on."

His teeth clenched, annoyed with her sarcasm, but reveling in her jealousy. Viktor was tempted to pull her into his arms and kiss the scornful look away. Unfortunately, before he touched her again, he needed to get this out of the way.

"My apologies. Let me back up a bit. Dmitri was a close friend of mine. He assisted me in disposing of the madman who used to sit on this throne, and he paid for it with his life. Shortly before Dmitri's death, his sieva was murdered. His revenge motivated him to take up my cause with one stipulation. If something happened to him, his daughter would have no one. He asked me to provide for her should anything happen to him. Our agreement was sealed with magic and, when he died, she became my responsibility."

Eden shuddered. "You raised her?"

"Goddess no. I never even laid eyes upon her until she was almost forty. At her request, she remained in the town where she was born. I sent guards to protect her. Eventually, she earned unwanted attention from a variety of males, and we agreed she would be better off here."

"Yes, I can see why men would be drawn to her."

Her fork dropped loudly onto the empty plate.

"She is nothing compared to you, Eden."

Eden rolled her eyes. One blink and Viktor was kneeling in front of her, the table crashing into the wall. He cradled her head and pulled it close to his, ratcheting her pulse higher and higher.

"She is nothing. *Nothing.* You are my sieva, Eden. There is no comparison to be made. The space you fill in me could never be touched by anyone else."

His mouth crashed into hers, giving her no time to argue. She groaned, fighting to pull him as close as possible.

Viktor ported them to the bed, shredding their clothing to rags. He spent the next few hours worshipping every inch of his mate, proving over and over she was his.

\* \* \*

"So, Eden, what do you think of Castra Nocte so far?"

Eden cleared her throat, running through possible diplomatic responses to Mariana's question. Yuri's wife was amiable enough, but it seemed she was also uninformed as to where Eden had been spending her time the past few days.

"Well, the view from Viktor's balcony—"

"*Our* balcony," he corrected.

Eden refrained from rolling her eyes. She knew where that would land her if she did so again—flat on her back in their bed. This was no place to encourage Viktor to make a scene.

She and Viktor were dining with the attractive couple in a small, formal room on the main floor of the castle. It was a comfortable space and far less lavish than Viktor's personal chambers.

"The view from *our* balcony," she amended, "is stunning, and I find that I enjoy hearing the ocean in the background."

"So does Viktor," Yuri added. "It's why he moved into those quarters. The main living quarters for the King and the Queen are on the other side of Castra Nocte."

Viktor shook his head imperceptibly, hoping to steer Yuri away from the topic. Eden didn't notice. Mariana, catching Viktor's wordless meaning, put her hand atop Yuri's.

"The King's quarters are wherever he demands they be, my husband. Let us speak of more interesting topics, like commanding magic," she teased.

"You find magic interesting?" Eden asked.

"Oh, yes. What's it like?"

Eden had never pondered it. It was like asking what it was like to have two arms. All elementals had some sort of magical control of an element. They were born with it and it required little conscious thought or effort.

"I'm not sure how to answer," Eden replied. "The Prajna have magic, too. The influence of hypnosis and sealing obligations with magic, oh, and teleporting around from place to place. I imagine those are all likely the same sort of feeling."

Mariana shook her dark head. "Oh, no. Those are boring. We can't hypnotize one another very well. Only extremely powerful vampires can affect another vampire's mind, so it's become quite useless to me. And I've not made any pacts, thanks to this one's," she pointed at Yuri, "extreme paranoia."

Eden grinned at Mariana's jab. She enjoyed how the couple interacted, with warmth and humor. They weren't the cold predators she'd been taught to fear.

Even more, she appreciated the fact Viktor had someone like Yuri in his life. During their handful of quiet talks, Viktor asked all sorts of questions about Eden. He truly made an effort to get to know her.

She had many stories to tell, most of which included her family. Sadly, Viktor spoke of no one, aside from his mother and Yuri. Even then he remained reticent with information.

She detested the hints of loneliness she detected in Viktor. No one deserved to walk this life alone. Yuri had Mariana, and now Viktor had Eden.

Eden's smile widened when Yuri snapped playfully at Mariana's finger, which was still pointed in his direction.

"I would think a female could forgive her sieva when acting in her best interest," Viktor said, a tad more fervently than intended.

He was looking at Eden when he said it. She could feel his regard, like butterfly wings dancing on her skin. It happened every time she had his focus, ever since the soul-bonding.

She could feel him whenever he drew near. She wondered if she would feel anything when they were apart. He hadn't left her side other than the time on the balcony with Bianca and a few moments of privacy in the bathroom, so she'd yet to fully test it.

Viktor's words affected her. He was a proud male. He would never seek Eden's forgiveness. He would demand it. She took comfort in the fact they were able to work through the issue with Bianca expeditiously, and that he did not want Eden to be upset with him.

Eden was still jealous, of course, but Viktor had made quite a case for himself. She chose to let it go and leave Bianca in the past, where she belonged.

They still needed to discuss the Komora. As soon as she figured out the best approach to dealing with her concerns, she would broach the subject. At least she was no longer afraid he would turn to them for his needs.

"But of course, Viktor. Yuri wouldn't be able to function if he thought I was cross with him," Mariana joked, breaking Eden's rumination.

Viktor laughed at the unexpected jest. Mariana was the only person, aside from Viktor and Luka, who had ever dared make fun at Yuri's expense. With his baritone voice, many Prajna thought him half-demon with the power to compel their minds.

"Yes, well, that is the way of sievas, as you well know, my wife," Yuri grunted, pretending to be put off.

"Don't worry, Eden, you'll get used to it," Mariana assured.

"Used to what?"

"To overbearing maleness," she winked at Yuri. "It's difficult for them to be so attuned to another. The soul-bond is new for you both, so it may take a period of adjustment. Just don't let the King bowl you over and all will be well."

"The King is sitting right here and can hear you," Viktor scowled.

"Which is why I said it," she quipped.

A second passed and then all four of them guffawed.

Viktor tilted his glass towards Yuri. "You are lucky, friend, that I admire your wife."

"No, my friend," Yuri said, bringing his wife's knuckles to his lips, "I am the one who is lucky."

Mariana leaned over and kissed her sieva fully on the mouth.

Eden lowered her gaze to her lap, feeling like she shouldn't be privy to the intimacy the couple so easily shared. Viktor reached for her hand and brought it to his thigh, leaving them joined.

"I guess I forgot to mention the upside of matehood," Mariana said.

Eden looked up, quizzically.

"Total and utter adoration."

Viktor squeezed her hand and Eden blushed.

"But seriously," Mariana continued, "tell us about you. I'm dying to know about your magic."

"You don't have to, Eden," Viktor assured her. "Mariana is merely curious. It's not often we have guests that are not Prajna."

He already knew she could control fire. She had other abilities, as well. He was guessing air or something to do with oxygen from the way she could control her pulse.

"Fire," Eden blurted.

She'd never discussed her magics with anyone outside her close circle. All of Gwydion knew she could produce fire, but the rest of what she could do wasn't well-known.

Father was adamant about the family's secrets remaining undisclosed. After Eden's mother, Elora, was murdered, he trusted hardly anyone, especially those who would think his children too powerful.

"You can set things on fire?" Yuri asked.

"Yes. Or put out a fire. Or I can do this."

Eden held up her right hand and small flames emitted from her palm.

"Fascinating," Mariana whispered, leaning forward, the orange flares reflecting in her eyes.

"Undeniably," Viktor agreed.

Eden felt the butterfly wings caress her face. This time, when her heartrate accelerated, she did nothing to slow it.

# Chapter 16

"Viktor, are you sure you want me with you today?" Eden asked.

"Yes. I find I am not ready to part with you just yet."

Her mood lifted slightly as Viktor led her through the King's passage leading to the throne room, his hand on the small of her back. He hadn't seemed very enthused to bring her with him today and Eden worried he'd only asked her to accompany him out of some sense of obligation to keep her occupied.

Viktor could feel Eden's muscles relax a fraction under his hand. He detested the idea she thought he might not want her with him. Even more, he detested the idea of being away from her.

Bringing Eden to court might not be the most sensible plan. However, he was discovering when it came to his sieva, he was anything but sensible. He'd been neglecting his duties and it was time to see to them once more.

Today, he was holding court and had insisted Eden attend. He knew it didn't sound like it would be much in the way of entertainment, but she told him she understood he'd been putting off his work in order to spend time with her.

Viktor kept his hand on her lower back and steered her to the right, towards a small alcove. He knew she had no real sense of where she was going, or how to get back to their room.

Eden had yet to have a tour of the castle. She had been to the private dining room, but nowhere else. Viktor kept her too busy in their bed chamber.

Mariana offered to show her around, but Viktor seemed put off by it. Eden asked if he wanted to be the one to show her Castra Nocte and he'd replied, "It would please me very much to share with you all that is mine, *moj vestica.*"

He often gave her such poetic words and she questioned if he could keep his Heartless nickname for much longer. With Eden, he failed to live up to it.

Today, however, she would witness how he interacted with his people. She mentally prepared herself to accept whatever persona he needed to take on. She had heard the Prajna court could be ruthless. If the Heartless moniker helped him achieve his goals, for the betterment of the kingdom, she could live with it.

They approached a small door in the center of the alcove. Viktor spun Eden to face him, both hands holding her shoulders.

"I will assume your father held court?"

"Yes."

"And I assume it was a peaceful affair?"

"Of course."

Viktor's thumbs stroked the base of her throat, measuring her pulse. Slow and steady without a hint of magic. *Good.*

"This will likely be far different. I've ensured word got out that you were my sieva. Vampires understand the sanctity of soul-bonding, but they can be aggressive by nature, especially the younger ones."

Her pulse increased slightly.

"No one will harm you," he assured, "but I want to prepare you for the possibility of … unpleasantness. I can be harsh. In fact, it's often necessary. When I am, some do not react well and I am forced to take measures to ensure my word is final."

"I understand what you are, Viktor," she replied. "You do not have to explain. I can handle it."

His green irises illuminated in the darkened nook. He brought her frame against his own and rested his chin atop her head.

"Yes, little witch, I believe you can handle just about anything." *I'm counting on it*, he wanted to say.

"Come," he broke away and opened the door, allowing her to step through as he held it ajar.

Eden wasn't sure what to expect. The tales of the Prajna court were all so dreary and bleak. She'd envisioned a gloomy hall, void of sun, with minimal furnishings.

Brushing past Viktor, she found quite the opposite. In fact, she had to shield her eyes from the brilliant light flooding the throne room. It took several hard blinks before her vision adjusted.

The room was absolutely glorious.

The stone inside was a much lighter shade of grey than the rest of the castle. It looked like it had been washed with a bleaching agent.

Twenty or so pews were placed on either side of a large aisle. The walkway was covered with a long red carpet, which ran the entire length of the chamber.

Dozens of stained glass windows adorned the far wall. They were full of reds, oranges, and yellows, depicting flames.

Eden held up the palm with her marking, allowing a small flame to form, then gestured towards the windows.

"Coincidence?" she teased.

"I'd say prophetic," he replied in a serious tone. "Did you know vampires are attracted to fire?"

"Can't fire kill you?"

"Yes. Interesting, isn't it? To be drawn to that which could easily take your life?"

"You just described the prey of all vampires."

Viktor shrugged unapologetically. "Every living thing has its vulnerabilities."

"Even you."

"Even me. I am, after all, soul-bonded to an elemental with control over one of my few vulnerabilities."

She held her palm between them. "But you trust me."

"Implicitly. The question is, Sieva, do you trust me?"

Eden grinned and closed her hand. "Absolutely."

Viktor let out a low growl, but refused to approach her. If he touched her, court might get postponed indefinitely.

Her cheeks pinkened, knowing what that low rumble meant. She reached for him and he shook his head.

"I regret there is no time for that. We have less than a minute before the doors open," he said.

"Oh," Eden replied, her arousal dying rapidly. "Where should I sit?"

The door had led them onto the dais. A large wooden throne sat in the center. It was painted black with gold accents along the arms and legs. The padding for the seat was dark red.

Sitting on the top of the high back was a large golden hawk with emerald eyes. It was the same figure on Viktor's bedposts. There was no mistaking this was the King's chair.

Back and to the left sat a smaller, daintier version of the same throne. It was obviously meant for the Queen.

"Here," he clipped, striding to the right side of his seat, clearly indicating she was not going to be seated on the feminine throne.

Eden hesitated, thrown by his tenor. She wanted to ask him why he seemed bothered by her question, but the click of the locks echoed across the stone and the large doors swung open.

She had not been crowned Queen, so it was presumptuous of her to take the sovereign's chair. She dismissed it from her mind and moved to the small bench next to him.

Viktor stepped in front of his throne and waited. Eden remained standing, as well. In Gwydion, one did not sit until the King allowed it. Not knowing the customs of this court, she decided to follow the rules of her own.

Castle guards entered first, taking their posts around the room. Dozens of Prajna began filing in soon after. No one spoke. The silence was broken up by the soft, periodic clacking of their shoes upon the floor.

Eden surveyed the small crowd gliding fluidly through the space. Vampires were such graceful creatures. They entered as though following the steps of an orchestrated dance, knowing exactly where and when to move.

A familiar white-blonde head of hair moved up the aisle. Once the vampires in front of her moved into the rows to take their seats, Eden had a clear view of Bianca.

The female vampire only had eyes for Viktor. When Bianca finally noticed Eden, she drew up short, her entire body blanching. It disturbed the flow of others moving around her and the spell of the dance was broken.

As if forced, Bianca woodenly performed an about-face and exited the room. It had to be the result of the pact Viktor made on the balcony. Eden was impressed with the effects of such a power. She was also wary of someone misusing it.

Viktor exhaled loudly. Bianca was lucky she'd noted Eden's presence when she did. He was close to leaping off the dais to deal with her. It wouldn't be the best introduction to the Prajna court, yet he would do it to prevent Eden from any level of discomfort.

Eden was going to have a hard enough time of it, as it was. If Bianca did anything to cause problems between he and Eden, he would be very tempted to break the contract he made with Dmitri.

It would likely mean forfeiting his throne, but what was his life without his sieva? He would gladly give it up now, if his successor could be counted on to deal with the Prajna's major issues.

Unfortunately, his brother was selfish and would not care to do what was necessary to find solutions. Luka had not once shown concern over the lack of new matings or live births. He only appeared to care about himself, choosing to spend his days with a vat of wine or between the legs of a female from the Komora.

The Prince of Prajna was irresponsible and shallow. Viktor thought Luka and Bianca might just be perfect for each other. *If only ...*

Luka hadn't always been like this. Viktor's heart grieved the close relationship he and his brother once had, before their father had twisted and broken them both.

In truth, watching his younger sibling's spirit die at the hands of their father was the breaking point for Viktor. It had spurred him into taking action when he did—and both brothers paid for the action gravely.

Viktor was fortunate. He now had Eden and was starting to forget what life had once been. Piece by piece, she was putting him back together.

Luka had no one to mend his soul. Viktor blamed himself, and he prayed to the Goddess he would find a way to set things right.

Seeing so many hopeful faces enter and take their seats, Viktor knew he needed to hang on to his position as King, if only to see if the birth of a child could break the cycle. He owed his people that much, especially since he might be the cause of their plague.

Theron seemed sure it was possible, once Viktor bonded and conceived, the rest of the clan would follow suit. *Could it really be so simple?*

He glanced at Eden, thinking of her carrying his young. He was staggered by how much he wanted it to be her. For if his sieva bore him young and broke the curse, he would never be forced to lay a finger on the Queen.

Guilt surfaced, pushing his organs into his throat. For the first time since he'd killed his father, Viktor felt nauseous.

* * *

Eden shifted her legs, trying to get some blood flow back into them. She'd been sitting still for hours, taking in Viktor's court.

A few of the vampires caught her stare, only to quickly looked away. It was the same behavior they exhibited with

157

Viktor. It reminded her of how the wolves behaved in front of their alpha.

All in all, it wasn't as cutthroat as she'd imagined. A handful of petitioners came across as brutish, yet did not question Viktor's judgement. He was firm but fair, and the Prajna appeared to respect his handling of things.

The bulk of the people had come for information, having heard he'd been seeking answers to the current birthrate issue.

Eden's heart broke for the couples, especially the mated sievas who had been together for hundreds of years. Viktor spoke vaguely of his visit with Theron. He told them only that he'd brought it to the priest's attention and they were actively seeking answers. It was enough to appease them for now.

He refrained from introducing Eden or even mentioning he had found his sieva. Viktor made it clear to her, early on, word had spread, and by his command. It was easy enough to decipher who the female elemental sitting next to him was.

She thought he might mention the details of how clans procreated in ancient times, but he didn't so much as hint at it. Eden wasn't sure she wanted an entire kingdom waiting on her to become pregnant, anyway. If it didn't change things, she'd prefer not to be blamed for the failure.

After each petitioner finished, he or she exited. A handful were escorted by the guards. Viktor had just finished with the last one as Yuri walked up the aisle, a small scroll in his hand.

"My liege," Yuri greeted as he went to one knee. He always held to protocol when acting in official capacities.

"Rise," Viktor gently ordered. His manner with his friend was far different than it had been with the people.

"Two things, my lord. A missive just arrived. The messenger said it was urgent."

Viktor held out his hand for the scroll. "And the second?"

Yuri's eyes darted to Eden, then back to Viktor. "There is one more petitioner. She, ah, cannot enter the throne room at the moment."

Eden could guess who it was.

"Any idea what she wants?" Viktor asked.

"No. I think it best if you speak to her sooner rather than later. In private."

Viktor sighed. "Very well. Please stay here with Eden while I go deal with the issue."

He rose and positioned himself in front of Eden. "Feel free to walk around, but please stay in the throne room until I return."

The odds of Eden being in any sort of danger here were extremely low, but Viktor would take no chances. Yuri and the other guards would suffice as protection until he returned.

"It's okay, I don't mind," she told him when he didn't make any move to depart.

Eden stood and waited for him to touch her or show some sign of affection. He did neither. Only a curt nod acknowledged her statement.

"I'll return as soon as possible." He jogged down the stairs and out the doors.

Eden's stomach dropped. She would have to come to terms with his prior life, which included a castle full of females. The sooner she did, the easier her life would be.

"Well, that was entertaining."

Yuri's head snapped towards the door at the back of the dais and two guards ported in front of Eden so fast she yelped at being startled.

A large and handsome male was sauntering towards her, ignoring Yuri's dirty look. His size, hair, and skin tone were almost identical to Viktor's.

"Oh, back off. I'm hardly a threat to my brother's sieva," he said.

"Careful, Luka. I would advise not pissing him off today," Yuri threatened.

"Such sound advice, Yuri. Thank you," he bowed mockingly.

The male turned to Eden. She could barely see him through the sliver of space between the guards.

"Hello, Eden. Allow me to introduce myself. I am your ... well let's see, I'm not your brother-in-law seeing as he's not your husband," he tapped his chin with his index finger.

"Hmm. Well then, what is Viktor to you, a being born to a faction who does not recognize mates?" his taunting grin widened at Yuri's snarl.

"Oh, alright, I'll stop with the teasing. I am Luka, second in line for the throne of Prajna."

This was the type of vampire who gave the Prajna a bad name. Viktor may have been hardened by life, but Luka was embittered by it. Those who clung to such acrimony were often dangerous. If he thought Eden an easy target, he thought wrong.

Eden placed her hands on the guards' arms to slide them apart. They didn't budge.

"Please give me space," she respectfully requested.

They were used to being ordered about. She would not treat them the same as others did. Eden was still very alone in Prajna and a little diplomacy might go a long way with Viktor's men. If only the same could be said for his brother.

Yuri nodded to the guards and they stepped to the side, one at each of her shoulders.

"Ah, there you are. Luka, second in line. Feel the need to say that aloud, did you? In case people don't have a clue who you might be? How frustrating it must be to have to announce it in order to earn recognition."

Luka's malicious grin fell away as he registered the insult. It took him a second to recover. Eden could tell he wasn't used to being spoken down to.

She knew she would be tested. It was disappointing, though, that the test was coming from someone who should be nothing less that completely loyal to Viktor. There was only one way to deal with a male like Luka.

"So, the witch can bite back. How very interesting."

Eden's hands flung to the sky and she allowed her power to shoot long flames from her palms. The guards recoiled, but Luka stood his ground.

"The *witch* can also burn you alive," she threatened. "I suggest you choose to act in a manner befitting of the second in line. Might I add that I have a tremendous amount of control and can burn very specific areas of the body?"

She didn't know how he would react. She half expected to have to burn off his eyebrows to prove her ability. What she didn't expect was his full-bellied laugh. Loud and rolling, and almost cheery.

Eden extinguished the flames and dropped her arms, nervously glancing at the others standing close by. The guards were eying her warily, while Yuri's jaw was hanging wide open.

"What in the bloody hell is going on in here?" Viktor bellowed from the doorway.

"Oh, someone's in trouble now," Luka winked at Eden, just before getting thrown across the room by one very angry Viktor.

# Chapter 17

"Viktor, stop!" Eden yelled.

He currently had Luka pinned to the wall by his throat.

"Do not worry, Eden. I don't think suffocation will kill him," Yuri supplied.

"Yes, well, hooray for that," she shot back sarcastically. "I had it under control, Viktor. This isn't your fight."

If he interfered, the Prajna might not believe she could hold her own. Eden refused to be seen as cannon fodder.

He stiffened, slowly swiveling his head towards his sieva. "I disagree. Adamantly."

She rolled her eyes and approached him from the side.

"He didn't threaten me. He didn't make any move to come at me. He was rude—," her eyes snapped to Luka, "*beyond* rude, but not physically aggressive."

Luka's face pinched, feeling his brother's claws slowly extend against his throat. He watched in awe as Eden put a hand on Viktor's arm and the claws retracted. Few dared to touch the King when he was in a mood, much less achieve in calming him.

Eden needed to diffuse the situation. She felt a hint of guilt having been the one who escalated it, but she would stand by her decision to teach Luka a lesson he would not soon forget.

"I was simply trying to put him in his place and assert my ... well, ah dominance, so he would know I wasn't to be trifled with. Can we not talk about it without killing him?"

"Not likely, my dear," Luka snorted.

Viktor ignored his brother and stared at Eden, replaying the scene he'd witnessed when he'd returned to the throne room.

*Guards surrounding his mate, fire coming out of her hands, and Luka. Laughing. His brother had been genuinely amused.*

Viktor had assumed Eden was in trouble. She wasn't.

He loosened his hold around his brother's neck. "Why were you laughing at my mate?" he accused.

Eden rolled her eyes again, risking Viktor's usual reaction. This was getting ridiculous.

"She threatened to burn off my manhood. No one's ever spoken like that at court. It was the grandest thing this room has ever witnessed."

"Is this true?" Viktor asked.

"No!" she retorted, while the guards and Yuri all replied, "Yes."

"Eyebrows. When I said I could burn specific parts of the body, I was going to burn away your eyebrows."

Viktor let go of Luka and the male dropped to the floor, coughing. The King pointed a finger in his younger brother's face.

"I never want to walk in on something like that again. She is my sieva. If I'd truly thought you'd been a threat, this would have ended very differently."

Viktor worried he was going soft. First Bianca, now Luka—the only two Prajna he really couldn't kill. The next person to upset him would not be so lucky.

"Yes, I'm aware," Luka panted.

"Good," Viktor punctuated, then crooked a finger at his little warrior. "Come here, little mate."

Eden advanced with apprehension. When she was within reach, he hooked her around the waist and pulled her against his frame.

"I think you scared every last guard in the room, as well as poor Yuri," he chided gently.

"I—"

"While I can appreciate your need to, how did you word it, assert your dominance? Let's keep the indoor fires to a small flicker unless there's real danger, shall we?"

Eden crinkled her nose, wanting to argue she could easily control her power. She could cover her own body in flames without so much as a twitch of a burn. It's not like she would have burned down the castle.

"Okay," she agreed instead of arguing.

Viktor kissed her cheek and whispered into her ear, "I panicked when I saw you. I did not like the feeling. Help me to never feel it again."

She squeezed his hand when he straightened. She understood how it must have looked. At least he didn't tell her she was supposed to let the guards manage things, should anything like this happen again.

"Yuri, please accompany Eden up to our chambers while I have a word with my brother."

"But, I was hoping to see the castle today," Eden protested.

Viktor held up the missive Yuri had handed him earlier. "Not today, *mala vestica*. You'll want to read this in private. I'll be up shortly."

Eden looked at the scroll worriedly.

"It will be okay, Eden. Take it. Yuri can stay with you until I get there."

Eden grabbed the parchment and allowed Yuri to escort her out.

"Leave us," he ordered the remaining guards.

Once the doors were closed, Viktor held out a hand to Luka and helped him off the ground.

"I take it you were your usual charming self," Viktor accused.

"I may have baited her a bit, yes," Luka admitted.

"Why? You knew I would not tolerate it."

"Yes, but I didn't know if *she* would tolerate it. She'll have to have a thick skin to survive here. And if I'm honest, I wanted to know what sort of female the Goddess created for you. And I must say, Brother, she is unequivocally sublime."

"Yes, she is, but you'll not do it again. Do not test me on this, Luka. I'll not act rationally when it comes to her. I'm not capable of it."

He was loathe to admit it, but Luka needed to understand the cold and logical King was anything but when it came to Eden's well-being.

The last thing Viktor wanted was to kill his only remaining family member, but he would do it. He would set the world afire if it made Eden safe, especially now, after reading the message from Theron.

"You care for her," Luka assessed.

"I do," Viktor admitted.

He'd never said as much to Eden, but their souls communicated and that would have to be enough for now. He wasn't sure why it was so easy to say it to his brother.

"The Heartless King has finally found his soulmate," Luka announced, as though addressing the room. He'd always had a thing for dramatics. "I bet that sent Bianca into a rage."

Luka felt a troubling cramp in his abdomen, thinking of the white-haired beauty. He'd studiously avoided her since she'd arrived decades ago, fearing his severe attraction to her would land him in trouble.

Viktor scratched at the scruff on his jaw. "She ported to my balcony to see for herself."

"And she lives?"

"You know I cannot kill her."

"Oh, you could, but you shouldn't. For once, I don't envy you in the slightest, Viktor."

Viktor sat down on one of the steps below his throne. He brought his elbows to his knees, suddenly feeling weary from the weight of his burdens, the regret of his life's choices.

"She doesn't know."

"Who doesn't know what?"

"Eden. She knows about Dmitri and that I agreed to take care of Bianca. I left it at that."

"You can't keep it secret for much longer. We're weeks past the solstice, Viktor. Time's almost up to make good on your end of the deal."

"I'm aware."

Viktor's hands fisted, furious with himself for allowing his affection for Dmitri to affect his decision-making. He should never have agreed to the last part of the contract.

He'd conveniently pushed it to the back of his mind, unwilling to spoil his time getting to know his sieva. It hung heavy in the background. As the days passed, he could no longer pretend all was well.

Luka sat next to Viktor, in the same spots they would sit as children. It was where they watched their immoral father hold court, painstakingly destroying their innocence. He scared the life right out of them, slowly shaping them into what they would eventually become.

Unfulfilled. Unfeeling.

Viktor didn't want to go back to what he had been. Eden was changing him, for the better. He would not entertain any option other than building a life with her, here at Castra Nocte.

What did a piece of paper and a ten-minute ceremony mean compared to the one who held his soul in her delicate hands? Nothing.

"What are you going to do?" Luka asked.

"There's nothing to be done."

Luka looked at his brother incredulously. "You mean to have your sieva bow to your Queen?"

"Never. Eden shall be exempt. She's not a vampire, so she won't fall under the Queen's domain."

Luka leaned towards Viktor, concern marring his handsome face. Viktor couldn't recall the last time he'd seen it be anything other than contemptuous.

"Something must be done, Viktor. I know I don't hold a place of esteem in your life, but listen to me. This is not going to turn out well for you."

"Breaking the contract is virtually impossible. You know this. And I'll never let Eden go. I'll chain her to my bed, if necessary."

"Right, and she'll allow it. Did you not see the flames coming out of her hands?" Luka's voice was laced with skepticism.

"I can be very persuasive," Viktor replied.

"And what of Bianca?" Luka questioned, locking down his reaction to the possibility she'd not end up married to Viktor. He didn't want to contemplate why he was having such ridiculous thoughts.

"She can live in the Queen's quarters on the opposite side of the castle. I've already ordered her to never enter a room where Eden might be if she cannot be anything but respectful towards her. If I have to, I'll send her to another residence."

"It won't be enough," Luka stated unwaveringly. "The kingdom has ceremonies and festivals, things the Queen must be a part of. You can't throw them together like that and expect all to be well. You cannot live two separate lives and you certainly cannot expect them to do it either."

Luka thought his brother was in total denial. He could not force this upon his mate and expect anything other than the destruction of their relationship.

The soul-bond would not save Viktor from Eden's wrath once she found out. Or, worse, his brother may very well break her indomitable spirit. Just as Nikolai had done to them and their mother.

"Then I'll not attend any ceremonies," Viktor countered, knowing how preposterous it sounded, yet unwilling to yield. "I don't have to be present at festivals. I'll hold court and leave the rest to Bianca. We'll split duties and I'll keep Eden out of court life as best I can."

"You'll not attend," Luka responded drolly. "What about your wedding? You plan to attend that? Plan to invite your *sieva* to watch you pledge yourself in matrimony to another? I'm sure that will go over swimmingly."

Viktor's eyes flashed bright green. He was tempted to hit his brother again, preferably break the nose on his sarcasm-laced face. He hated that Luka was right. There was no positive outcome in this scenario.

Luka shook his head irritably. "There is no peace for us, is there, Brother?"

"No, I suppose there isn't. It's the burden of those who rule, Luka."

"No, I refuse to believe that. And I wasn't just referring to you, you conceited ass. You think I don't want to find my own sieva? For the vampire race to once again bear children? We've brought a plague upon our heads and every last one of us is paying for it," Luka's voice rose as he stood, resolutely straightening his tunic.

Viktor opened his mouth, stunned at Luka's words. It was the first time Luka had ever inferred he was personally invested in the kingdom's struggles—the first time he'd acted like the male Viktor had known before Nikolai had broken him.

Perhaps there was hope, after all. It was a last resort, but handing over the crown might be an option if Luka could prove himself capable.

The chance was small, but the flicker of hope remained. Viktor didn't dare fuel the flame, but he allowed it to burn within.

A fraction of Viktor's burden lifted the tiniest bit. He needed a miracle. If Luka could find his way back to his old self, Viktor might just get one.

Viktor stared hard at his brother, measuring the odds, thinking through the fallout from abdicating. Theron's words about the leader needing to produce offspring hung heavy in his mind.

Viktor sighed. Until he could confidently place the care of all Prajna in Luka's hands, he needed to explore every other possibility. He was furious with himself for letting it go this long.

For five years he'd lived with the knowledge his sieva would be crossing his path and he'd dismissed it as an inconvenience. What a fool he had been.

Viktor stood to face his brother. "I've limited options, Luka. If you have any ideas, I'm listening."

Luka bowed his head. He didn't have any ideas, not any that would end without someone dead or his brother dethroned.

"You still have a few weeks. I'll think on it. We'll come up with something. I'll not rest until I do," Luka promised.

Viktor clasped Luka's shoulder and squeezed, touched by his pledge. "I appreciate the sentiment, but this burden is mine to carry. Do not waste time worrying on my behalf. Seek answers or alternatives, but do not take on personal responsibility for my mistake."

With that, Viktor ported away before Luka could respond.

\* \* \*

Eden rolled up the message and sat it on the table next to the chair. She closed her eyes and her shaky hands rubbed her temples, trying to stave off the migraine she felt coming.

"Here, have some tea," Yuri insisted, pouring her a cup. When she made no move to reach for it, he sat it on the table next to the scrolled parchment.

"I don't want to burden you further," he said, "but I wanted to make a comment on your ... introduction to Luka."

Eden opened her eyes.

"First off, kudos to you for the display of power. It earned you the respect of the royal guard and I dare say of Luka."

"Do you think?" she asked uncertainly. She couldn't picture Luka respecting anyone if that was his normal behavior.

"Oh, yes. You acted as Viktor does when dealing with his brother. The other males were terrified. I greatly enjoyed it."

Eden didn't want them to be terrified of her. She only wanted some degree of respect.

"I also wanted to warn you," Yuri continued, "should you, in the future, feel the need to turn those flames on him—and not just to singe his eyebrows—if it is not done in self-defense, it is considered attempted murder."

Eden snorted humorlessly. "I can assure you, Yuri, if I'd wanted him dead, it wouldn't be *attempted* murder."

She didn't actually think she would do it, but she was in a foul mood and her headache wasn't helping.

"I believe you. Nevertheless, you should know attempted murder carries an automatic death sentence. If unprovoked, of course."

Eden wanted to reply that Luka had done nothing other than provoke her with every insulting word he flung at her. But she could see Yuri was concerned and only trying to warn her.

"You mean don't try to kill anyone unless my life is in danger."

"Yes."

"Fair enough."

She picked up her tea and held it up towards him. "Thank you for this."

"You're welcome. Now—" he cut himself off. Something caught his attention at the balcony.

Eden followed his gaze. Viktor was opening the glass doors. He marched to her chair and knelt in front of her, his warm palms settling on her knees.

It was humbling watching the King of Prajna kneel before her. He'd done it multiple times now and she didn't think she'd ever get used to it.

"Are you alright?" he asked.

She nodded, but she wasn't alright. Her bottom lip trembled.

"Thank you, Yuri. That will be all for now," Viktor dismissed his friend, taking the teacup from Eden's hands and setting it aside.

"Of course," Yuri replied as he went to the door. "Send for me if you need anything," he added before shutting it behind him.

Lines formed on Eden's forehead and her lips pressed tight. She looked pained, but she did not weep. Viktor knew she'd read the message. His sieva was barely holding herself together.

The message had come from Theron with news of her sister, Nora, and their father. They had all been betrayed by the girls' governess, Mara. She was the elemental member of the Sephtis Kenelm.

Mara had made an attempt on Nora's life, along with the help of King Kellan's healer, Agatha. It was unheard of for healers to take a life. Viktor was certain the betrayal had rattled the wolves.

They would be out for blood and they would want to hunt, possibly on Prajna soil. Kellan wouldn't do it without Viktor's permission, but he would expect Viktor to cooperate.

Viktor would normally refuse. This time, he couldn't, not when he'd promised to help find the remaining members of the brotherhood. One of whom was Prajna.

It was assumed the group had four members because that was how it had always operated. Currently, it appeared two members were still alive.

The demon member, Bogdan, had been caught a week ago and dealt with in a manner fitting an assassin—his heart had been removed from his chest. Mara was already dead, by Nora's hands, if Theron was to be believed.

The demon and the elemental were dead. Agatha, the she-wolf, was on the run. That left one unknown member, a vampire.

Viktor crushed Eden to him. He'd believed she would be safe here. She should be safe here. Regrettably, she might not be, not with the fourth unknown member on the loose.

To top it all off, her father and some other men had been attacked on their way to Castle Burghard to see Nora and Kellan. The Sephtis Kenelm were getting bolder, likely growing desperate in their mission to prevent what they perceived to be an imbalance of power.

He waited for the tears to come, for Eden to show her distress. The only outward sign was the tenseness in her body. He admired her tenacity, but he'd comfort her anyway.

Viktor picked up his mate and sat down in her place, wrapping his arms around her tightly. He adjusted her to sit comfortably in his lap.

Eden pressed her face into Viktor's neck. She inhaled deeply, comforted by his unique, earthen and spicy scent.

He held her for long minutes before speaking. "I sent word we would arrive at the temple in three days. I asked Kellan and Nora to join us."

"Is that safe?"

"Sanctus Femina is probably the safest place to be. I'm thinking of sending you there to stay until this is all over."

Eden sat up, scowling.

"By myself?"

"Of course not. Evelyn is staying there. I'll make sure you have more than enough guards."

"I meant, alone, without you, Viktor."

"I cannot be gone from the kingdom for long."

"That's fine. I'll just stay here, then."

"Eden—"

"No," she replied vehemently. "I won't feel safe without you near. Do not ask it of me."

Warmth spread through his chest. She was a balm to his wretched soul. He wanted to tell her as much, but he couldn't. He was afraid to say such things aloud, terrified of her owning his heart when he was only going to hurt hers in return.

He needed to tell her about Bianca. He was running out of time, but he couldn't bring himself to do it. Viktor knew Eden. She wouldn't want to stay with him and he would never allow her to leave.

Goddess willing, he and Luka would figure out a solution before his magically enforced deadline. If they did, maybe Eden wouldn't need to know.

At the thought of losing her affections, he ported them to the bed, stripped them of their clothing, and held her tight against the length of his body until dawn.

# Chapter 18

Three days later, Viktor ported with Eden to Sanctus Femina. They didn't bring any luggage, having decided not to stay overnight.

He'd tried multiple times to get Eden to agree to stay longer, a month at most, thinking it would be an ample amount of time for things to blow over. It would give him time to help with tracking the remaining members of Sephtis Kenelm and to deal with Bianca.

Selfishly, he didn't want Eden anywhere near Castra Nocte or the looming ceremony being planned. He was trying to protect her both physically and emotionally. He feared he would only succeed in one of the two.

Eden still didn't know the entirety of what was in the contract with Bianca. If Viktor couldn't find a way out of it, he would tell Eden. He was starting to cling to hope he would find that miracle. It was a dangerous way to think.

He wanted to have faith in his brother. It was starting to look as though Luka might be his only way out. Yet again, he tucked the idea away as an absolute last resort, unsure he could actually go through with handing over the kingdom.

Viktor had considered bribing Bianca. He doubted there was anything more she wanted than the title of Queen, but if there was, he would give it to her. He would have to approach her soon. He loathed the very idea of the female having any sort of leverage over him.

He'd spent some time the past two days with both Yuri and Luka, trying to brainstorm ways out of the contract. They only came up with two options.

One, Bianca could refuse to marry him. Dmitri had added the clause in case she had major issue with Viktor and could not be happy with him. What Dmitri didn't know was that Bianca would grow up into a selfish adult who would do just about anything to sit on the throne. She would likely never refuse to marry Viktor, even if he could never love her.

Two, Bianca could die. She was barely over one hundred years old, so old age wouldn't take her. Luka adamantly offered to take care of it, but Viktor brushed off his absurd idea.

If Luka killed Bianca without provocation, Viktor would have to take Luka's life. It was the law and no vampire was above it, especially when the King was magically compelled to enforce it. It was the ultimate contract required of every sovereign of Prajna who was crowned.

Neither Yuri nor Luka had suggested Viktor step aside. They weren't aware of the loophole Viktor realized he'd been given. He kept it quiet, unwilling to tease Luka with prospect of being a king.

Viktor did his best to hide his tension, but Eden could sense it, just as he could sense when she was out of sorts. There was no hiding such things when one was soul-bonded.

She didn't pry and he appreciated it. He would not lie to her if he could avoid it. He just needed more time.

He might try once more to ask her to stay here. Perhaps she would be more inclined once she saw her sisters.

Brushing aside his worries, he focused on his mate, who needed a second after teleporting. It always made her a little dizzy and he kept ahold of her shoulders until she was steady on her feet.

"Better?" he asked once she stood straight.

"Better."

He offered his arm and she took it. They walked in tandem from the small clearing towards the temple. She slowed the closer they got.

Viktor put his hand at the small of Eden's back and nudged her towards the stairs. She allowed him to lead her up the steps and into the temple.

"I'm almost afraid to see them," Eden confessed.

"Nothing here will harm you, Eden."

"No, it's not that," she insisted, "it's just ... seeing Nora solidifies the news. It's all real. We were betrayed. We are still being betrayed. I can defend myself. Evelyn, can as well. Nora's never had magic so she's practically helpless."

A twirling gust of wind appeared suddenly, surrounding Eden and lifting her slightly off the floor. Viktor growled and turned to face the threat, straightening when he saw the perpetrators.

Nora and Kellan were standing at the edge of the hall that led to the library. They both wore toothy grins.

"Nora? Is this—is this *your* magic?" Eden asked suspiciously.

"Yes," Nora laughed. "Do you like it?"

Eden shook her head, her jaw almost dragging the floor. Nora had never been able to control magic. Her entire life, she'd had to syphon it from her surroundings to continuously replenish her life force.

"If you don't mind, please release my sieva before explaining," Viktor requested sternly.

"Oh, you're no fun," Nora pouted.

He lifted a brow. All three sisters spoke to him as if … as if he wasn't the Heartless King.

"Wife, I think you've had your fun," Kellan chastised slightly, kissing the crook of her neck.

Nora sighed and released Eden from her hold. Eden dropped back to the ground. Thankfully, she'd only been a couple inches up.

"Sorry," Nora apologized running to hug her sister. "I'm still working on control."

Eden squeezed her hard. "No apology needed, Nora. I'm thrilled for you! The mating worked, didn't it?"

Nora nodded enthusiastically. Not only had mating with Kellan repaired her soul, it had brought forth her magic.

They grinned at each other. Viktor watched, fascinated. The sisters loved one another and were treasured by their father. They were the epitome of familial love.

He scratched at the area over his heart, unsure what he was feeling. Had he and Luka ever been this close?

Eden spun her sister to face Viktor. "Sister, I'd like you to meet The King of Prajna. Viktor, this is Nora."

"A pleasure to meet you," Nora said as she curtsied.

Viktor bowed to Nora in response, then turned his attention to the wolf.

"Viktor, it's been a while," Kellan stepped forward and they shook hands.

"Yes, it has ..." he trailed off, watching as a flash of dark red hair went flying by.

"Slow down!" Nora shouted a second before Evelyn barreled into her sisters, hugging them tightly. The three of them giggled like little girls and Kellan's mouth quirked.

"She-wolves do not act like this," Kellan commented, tilting his head while observing the trio hop around with joy.

"Neither do female vampires."

"I feel like I'm intruding," Kellan bluntly admitted.

"I feel the same," Viktor agreed, noticing how young Eden looked surrounded by her sisters. Or was he just old?

"Well, come on then, men," Theron called from down the hall. "I've got whiskey."

"Thank the Goddess," Kellan mumbled. "Come on, Wife."

Nora immediately turned from her sisters to clasp Kellan's hand. Kellan nuzzled the crook of her neck, inhaling sharply, then straightened and led his mate down the hall.

Viktor reached for Eden with his left hand and she readily took it. A small hand snuck into his right. He looked up the length of the arm to its owner.

"What?" Evelyn asked innocently. "I've no mate or husband to speak of, but now I've got two brothers. Don't you know siblings hold hands?"

Viktor blinked.

Evelyn waved a hand in front of his face. "Are you okay up there?"

Eden pressed her face to his arm. He could feel her shaking with laughter at Evelyn's antics. She must be the mischievous sibling. One who now thought of him as her brother.

He cleared his throat, shocked by his reaction to her previous statement. Brother. She'd claimed he was her brother.

He'd never had a sister and he hardly knew this female aside from a two-minute introduction. Yet, here she was calling him family despite his not being married to Eden.

"It's okay, Viktor. I didn't mean to scare you." Evelyn started to pull her hand out of his, but he held firm.

"I'm not scared of you, little one."

"Really?"

"I'm terrified."

The sisters laughed and Viktor felt his chest tighten as he escorted them down the hall.

* * *

"This is insane," Evelyn announced to the group.

The jovial reunion had turned somber in the past hour while Nora and Kellan recounted the events having occurred since Nora had gone off to live in the Northland.

Most of the information they already knew. What Viktor was surprised to hear was that a second vampire's scent was picked up when Kellan's men found the wolf who had poisoned Nora.

It seemed that the she-wolf, Isla, had been under compulsion from the demon named Bogdan. At least Kellan could take comfort in the fact she hadn't acted on her own accord. Betrayal was a bitter pill to swallow.

"What's our first move?" Eden asked.

"I need to find Agatha," Kellan replied. "I'd also like to bring my trackers to the Eastland, the ones who have scented the vampire involved in the attack on Edward, as well as the vampire from the area where Isla was found."

Viktor knew this was coming. Only the wolves knew the scents of the two Prajna. It only made sense they would be the ones to track them down.

It wasn't Kellan's request, though, that was bothering Viktor. It was the fact there were two different suspects from his kingdom. The likelihood of it being mere happenstance a vampire stumbled across the area where Bogdan and Isla had ended up was next to nothing.

Sephtis Kenelm had never deviated from its original grouping of only four members. He would have to start dedicating his time to finding the perpetrators instead of remaining holed up in his chambers with Eden.

"I'll allow it," he told the Wolf King, "but you'll have to have either myself or a Prajna of my choosing escorting you."

Viktor worried his people wouldn't take kindly to wolves running free across their land. Plus, if they did come across the vampires in question, Viktor wanted to be the one to deal with them.

"Understood," Kellan responded, pleased Viktor was being accommodating.

"Does anyone have any *good* news?" Evelyn griped. "All this doom and gloom is extracting any happiness I might have right out of me."

"Well," Nora hedged, glancing at her husband, "we might have come across something positive."

"You are with child?" Evelyn probed hopefully.

"What? No!" Nora exclaimed, her cheeks reddening.

Evelyn shrugged. "Worth a try."

Kellan and Theron both chuckled while Viktor shook his head. Evelyn was a very strange female. If not for her exquisite looks, Viktor would believe she was a juvenile male with the way she spoke and behaved.

Nora rubbed her forehead. "What I was going to say was we've received reports from the far north that some of the forest is recovering. Rather quickly, in fact."

"This is wonderful news," Eden replied buoyantly. The drain on Gwydion's powers had ceased and the forest of Burghard had experienced some degree of recovery. With any luck, these were signs the tide was turning.

She reached for Viktor's hand and squeezed. He was the first vampire to find his sieva in a century. She hoped their mating was the first of many and that some vampire pair would finally be blessed with a child.

Viktor returned his mate's warm grasp, but he didn't allow himself to read into this new information. Ever the cynic, he refused to allow false hope to bloom. It made avoiding disappointment much easier.

"Let us hope the healing of your land continues," Viktor toasted, raising his tumbler towards Kellan.

"Thank you." Kellan lifted his glass in response.

"Well," Theron said, "this seems like a good time for a break. I've had brunch prepared in the dining area, so let us finish this discussion with full bellies, hmmm?"

"Thank the Goddess, I'm starved," Evelyn proclaimed, dragging her sisters out the door.

Kellan and Viktor made to follow when Theron reached for Viktor's elbow.

"A minute, if you will?"

Viktor eyed the old man, then nodded.

"Kellan, please inform my mate I'll be along shortly."

"Of course," he said and exited the study.

Theron closed the door and moved back to his chair. Viktor moved to the closest seat across the desk. The priest's multi-colored irises swirled and spun as they stared at one another.

Viktor held very still, in that way only the Prajna could do. They could become motionless, even in respiration, when sensing a threat. Theron wouldn't attempt to harm Viktor, but the priest often saw too much and Viktor suspected he wouldn't want to hear whatever Theron was going to say.

"I am pleased you have found your sieva, Viktor. Happy for you, even."

"Thank you."

"Are *you* happy you have found her?"

A crinkle formed across Viktor's brow. "I do not understand what you're asking."

"It wasn't a difficult question."

"No, but it was an unnecessary one. What vampire would not find happiness in bonding with his mate?"

"Oh, I could name at least one," Theron replied giving the king a pointed look.

"She pleases me, immensely."

"I'm sure. But there is more to it, is there not?"

Viktor leaned forward, putting his elbows on the desk. His hulking form did nothing to intimidate the old man.

"What do you know, Theron?"

"I know you cannot continue the path you are on."

"And what path might that be?"

"The one where you keep secrets from the other half of your soul."

Viktor's teeth ground.

"You need to tell her and you need to tell her soon."

Viktor exhaled a harsh laugh. "Right."

He started to pull away from the desk when Theron's bony hands reached for his, holding him in place. The priest was much stronger than he appeared.

His eyes were eddying like the whirlpools near the cliffs. Viktor tensed but didn't fight him, caught in the hypnotic hues of Theron's gaze.

"Truth is the way forward. You cannot see it, but I can. Tell her. Before the next blood moon. No matter what course you end up taking, Eden must know the truth."

Viktor jerked away, needing reprieve from Theron's probing stare. The King was rattled. Theron had never touched him before, nor had he ever used whatever powers he possessed to force Viktor into anything.

It had felt like the priest was attempting a sort of compulsion. No one had been able to compel or hypnotize

Viktor, not even his own father who matched him in strength.

He wanted to retaliate, or at least rage against the male, to force him to agree never to do such a thing again. He knew he could not, not here on hallowed ground where Theron ruled.

When Viktor felt a little more in control, he met Theron's eyes, which had softened.

"The future is not a fixed point on a predetermined line, Viktor. Every decision affects the trajectory of what is possible. I cannot always see clearly, and I can rarely intervene. But in this, I advise you to listen or be prepared to lose."

"To lose what?" Viktor asked.

"Everything."

# Chapter 19

The sun was setting. The ocean below had turned to wondrously bright shades of orange and pink, courtesy of the fading light. Viktor was sitting in his usual chair on the balcony, with Eden in his lap.

To their right was the chair he'd had made for her. It was a cushioned lounger and far more comfortable than his own. Eden glanced at it, thinking Viktor should have sat in it instead of his iron one with no padding.

She'd yet to sit in hers for longer than a few minutes. Each time they came out to the balcony, Viktor would grow impatient with mere handholding. He'd scoop her up and drop in his chair, sighing contentedly as they watched the waves crash into the shore.

When Eden suggested a larger chair, built for two, he'd gotten a novel idea. He told her he'd have an outdoor bed made and they could make love on the balcony.

Eden's eyes twinkled when she'd replied, "We don't need a bed for that."

That was the first time he'd taken her against the wall, right there on the balcony. He informed her he was still going to have the bed made because it was good to have options.

Eden smiled thinking back to his jest from two evenings ago, having very much enjoyed the cold stone at her back and the hot vampire at her front. He was turning her into a lustful creature.

She'd considered offering to go into his feeding room. Each time, however, she couldn't bring herself to be in a place where he'd had so many others.

Judging by the apparatuses in that room, she knew he must have enjoyed acts she had long thought taboo. Being intimate with him so many times now, she no longer thought the contraptions distasteful.

A sort of morbid curiosity had been niggling at her more and more. Eden wanted to fulfill those needs for him. She need only be brave enough to voice it.

Eden also wanted to tell him how she felt. He'd stolen her heart and she'd gladly relinquished it. Viktor had never professed his love, but she could feel the connection to his soul and knew he cared for her deeply.

Several days had passed since their trip to see Eden's sisters. After they'd returned, Viktor had been even more attentive than before.

When she'd asked him if he needed to be somewhere else or preparing for the hunt, he'd told her he was where he needed to be. Soon he would be meeting Kellan at the border to start tracking and he wanted to spend every second he could with Eden before he left.

They hadn't been apart since the day they'd met and Eden found she didn't want to be apart from him, either. She didn't think it was normal to crave someone in the way she craved Viktor, and not just sexually.

She loved waking up with his large body wrapped around hers. He was overly affectionate, especially when they were alone, like now while they were sitting on the balcony. He made her feel safe and adored.

They hadn't been around the other Prajna since that day at court. At dinner tonight, Eden asked Viktor if they would be returning to the throne room anytime soon. He responded that he wasn't ready to share his time with anyone else besides his sieva. Eden worried he was sacrificing important duties in order to be with her.

She also had a hunch he believed himself to be protecting her. He'd been disturbed by the news of two possible suspects from his kingdom.

Not wanting her own anxieties to push through their bond, she concentrated on how much she enjoyed the past couple of days.

Viktor had started taking her on walks in the surf, telling her about Prajna. He promised he would take her around to his favorite places once he was sure the danger had passed.

It was the one blight on her happiness. Eden was beyond content here in Prajna. She missed her family, but she wouldn't give up Viktor for anything, not even for some sinister group who may very well be trying to kill her solely because she was his mate.

Her muscles must have tightened because Viktor shifted to get a better look at her face.

"What is it?" he demanded.

"Nothing."

"Your entire body is stiff as a board, *mala vestica*."

"Nothing, I just was thinking."

Now it was his turn to go rigid. "About?"

"Sephtis Kenelm."

He growled. "Do not waste your precious thoughts on such things. I will take care of it."

She nuzzled his jaw.

"I know. I'm not exactly worried. I feel better now that Nora has some ability to protect herself. I just want it to be over, so everyone can go on with their lives. Also ..." she paused.

"Also?"

"As much as I love being alone with you, it would be nice to feel safe enough to walk around by myself. Or to see something outside of your chambers."

"*Our* chambers," he corrected.

She laughed. "Yes, I meant our chambers."

Viktor slid his lower lip across his upper teeth. It was something he often did when thinking through a problem. Eden didn't think it was very kingly, but she liked how it made him seem more approachable and less intimidating.

"You're right. You shouldn't be cooped up in here." He stood with her still in his arms.

"I shouldn't? I thought it was too dangerous for me to explore."

"It is, but I think I know something you'll like and it's not a place where anyone lives or would likely be visiting."

He ported them away and Eden closed her eyes. It always made her so dizzy she worried she'd get sick.

"A little warning, next time," she gasped.

"Ah, yes, I apologize. Sometimes I forget."

Viktor set Eden on her feet and cupped her head with both hands, waiting for her to feel steady. His thumbs caressed her cheeks and she exhaled softly.

"That's nice."

"My touch?"

"The way you ground me. After ungrounding me," she smirked as her eyes opened.

"I like ungrounding you."

He kissed her languidly, drawing a groan from her mouth. She pushed against him, trying to press close. Viktor broke the kiss and gently nudged her back a few inches. Her lips puckered in a full pout and he chuckled.

"My apologies, Sieva. You drive me to distraction. I should know better than to start something I cannot finish here."

Eden glanced around at her new surroundings. She'd been so engrossed in his kiss she'd forgotten he'd ported them off the balcony. He was the master of distraction.

"Where are we?"

He grabbed her shoulders and turned her body to face away from his. Without letting go, he pulled her back to rest against him and his arms went down to her waist.

"I've brought you to our southern coast. To the lagoons. We call this area the Emerald Isle."

She expected to see shades of green, with such a name. However, the ocean looked much the same as it did from Castra Nocte. The water glimmered with the same shades of orange and pink, reflecting the fading sun.

The noticeable difference was the terrain. Castra Nocte was built high on the cliffs. The sounds of the ocean crashing into the rocks was a constant background.

A little further south of the castle was a stretch of beach where they could walk. The sand was dark, similar to the rocks of the cliffs. The shoreline was a large arc and the beach was narrow. At high tide, it was barely a sliver of land between the dunes and the water.

Here, the sand was a light tan. The shoreline snaked in and out, with shallow, elongated bodies of water abutting one another up and down the beach.

"My mother used to bring me here as a child. It was my favorite place to play and swim. Away from court, away from ... well, just away. She always knew when I needed a moment," Viktor said wistfully.

"It's beautiful."

"It is."

"I'm surprised no one lives here."

"The ground here is not conducive to building any sort of dwelling."

"That's unfortunate. The view is stunning. Do others come here just to sight see? Or get away, as you did?"

"No. Most Prajna are old enough to have been here many times over. It was once a rite of passage, being brought here by a parent to witness its splendor at nightfall. There are no longer any children to whom we can teach our geography or history. I haven't seen another here in a decade. I think it is too much of a reminder of what is now missing."

Eden spun in his arms. She lifted her hands to hold his handsome face, a doleful smile lifted her lips when he had to bend for her to reach him.

"We will bring *our* children here, Viktor."

Her words hit him square in his chest. A painful longing spread through his body, deep into his very soul. His hands shook as they rose to mimic hers, pressing his palms softly to the sides of her face.

Viktor looked back and forth into each of her eyes, memorizing every facet, every subtle change in the waning light. The sun was almost down, reminding him he was running out of time.

The next blood moon was only days away. The wedding two weeks after. Theron's warning plagued his conscience. He thought of little else aside from killing off the Sephtis Kenelm.

He'd been turning it over and over in his head. This morning, he decided to tell Eden the full truth when he returned from his hunt. He could not do it prior and then leave it to fester while he was with Kellan and Eden was alone in her anguish, or worse, her hatred.

His sieva could be logical and rational, but no male would make the mistake of assuming his mate could accept a marriage to another. It only added insult to injury that this marriage would put the other woman on the throne of Prajna.

It wouldn't matter that Viktor had no intention of living his life as Bianca's husband or to ever taking her to bed again.

Eden's smile dropped. She felt his troubled emotions radiating through their bond.

"What is it?" she asked.

"I was just looking at your eyes, at the differences in them."

It wasn't a lie. He was studying her raptly, committing her to memory, terrified she would never look upon him with the same regard once he confessed.

"Oh, yes, my sisters and I all share this trait. Our eyes don't match. We're ... strange in this way."

"*Unique*," he corrected.

"Unique, hmm?"

"Nora has one blue eye. Have you noticed it's the same shade as her husband's?"

Eden nodded.

"And what of this one, Eden?" his thumb brushed under her right eye, the emerald green one.

Eden inhaled. Neither had ever acknowledged it, but it was obvious.

"It's yours. I mean, it's the same color as yours."

"It is. It marks you as mine. As does this," he pulled her right hand up to his lips and kissed her cicatrice.

"And even this."

Viktor placed his palm over Eden's heart. He could feel the steady beat increase slightly.

"You feel it, don't you?" he whispered.

"Feel what?"

"The soul-bond. The connection. Your soul tethered to mine and mine to yours. We are united forever, Eden. There is nothing that will change it, there is no one that can replace it or break it. No matter what happens, we are bound to one another for life. Tell me you know this, that you feel it."

"I feel it, Viktor."

He wrapped his arms around her waist and lifted her so she was eye-level with him.

"Good. Promise me you'll remember. If ... when things become complicated or I do something you don't understand, promise me you'll remember I am just as bound to you as you are to me."

Eden's thoughts filled with worry. He was going hunting for the traitors very soon. He would probably be the one to kill the Prajna involved. She understood.

"Do you think I do not understand your duties? All they involve?"

"Eden—"

"I love you. No matter what comes, my heart is yours. Nothing can change that."

Her words, like the sharp blade of a knife, tore across his heart, leaving behind a jagged rift. Viktor did not deserve them, yet he craved them. No one, aside from his mother, had ever professed love for him. It was too much. He felt unworthy.

"Eden, I ..." his voice cracked, overcome by the storm of sentiments battering his undeserving soul.

"Shh, do not say it back. It is enough for me to know our souls are joined. I can *feel* you, through the bond. I know how you feel about me. It's more than enough."

Viktor opened his mouth to speak and Eden quieted him with a slow, simmering kiss. She put as much love and feeling into it as she could, showing him he shouldn't worry over how she felt.

He returned her ardor, holding her tight, swaying back and forth, dancing without music. In this moment, with just the two of them and no one for miles around, his life was perfect.

On and on they went, neither rushing or making any move to stop. Viktor was basking in the love of his mate. It was the sweetest, most precious moment of his life, living inside that kiss.

He slid his hand to the back of her neck and buried his fingers in her hair. After one more kiss, he tenderly tugged her head backwards.

The sun had dropped below the horizon and night had crawled across the shore. Her one emerald iris blazed in the dark, as he knew both his were likely doing.

Viktor hated to break the spell, but he would need to take her back soon. First, he wanted her to see why he'd brought them here.

"Look, *mala vestica*," he motioned with his head.

Eden turned and gasped. No matter what age a person was, this was the reaction the first time someone saw the Emerald Isle at night. It was the same for him when he was a boy.

The lagoons were covered in tiny green lights, floating on the surface. They undulated slightly in the water, emitting a stark emerald luminescence so brilliant she could easily see her environment in the dark.

"What is all of this?" she asked.

Viktor set her on her feet. His hand clutched hers and he pulled her towards the closest lagoon.

"It's algae that glows at night."

Eden tried to stop but Viktor continued tugging.

"It's perfectly safe, Eden. I've walked in it my entire life."

She didn't reply, but she did allow him to guide her to the lagoon. Viktor dropped to his knees and removed her boots and stockings, then he did the same to himself.

"The lagoons are shallow, but we'll stay close to the edges in case there are any predators in them."

"What predators?!"

Viktor laughed. "I'm joking, Eden. There's nothing in there scarier than I am."

"Really?"

"Truly. You think I'd go to all this trouble just to throw you to some hungry beast?"

"No. I think you like having me around too much to let me get eaten."

"Indeed," he replied, guiding her to the edge of the water.

Hand-in-hand, they traversed in and out of the shallows of the lagoons. Viktor watched happily as his mate giggled and splashed with her feet. It was a wondrous sight, and not just because of the glowing algae.

Eden was content, joyous even, despite the dangers she knew were looming over their lives. She was a miracle to a male such as he. It suddenly struck Viktor he was a danger to his mate's happiness.

A plan began to form, one he'd readily dismissed shortly after he'd found Eden. The one which played at the edges of his mind constantly. The flickering flame he'd allowed to burn. His last resort.

Viktor had never really believed he could go through with it. Seeing his mate blissfully enjoying the life he so wanted to give her changed something inside him. It did not matter if Luka was ill-mannered, ill-suited, and ill-prepared. Viktor's life was worth nothing without Eden's contentment.

His path was suddenly very clear to him.

When he returned from the hunt, he would offer Bianca a bribe. If she didn't take it, he would enact his plan. Goddess willing, the female would be reasonable for once and he wouldn't need to upend Luka's world.

Eden's loving gaze fell upon him and he knew he'd made the right decision. He grabbed her and ported directly to the side of their bed, uncaring he'd left behind their boots.

"Undress for me," his hoarse voice demanded.

Eden slowly removed her dress, lifting it over her head and throwing it aside. She stood in her lace undergarments, taking his breath away.

Eden sparked a carnal desire in him he could scarcely control. It was more than lust. He wanted to claim her, to own her. He would spend every waking moment buried inside her if he could, if only to feel her need for him through the bond.

Viktor's eyes raked over his mate. He would need to have more underthings made for her. He liked unwrapping her like a present, but his impatience typically resulted in him destroying the delicate garments. Tonight he would be patient.

"Remove them, Eden."

Eden reached behind her to unhook her bustier. She let it drop. Her nipples pebbled when the cool air touched them. Goosebumps broke out across her heated skin.

Hooking her thumbs in her panties, she slowly pushed them down. Viktor especially loved her underwear so she kept a sluggish pace getting them off, teasing him. Stepping out of the lace, she straightened and waited for his command.

"Come here, *moj vestica*."

Eden stepped up to his body, the silky fabric of his shirt rubbing against her chest. She licked her lips.

"Remove my shirt."

Eden lifted her hands between them and untucked his shirt. She unbuttoned efficiently, growing needy the longer she stood close to him. Viktor shrugged out of the sleeves and the shirt slipped to the floor.

"Now the rest."

Keeping her eyes locked on his, she grazed the front of his trousers reaching for the button. Viktor inhaled sharply. His mate was growing more confident in their bed play.

Eden used one hand to unfasten the top while the other lowered the zipper. His hot exhale skimmed across her face.

Eden pushed his pants down over his hips until they hit the floor. She was kneeling at his feet, a position she had yet to find herself.

Viktor often brought her pleasure with his mouth. Not once had he asked her for the same. Feeling bold, Eden reached for his shaft.

His hardened length flexed as Eden's hand wrapped around it. A shiver rippled down his abdominal wall. He'd not broached this act before.

Few had ever been allowed to put their mouth on him. Viktor never trusted the sharp teeth of an ambitious female Prajna who might "accidentally" trigger a mating bond by drawing his blood.

With Eden, it was different. He'd considered directing her to this a number of times, yet every time he stripped her bare, he could hardly think beyond his need to be inside her.

If Eden was curious, he would only encourage her. Viktor was dying to feel her hot mouth around him. He caressed the side of her face, rubbing a thumb over her bottom lip and opening her mouth.

Eden tentatively licked at the crown. The salty taste made her mouth water. She licked it again, this time with more enthusiasm.

"Take me into your mouth, Eden."

She closed her mouth around him and Viktor slid his hand into her hair to hold her still. She may have him in hand, but Viktor was the one in control.

"Go slowly until I say otherwise."

Eden was gazing up at him, her eyes blazing with desire. Her look alone was going to unman him.

She slid her mouth up and down his length, stroking with her small hand. Viktor shuddered violently. It thrilled her and she picked up her pace. This time he allowed it.

"Goddess, you undo me, Eden," he gritted.

She moaned around his flesh. Viktor could feel her little pink tongue pressing against the pulse of his cock. On the verge, he used her hair as leverage as he thrust into her mouth, careful not to go too deep.

"You're going to take me down your throat, little mate. You'll swallow it all, won't you?"

Eden hummed in agreement, agonized in her arousal. Pleasing him was intoxicating. She felt drunk on feminine power.

"Swallow," he grunted.

His hips rocked forward and his essence exploded across her tongue. She swallowed around him, feeling his pulsating release. He tasted like the ocean.

His grunts eased and his thrusts slowed. Once Viktor was spent, he reached down for his mate and threw her on the bed. She giggled in delight as she bounced. Viktor prowled towards her, the predator inside consumed with need to be inside his sieva.

"I promised myself tonight I would be patient. I promised tonight I would go slow and love every inch of your delectable body."

He crawled up onto the bed and loomed over her small frame. Her chest rose and fell, excited to discover whatever he was going to do to her.

Settling in the cradle of her thighs, his blunt head nudged at her entrance. Eden lifted her hips.

"Now ..."

"Now?" she prodded.

"Now I realize there is no going slow with you, not when I want you so."

"I feel the same, Viktor." Her voice was pleading. He was holding himself back, not pushing inside as she wanted.

"Good. Are you wet for me, my mate?"

Eden nodded as his fingers skimmed her folds.

"Ah, you are. My kisses down there will have to wait until later."

With that, Viktor plunged into her tight channel and Eden cried out. He withdrew and did it again. Eden's nails scored down his back, her heels dug into the back of his thighs.

"That's it, Eden. Mark me. Mark me as I mark you."

She exposed her neck and Viktor sunk his fangs into her throat, causing an immediate orgasm to rage through her. He swallowed her lifeblood, feeling it's powers fuel his body. Another pull on her vein and she peaked again, sobbing this time.

The smell of their joining and the flavor of her blood overwhelmed his senses. Viktor erupted, his ejaculate filling her womb. She was writhing and scratching at him wildly. He struggled to close the punctures in her neck as he groaned with his release.

Conflagration. It was the only way to describe what they shared every time they were joined. It was good he could recover quickly because he could never last long in Eden's arms.

Finally, their combined passion eased. Viktor collapsed over her, careful not to lower his entire weight. He was panting from his exertion. Eden's arms encircled his back and pulled him closer.

"I'll never let you go," he whispered into her ear.

"Good," Eden sighed contentedly. "I don't want to be let go."

Viktor prayed she could say those words again when he confessed his sin tomorrow night. Needing a distraction, he lowered himself down her body and lazily kissed her wherever he wanted.

# Chapter 20

*Western Border of Prajna*

Viktor yawned and Kellan slapped him good-naturedly on the back.

"Long night, my friend?"

Viktor scowled. They were currently resting against a boulder a few miles from Sanctus Femina, waiting for several scouts to return. Kellan had sent his wolves in different directions to see if they could pick up any trace of Agatha.

Kellan lifted his hands in surrender. "I meant no offense, Brother. I, myself, was kept up late by my wife. We've not been apart and she wasn't keen to let me sleep."

"Brother?" Viktor scoffed.

"Well, my mate is sisters with your mate. It clearly makes us family."

"You've been spending time with Evelyn, I see."

Kellan chortled. "Yes, she's not afraid to force people to come into the fold."

"Agreed. It is not normal."

Kellan snorted and shook his head. "Not used to it, eh? I thought you had a brother."

"I do. We do not act so ..." Viktor hesitated, debating how much he could trust the wolf. "We do not behave so informally. We have not been close since the last King's passing."

The confession had left Viktor's lips before he could even think to stop it.

"You mean your father."

"Yes, that King," Viktor grumbled, uncomfortable with the topic.

"Well, if it's any consolation, you're the preferred sovereign."

"Pardon?"

"You. Edward and I, as well as Theron, think you're the better choice. Nikolai's nature was worrisome."

"You have no idea."

"I could probably guess, not that it's any of my business. Not much news of Prajna reaches beyond your border. You vampires are good at secret-keeping."

Viktor shrugged.

"I met Nikolai twice, briefly, when I was young," Kellan continued. "My father occasionally took me to Theron's meetings. A few minutes was more than enough time to pass judgement on Nikolai's state. He wasn't just being an ass. There was something dark inside him, twisted. I think he was going mad."

Kellan eyed Viktor, who hadn't responded. The Vampire King wasn't exactly verbose. Kellan couldn't blame him. Kellan was raised by two loving parents and, despite the heartbreak he felt over his father's murder decades ago, his life had never been anything short of a blessing.

He wondered what sort of life Viktor had lived. Certainly not a happy one. Those feeling blessed by the Goddess do not earn nicknames such as *Heartless*.

Then again, Viktor had done what was necessary to secure peace for his people. Killing his father would have left a mark, but in the end, the entire kingdom was better off.

Viktor's reticence was indication enough he did not want to discuss Nikolai, so Kellan changed the subject. "Speaking of not my business, when's the wedding?"

Viktor froze, unable to take a breath for a moment.

"Wedding?" he coughed.

"Nora and I only did a binding ceremony, but if you're going to do anything, no matter how small, I would request you include her sisters. They're close and would want to be there for Eden."

Viktor thought how to construct his response. Wolves could smell untruths. He wasn't prepared to share his predicament, especially not when Eden was still unaware.

The truth was, he wanted to marry Eden. He simply couldn't, not with how things were. Goddess willing, he'd be able to fix the mess. He was banking on his perceived loophole actually working.

"If Eden and I were to ever have a ceremony, of course her family would be in attendance."

It was the absolute truth. He'd give Eden whatever she wanted if they could marry.

"Good. I can't wait to see where you live," Kellan cackled, knowing it would rile the vampire.

The Prajna had always been guarded about the location of the royal family's residence. Kellan was dying to know where it was.

"Very funny, wolf. You know I could port you there and you wouldn't actually know where you were."

"Sounds fun."

"Are you always like this?"

"Like what?" Kellan asked, not at all affronted.

"Nosy? Incorrigible?"

"Absolutely. Wolves are inquisitive, didn't you know?"

It was Viktor's turn to chortle. The annoying male was surprisingly likeable. He reminded him of Luka, minus the bitterness.

He'd never spent time with wolves outside of Theron's meetings at the temple. Viktor had always thought wolves to be unstable, looking to tussle whenever possible.

He hadn't expected Kellan to be so entertaining or jovial. It went against the Burghard's brutish reputation.

Viktor wished the circumstances of their time together today were different. He'd never imagined any sort of extended family in his life. Eden waltzing into his world had changed that.

"Would it make you feel better to ask me questions?" Kellan inquired.

"No."

Kellan laughed.

"Fair enough. There is one thing I did want to address, to make sure the air was clear between us."

Viktor's right eyebrow rose.

Kellan cleared his throat and blurted, "You do know I was to marry her, right?"

"Who?"

"Eden."

Viktor growled low in his throat. His claws lengthened as he fought his desire to lash out at the King of Wolves, perhaps remove his jugular and feast upon his marrow.

"Easy, vampire. It wasn't as if I wanted to marry her. It was arranged when she was just a babe. When she turned eighteen, I was invited to visit. That's when Fate intervened. Nora swept into the room and my life changed forever, yours, too, in a roundabout way."

"And you thought it prudent I know Eden was your betrothed?" His words were curt but his claws did retract. The wolf would live to see another day.

"I would want to know, if it was Nora. There should be nothing but truth between mates, no lingering secrets that might bring forth negative emotions. I wasn't sure if Eden had told you and I didn't want to risk any animosity between us over it."

Viktor resentfully acknowledged the truth of Kellan's response—though it had nothing to do with the betrothal. The blood moon was tomorrow night.

Even if he managed to get Bianca to agree to what he wanted, he'd still have to tell Eden he'd kept something from her. If he didn't get Bianca to agree, Luka was in for the shock of his life.

"Kellan—" he started when he heard movement.

Both males jumped to their feet, scanning the tree line. One of Kellan's men, Bran, burst through the foliage in a dead sprint. He shifted in the air and came to an abrupt stop ten yards away.

"We found her," he panted.

"Show us," Kellan growled as he hurriedly removed his clothing and shifted, bounding off after the other wolf.

Viktor sprinted after them.

For miles they ran, skirting the border between Prajna and Burghard. They weaved in and out of the underbrush, following the tracker at a rapid pace.

Viktor could make out a very faint scent of wolf not belonging to any he knew. The trail was weeks old and disappeared in spots, but an unknown wolf had definitely been here.

Eventually, the scent disappeared completely. Viktor could hear a running brook nearby. It would have been smart of Agatha to travel in the water where no scent could be traced.

They followed the sound of the stream until they came upon a small waterfall emptying down into an oval basin. Halting on the ridge beside the water, Kellan and the other wolf shifted to human form.

Viktor stopped beside them. Peering over the edge, he could see a bloated body at the edge of the shallow pool, two Burghards were standing a few feet away with their arms crossed.

"Is it her?" he asked Kellan.

Kellan raised a questioning brow to Bran who nodded slowly.

"How did she die?" The Wolf King hissed bitterly, disappointed he was now unable to dispense justice for his wife's attacks by one of his own.

Bran glanced at his king. "We assume she drowned. There are no marks on her, nothing's broken as far as we can see. She's been dead a couple of days."

"I'm surprised scavengers haven't gotten to the body," Viktor remarked.

"They wouldn't have scented her. She was under a rock, just heavy enough to hold her down. We were lucky we came up this ridge. Alec caught the glint of her necklace under the water."

Kellan snarled in frustration. "She would have been strong enough to get out, even if she'd somehow fallen with a rock atop her."

"Not if she'd chosen to stay under," Viktor interjected.

"Suicide?" Bran huffed. "Not likely."

"No, not suicide. Hypnosis," Viktor deduced. "The demon is dead. The elemental is dead. Now the wolf. That leaves the one person who happens to be capable of hypnosis."

"The vampire," Kellan sniffed and lifted his head, no longer interested in the body.

"Bran, I don't suppose there was any scent on Agatha, strong enough to identify who she was with?" Viktor knew the answer, but asked it anyway.

"No. She's been in the water too long."

They stood in silence for a long minute. Bran shifted restlessly.

"My liege?" Alec called from below.

"Alec."

"Your orders?"

Kellan raised his chin and howled fiercely into the air. The other three wolves joined in, creating an ear-splitting chorus of song soaring out across the land.

\* \* \*

*Castra Nocte, Eastern Shore of Prajna*

"So you've been put on babysitting duty, then?"

Yuri tried not to choke on the bite he'd just swallowed. He and Mariana were currently having lunch with Eden in Viktor's private dining room.

"My King requested I spend some time with his sieva this day. I was happy to oblige."

Mariana beamed. "Yes, we both were. Especially since Yuri said I could take you exploring today."

The male gave his wife a pointed look. "Only to certain areas, Mari, and with either myself or a guard."

"Yes, yes, I know," she waved him off.

Eden grew excited at the prospect of finally seeing her new home. "Thank you, Mari. Viktor failed to mention this before his departure. It's a lovely surprise. I can't tell you how boring it is spending day after day in our chamber."

"Do not let the people of Prajna hear you say the King is boring in his own bed chamber."

Eden's head whipped around to see a smirking Luka leaning against the archway.

"Luka," Yuri warned.

Luka lifted his hand, "It was only meant in jest, Yuri. I'm not here to cause problems. I only wanted to see how my brother's sieva was faring without him. It is not easy for mates to be apart for long."

His eyes were on his boots when he added softly, "Or so I've heard."

His statement took Eden by surprise. It tugged at her heart, a complete contradiction to her first impression of the male. He looked almost vulnerable, hovering and unsure of himself.

*Was there more to Luka than the taunting display he'd shown in the throne room?* Eden considered. His demeanor and comment pointed to the same thing. Apparently, Luka mourned the sieva he could not find.

His tone was sincere, and she did feel a smidgen guilty over the way their last encounter had ended with Viktor's hands around Luka's neck.

Eden wanted the gap between the brothers to be bridged. For Viktor's sake, she would not be the cause of further discord.

"It's fine. Luka, please join us for lunch," Eden asked him, patting the chair to her right.

Luka, to his credit, appeared flummoxed.

"I don't want to intrude."

Eden disliked the insecurity of his tone. It was easier for her to handle someone she found deplorable. This did not sound like the same Luka she'd met last week.

"Nonsense. We are basically family, now, and it is high time we begin acting like it."

Luka gawked at Eden. She wanted him to sit and share a meal with her, despite his disgraceful behavior at court. His brother was a lucky bastard, despite Luka's previous assertion over the situation Viktor was in with Bianca.

217

Clearing his throat and acting with more bravado than he felt, he took the seat to Eden's right. One of the servants immediately brought an extra plate and served the Prince of Prajna.

"Looks divine," he commented, digging in. He could feel the three sets of eyes on him, likely waiting for him to do something unseemly.

Luka supposed he'd earned their wariness. Acting out had become easier than dealing with the ugliness he felt inside. Eden didn't deserve his animosity, so he'd do his best to reign in his antagonistic nature.

She'd not been the one to bring forth the problems in Prajna. Goddess willing, she'd be the one to help end them. At least, according to Theron.

Viktor wasn't the only one who sought the priest's counsel. Luka had meant what he'd said to his brother in the throne room. He had been travelling, researching, trying to find a way to break the contract without anyone getting killed. When he reached a dead end, he went to the temple.

Theron didn't have exact answers. Though, he did tell Luka to trust Eden, that she was the way forward. Luka didn't see how, but he accepted the advice and returned to the castle to find her.

He was surprised to discover she was in the private dining room and Viktor was nowhere to be found. His brother hadn't once allowed Eden to move around Castra Nocte without him.

"So, where is my illustrious brother this fine day?" Luka asked, curious what had kept Viktor from his sieva.

He also wanted to break the group's silent judgement of his presence.

"He's in the forest," Eden replied, picking up her silverware again.

"Doing what, hunting?" Luka scoffed.

Eden paused, her knife and fork hovering over her meal.

"Eden, perhaps—" Yuri started to say.

"What in the name of Imperium would the King of Prajna be hunting?" Luka interrupted.

Eden straightened in her chair, searching her mind for an appropriate response. Viktor never shared with her whether or not he'd told Luka about Sephtis Kenelm.

Yuri knew. He'd seen the missive from Theron.

Eden caught Mariana's nervous eyes, shifting from Eden to Luka. Eden doubted Yuri's wife knew the full situation. Yuri went to great lengths to keep her out of trouble.

Since Eden arrived in Prajna, Yuri and Mariana had been her only companions outside of Viktor. Luka had yet to prove his worth, but he was Viktor's only sibling. She wanted to trust him, to trust all three of them.

Eden wasn't Queen, nonetheless, she needed to act the part if Viktor wasn't around. Trust should be earned, but there wasn't time to forge such bonds in a short period of time.

Viktor should have shared with her who knew the truth of what was going on. Eden should have asked him.

219

It was far too easy to be distracted in their bed and she'd ended up putting her desires before what should be her due diligence with matters of state.

It was very unlike Eden to allow her heart to lead her head.

She laid her utensils down and pushed her plate away. Crossing her arms, she set her elbows upon the table, taking her time to show each of her companions her serious regard.

"I find myself at a disadvantage," she stated. "I realize, remaining circumscribed to the royal chambers, despite it being Viktor's preference, has done more harm than good."

"It's not safe, Eden," Yuri insisted.

"Yes, I know. I'm not saying I should be walking around and doing as I please. I'm saying I don't know anyone here. Not really. And no one knows me. One must have interaction in order to build a foundation."

Mariana's brow furrowed. "A foundation of what?"

"Trust," Eden replied.

"What are you trying to say?" Mariana asked.

"She doesn't trust me."

Mariana snorted at Luka's statement. "Do you really find that surprising?"

Luka ignored the barb, staying focused on Eden. "What is Viktor hunting?" he asked again.

"For goodness' sakes, she just admitted she doesn't trust you," Mariana scolded.

Luka's dark head slowly swiveled menacingly towards Mariana. "Do *you* know what Viktor is doing in the forest?"

"Well, no, but I hardly see how that matters."

Yuri patted his wife's hand and shook his head. His sieva pursed her lips, but remained quiet.

"What are you getting at, Eden?" Yuri inquired.

"I want a promise ... no, I want an unbreakable oath, that you'll not disclose, discuss, or share what I tell you in confidence with anyone under any circumstances, without my express permission."

"Done," Luka promised. He didn't need to think about it.

"Oh, good show!" Mariana complemented Eden. "Yes, very clever to extract a contract from Luka."

Eden hid her grimace.

"I'll need one from you, as well, Mariana. And Yuri."

Mariana sputtered indignantly and Luka laughed, clapping his hands in delight. Yuri remained very quiet, stroking his wife's hand with his thumb, thinking he may very well have to kill Bianca so the better woman could be Queen.

# Chapter 21

*Western Border of Prajna*

Viktor was restless. The longer he was away from Eden the more on edge he became. Couple that with the dead end they'd run into, and the impending blood moon, and Viktor was fit to be tied.

"How much longer?" he asked.

"They should be here any minute. They weren't very far away," Kellan replied.

The group howl had been a summons for the other wolves to return to their king. Kellan was going to have them concentrate their search in all directions, spreading from the pool where they'd found Agatha's body.

Unfortunately, Alec and Bran had been the only wolves to scent both the Prajna who had attacked King Edward and the one who had been in the clearing where they'd found Isla.

They would have to break into two groups and move in concentric circles. Any of them could scent a vampire, but they needed Alec or Bran to confirm it was the right one.

After taking a closer look at the she-wolf, Kellan ordered the men to burn her body while they waited for the others. Agatha would not get the burial rites of her people. It was the only act of retribution Kellan could now extract.

Viktor could feel the pain of disloyalty radiating from the wolf. He was taking it as a personal offense against him, not just against his people. Agatha had been a friend. Or so he'd believed.

Viktor knew the feeling all too well. It would affect the wolf's ability to trust—which might not be a bad thing considering there had been a murderous group of assassins on the loose.

"While we wait, I'm going to retrieve one of my men. If we're in two groups, I'd like to have at least one Prajna with each."

Kellan licked his upper teeth. "Isn't your home on the coast?"

Viktor rolled his eyes, a habit of his mate and her sisters. One that was now his, evidently.

"I'm just saying that's an awfully far distance to travel. My men will reach us soon."

The wolf's eyes were sparkling mischievously and Viktor grunted.

"I find you very annoying, wolf"

"Tis the way of families, is it not?"

"You're digging for information. Where I live. How I travel. I'm certain you already know the latter."

Kellan flashed a big, toothy grin. "Nora said you were smart. Don't worry. I've not been broadcasting your abilities to the world at large. My father saw you arrive at the temple once. 'Appeared right out of thin air!' he'd exclaimed. He was quite impressed, if it helps."

"Bloody wolves," Viktor muttered, earning another slap on the back.

"Go on, get your man. We'll eat while you're gone. I'm sure my wolves are hungry."

"You've brought food?"

Kellan unsheathed his claws. "No. We'll hunt food. With your permission, of course."

"Just don't eat any of my people."

Kellan's grin widened. "I'll see what I can do."

Viktor assumed Kellan was joking. He'd hurry, just in case.

Even though Kellan knew about Viktor's ability to port, he didn't think the others did, so he walked some thirty yards into the thick of the forest before tracing away to Castra Nocte.

\* \* \*

"I swear upon my name, I will not discuss, disclose, or share anything you tell me in this room without your express permission. Unless it is an absolute matter of life and death or could bring harm to an innocent life."

The magic of Yuri's oath zapped across Eden's skin. He was the last of the three to pledge. He'd instructed Luka and Mariana to add the last caveat, just in case.

Yuri had insisted there needed to be a way out in the direst of circumstances, especially when dealing with something so serious. He also told her to be very wary of demanding pacts for they all had magically-enforced consequences. Eden fully intended to heed his warning.

"Now," Luka said, "what is so important you demanded an enchanted oath?"

Eden took a sip of wine, a deep breath, and let the story unfold. She started with the death of her mother and the fact it had been poison that took Elora's life. When Eden mentioned Sephtis Kenelm, Mariana's face went white.

She kept the details succinct and refrained from displays of emotion, even when revealing the attack on her father. When her story ended with where Viktor was today, Mariana was shaking her head and Luka's face was pinched. Yuri's expression gave away nothing.

"That was quite a tale," a deep voice rumbled with disapproval from the door.

Eden pushed her seat back, launching herself up and throwing her arms around Viktor. She buried her head in his chest. He'd only been gone for half the day, but she'd missed him terribly.

Guarded green eyes fell upon her face when she lifted to offer a kiss. Viktor simply glared.

"Are you angry with me?" she inquired cautiously.

"Angry? No."

"Oh, good—"

"I'm beyond furious. What were you thinking, Eden? There are reasons I do not disclose certain things to certain people."

Luka pointed a finger in the air. "If I may—"

"You'd do well to remain quiet," Viktor spoke sharply.

"—your sieva took precautions," Luka continued, ignoring his older brother's threatening tone. "Brilliant precautions, if I might add."

"Thank you, Luka," Eden said. She pushed away from Viktor, scowling. "I am neither dim nor inexperienced with handling sensitive information, Viktor. *You* would do well to remember that."

Viktor's eyes crinkled in the corners. He loved the fight in her. She was the only person he allowed to speak to him in such a manner. Others had tried and paid for it with their lives.

He wasn't really furious with her, but he thought she had been careless with information. He reached for her arm and jerked her forward into his iron embrace. Eden didn't struggle.

"I don't like it when you speak to me thus."

The corners of her mouth lifted. "I think you do."

A soothing vibration ran up and down their bond. Viktor sighed and bent to kiss the corner of her mouth. If they'd been alone, he'd have her pinned against the wall.

After inhaling her essence at the crook of her neck, he straightened and escorted Eden back to her seat. Viktor stood behind her chair and rested his hands on her shoulders.

Mariana, Yuri, and Luka were gawking at the pair as if they had suddenly sprouted extra heads. Viktor knew he was losing his reputation as someone to be feared. So long as it didn't spread past this group, he could live with it.

"Tell me, Brother, of these brilliant precautions."

"She forced us to swear on our names to never disclose, discuss, or share what she told us without her permission."

"All of you?"

"Yes," Mariana complained, "all three of us."

"Come now, wife, don't be so cross. It was the best way to trust us," Yuri chastised as kindly as he could.

Viktor massaged Eden's shoulders affectionately. "Well done, Eden."

"I know," she chirped. She could feel Viktor's mirth through the bond and it felt wonderful. She was growing tired of his newfound apprehension, which was getting worse by the day. It only fed her own anxieties.

"Join us," Yuri pointed to Viktor's seat at the head of the table.

"I cannot. I must return. I only came here to retrieve you. I need your assistance."

"But of course. Is everything okay?"

"We found the wolf."

Eden's breath caught.

"She was already dead, under the water in a shallow pool. We're guessing the vampire used his or her power to force her to drown herself. Aside from the obvious, nothing else was wrong with the body."

Mariana covered her mouth and Yuri rubbed her back.

"And then there was one," Luka whispered.

"Isn't that good news?" Mariana asked.

"We're not sure the vampire was working alone. The wolves picked up on two different scents in Burghard during two different attacks. Both were vampire," Viktor responded.

Yuri kissed Mariana on her cheek then rose from his seat. "I'm at your service, Viktor."

"You might want to change your clothes. We'll be navigating the edge of the marshlands. I can meet you outside the guardhouse in, say, twenty minutes?"

"Of course. Wife, don't wait up."

Marian nodded and bit her lip nervously.

"Eden, I have a couple of things I need to do before I meet Yuri. I apologize I cannot give you any time today."

Eden put her hand on his and craned her neck. "Do not apologize for doing your job, Viktor."

Viktor knelt beside Eden and kissed her firmly, yet briefly, on the lips. His knuckles brushed her cheek just before he rose.

"Take care of my sieva, Luka. I'd like someone with her until I return. Goddess knows why, but she seems to be enjoying your company."

"I will guard her with my life."

"I know," Viktor answered, shocking Luka with his faith in him.

"Can we still explore today?" Eden asked.

Viktor really didn't want her to, but he'd promised. He'd already taken measures the past week to tighten security by limiting who was allowed in and out of the castle. He'd even sent some of the more jealous females in the Komora away to another property.

It wasn't much, but his order had delighted his mate. She'd been very obliging and patient with him when he'd told her he couldn't simply send them back from where they came. It would have been an insult to their families and the females might be shunned for it.

Though, he didn't actually believe anyone in the Komora was a member of Sephtis Kenelm. He had seen each of them in various states of undress and not one had the marking the members carried on their chests—not that he'd ever tell Eden how he knew. She was smart enough to guess and he was smart enough not to call attention to it.

Members of Sephtis Kenelm had a tattoo-like brand over their heart with the brotherhood's name in a swirling script. Viktor had Yuri check every royal guard. None carried the mark.

All signs pointed to the traitor being somewhere near the border. He doubted any fool would come to Castra Nocte and raise so much as a finger against Eden when

229

either Viktor or Luka was around. Their grisly reputations were rooted in truth.

"I'd prefer not, *mala vestica*. Not unless you can talk Luka into showing you some of Castra Nocte."

She turned a hopeful face towards the male.

"It would be my pleasure, Eden."

Mariana clapped, eager to show Eden the beauty of their home.

"Do not leave the castle," Viktor ordered.

"We won't," Eden promised.

Viktor brushed his lips across hers and headed for the door.

"Oh," he turned towards Luka, "stay out of the kitchens."

Luka cocked his head, as if waiting for Viktor to explain. Viktor held his tongue, preferring to cut it out before he announced Bianca had decided to invite several chefs today to finalize wedding fare. He was looking forward to ruining it for her.

Viktor disappeared before anyone could question him on it, confident they would obey.

# Chapter 22

Viktor ported straight to the kitchens. He'd expected a flourish of activity, but the area was calm. Bianca sat at a large table covered in a variety of dishes.

She stood the second she saw him, wiping her hands down the front of her dress. It was a nervous trait she'd never shown before.

Viktor's eyes darted to just above her cleavage, half expecting to see a black brand. Or maybe it was hope? Treason carried penalty of death, which would unquestionably solve all of his current problems.

He cursed himself for such foolishness. He'd seen that skin a thousand times. Nothing blemished her skin. She was virtually flawless—physically, that was.

"Come," he commanded, holding out his hand.

Bianca blanched. Viktor hadn't sought her out since she'd returned to Castra Nocte. The only contact they'd had was the night she'd stupidly gone to his balcony and then again, briefly, when she'd asked to speak with him at court.

He'd only learned of her meetings today after a guard alerted him upon his return from the forest.

Schooling her surprise, she rounded the table and lifted her hand to grab his. She'd barely touched him when he ported them to her rooms.

As soon as they landed he jerked his palm from her grasp. Viktor did not want to touch her any more than he had to.

"I'm guessing you didn't come to taste the food," she commented dryly.

"Sit." Viktor pointed to the chair next to her dressing table.

"I think I'll stand, unless ..." she nodded to the bed.

"I am not in the mood for your games, female," he snarled.

"Very well."

Bianca lowered to the chair and crossed her arms. Viktor was in a mood. He was never cheerful, but he could usually be pacified with sex. His sieva had ruined that for Bianca.

She wished she could say her poor reaction was due to jealousy. On some level, it was. Mainly, Bianca was terrified Viktor intended to force her to leave the safety of Castra Nocte. Without his protection, what would she do?

"Release me from the contract, Bianca. Name your price and you'll have it. But release me."

She inhaled sharply, her features hardening. Swallowing, she dared to defy The Heartless King.

"No," she spoke softly, but with conviction. "You know I cannot. I am not the one who created the agreement."

"You can and you damned well know it. Dmitri loved you. He gave you an out."

"Only if I did not want you. So long as I do, I'm just as bound to this as you are."

Viktor's mask slipped. He knew she would refuse. However, he never believed she actually wanted him, only the title he could offer her.

"Do not look so surprised, Viktor. It doesn't suit you."

"I have my sieva. We are bonded. How could you possibly want someone who could never have interest in you? We will never live as man and wife. *Never*. All you would get from this is a title."

A humorless laugh escaped her lips.

"You think I only ever wanted to be Queen?"

"Don't you?"

"Of course I do! But you are very foolish if you think you're not the reason I ..." her voice trailed off, unable to finish.

"The reason you what?"

"It doesn't matter."

She knew he'd never feel the same, but Bianca didn't care. He offered her a safe place to live. The marriage would give her a position of power, of control. It was the one thing she would never willingly relinquish. She refused to ever be vulnerable again.

"Last chance, Bianca. Give me what I want or I'll be forced to take drastic measures."

Seconds ticked by slowly. Bianca bore his glower, feeling thousands of tiny daggers stab the back of her eyes. She'd never let it show, but she did care for him. It wasn't love, but it was something.

"I—I cannot," she finally responded.

"Then you leave me no choice."

"Viktor ..." She wanted to ask him what he meant. She was too afraid of his response to follow through.

"You are to remain in your rooms the rest of the day."

"Gorlind is coming today."

"He can attend to you in your rooms. Better yet, send him away. I'll never see you in that dress. *Never.*"

With his final declaration, Viktor ported out of her room. If he'd stayed but a second longer, he'd have seen the cracks in her icy demeanor break wide open.

* * *

"You were right, Mariana, Castra Nocte is a marvel. Truly," Eden stated.

Yuri's mate beamed proudly and continued chattering away as they headed towards the throne room.

Luka had led the trio around the castle and allowed Mariana to show off her knowledge of history. It was a fortress decorated in antiquity.

Priceless vases and urns lined the halls. The weapons room was a museum of sorts, where long-outdated armaments were hung in neat rows, gathering dust.

Eden had been especially impressed with the enormous tapestries in the main hall, telling stories of battles and wars fought over the millennia. Some were the only archives remaining after a fire had wiped out a large part of the library centuries ago.

She now understood Viktor's reluctance to allow Eden to use her powers inside. Fire was her favorite power, and it was the easiest to wield. It also scared a lot of people. She should probably tell him she could also control other elements.

It was hard being forthcoming with such information after a lifetime of being forced to keep it hidden. Eden knew her father's concern was warranted, but hiding it was starting to feel like she was lying.

She doubted Viktor would be upset. It's not like he set aside a lot of time for conversation when they were together. It wasn't an excuse, per se, she was just easily distracted by the male.

It had only been hours since Viktor left the dining room and Eden was once again pining for his touch. He might not return until tomorrow, so she needed to focus on something else.

Eden watched Luka open the doors to the throne room. From behind, the two males were almost identical.

She forced her attention to the room they were entering, wondering what she would learn from Mariana.

"It's beautiful, is it not?" Mariana sighed.

"It is. Viktor brought me here once before."

"Yes, I remember it well. Wonderful first meeting," Luka added sarcastically.

"Not my fault," Eden countered.

Luka's shoulders shook as he bit his lip. He really did like his brother's little mate.

"It's known for its windows. The stained glass took years to create," Mariana informed Eden, changing the subject.

The three of them walked closer to the far wall. The sun was low in the sky, bringing out the darker hues of orange and red in the glass. The prismatic effect spread across the shining floors, making the room look like it had been set aflame.

"Why fire?" Eden questioned.

"It's one of the few things than can kill us, yet we do not fear it as we should. Something in the Prajna make-up is intrigued by the flame," Luka replied.

"Why put it here, as décor in the throne room? It seems ... I don't know, like a reminder of your weakness. This is a room where the Prajna must stand strong."

Luka looked to Mariana who sighed dreamily. She'd always loved this part of Castra Nocte.

"We're not sure," she told Eden. "I always thought it was because these were the only colors the glass makers could manage all those years ago."

Luka snorted. "Perhaps. I see it more as a poetic show of strength and courage. It's saying, *Here we are, surrounded by flames, and yet we continue on our path*."

"I like that assessment," Mariana complemented Luka. "It's much better than my guess."

Luka dipped his chin bashfully, making him look far younger than he was. He clasped his hands behind his back and walked towards the dais.

"I used to despise coming in here, when my father was king. Viktor and I used to pretend the flames were real and they'd eventually crawl up the steps and destroy him."

He scratched at his head, ghosts of his past dancing across his mind. "In the end, I guess *we* were the flames."

Eden tried to keep the pity out of her eyes. She'd never experienced such depravity as Luka and Viktor must have. Nikolai was a monster.

"You and Viktor did what was necessary, Luka," Mariana contended. "When you were old enough and knew things could not continue, you saved Prajna from a wicked man."

"We did not do it alone. Others were not as lucky to live long enough to see it through.

He opened his palm and ran his finger along the edges of his cicatrice. His had an irregular shape. It was serrated, somewhat similar to a lightning bolt. Or, it had been.

Nikolai had purposefully defaced it by forcing Luka to hold the wrong end of a blade. He'd splayed it open and refused to allow Luka to seek the healer. His father had laughed maniacally, taunting him by saying Luka would never find the match.

"Sometimes I wonder if it was worth the price," he mused remorsefully.

Dmitri's death. The lack of sievas. No live births. It was a hefty fine to pay. Luka didn't regret assisting Viktor in usurping the throne. It didn't mean he rejoiced in it either. Patricide was a ghastly deed, no matter the circumstances.

Eden moved close to Luka and put a hand on his shoulder.

"I'd like to think you were the flames, as well," she said. "After a fire, everything is blackened. Charred. Lifeless. However, under all the devastation, under the ash and ruins, life blooms anew. It might only be the tiniest of seeds, but it can grow and thrive. A life that would never have stood out among the invasive weeds had the fire not extinguished what should never have been allowed to take root."

She held up her palm, showing her crescent-shaped birthmark. "It's taken a century, but this might be the start. Let us have hope, Luka. Without it, life becomes inundated with weeds."

Luka's mouth twisted. "You'll not allow me to wallow, will you?"

"No. It's not in my nature to put up with such nonsense."

Mariana giggled, enjoying how easily Eden pulled Luka out of his forlorn reverie. The Prajna simply did not speak to the royals like this. Eden was special.

"Well, I for one ..." Mariana began when a commotion of voices echoed into the room. Three heads swung towards the opened doors.

"She's kept me waiting for hours. I'll not be blamed for the disaster this dress shall become!" a male voice boomed.

"Stay here," Luka ordered and jogged towards the entryway. Just outside was a good-sized space where people typically congregated while waiting to enter the throne room.

Eden followed and Mariana grabbed at her arm.

"We should stay in here," she firmly suggested.

"I'm not leaving. I just wanted to see what was going on. It sounds like some male crying over a dress."

"Then we really should stay put. I'm serious, Eden. You shouldn't follow Luka."

Eden's eyes narrowed at her friend's reproach. Her head twisted towards the door. She could see Luka and two others arguing quietly. She wrote off Mariana's suggestion and strode towards the doors.

One of the men was rather portly, waving a blood-red dress around in both hands. His face was ruddy, giving him an even angrier appearance. The thick leather belt around his large midsection contained a variety of scissors, threads, and other tools for sewing.

The other two, Luka and a palace guard, had their hands up in a placating manner, but the dressmaker was having none of it.

"Please don't go out there," Mariana implored, tugging on Eden's hand.

"He's not going to sew me to death. Calm yourself," Eden reprimanded, deciding not to leave the doorway since Mariana was getting so worked up. The female's grip tightened.

"Tis the Queen's dress. I've not finished it because it needs a final fitting. She was to meet me here and I've seen neither hide nor hair of that female. How can I finish this before the ceremony if she'll not give me the time of day?"

Eden stilled. Someone had made her a dress? While thoughtful, it was not something she'd expected—and she'd never have chosen to wear such a garish shade, not with her coloring.

"Prajna has not crowned a Queen, Gorlind. Do not refer to her as such until it is done."

Eden flinched at the vehemence in Luka's tone. *Maybe he was still upset about earlier?*

"Forgive me, Sire, but the ceremony is in two weeks. I only meant this is the dress for the wedding which will give Prajna its new Queen. I need to finish it."

Eden cleared her throat and Luka spun around.

"What ceremony?" she asked.

Eden had never broached the subject of a binding ceremony or a wedding with Viktor. He had a lot to deal with and she'd put it off, accepting the soul-bond was far more significant than any legal commitment.

It was sweet he was planning something. Though, she would like to have been involved. She'd need to reach out to her family and make sure they could attend if it was only two weeks away.

Butterflies fluttered and she suddenly felt very excited at the prospect of walking down the aisle towards her love.

"Mariana, take Eden back to her rooms."

Mariana pulled on Eden's hand, but Eden shook her off, confused over the sharpness in Luka's voice.

"What ceremony?" she repeated. Everyone was acting very strangely, like she was not to know anything of her own wedding.

"The King's wedding, of course," Gorlind chuffed. "It's been planned forever, nearly a century. Why people plan these things so far in advance is beyond me, but to each their own."

"But ... I've only known Viktor a short time."

Gorlind coughed, "Yes, well—"

"Eden. Go back to your chambers." Luka's voice whipped through the air, interrupting the dressmaker.

"Absolutely not," she denied him, the fluttering in her stomach turning to apprehension.

When Luka made to step towards her, she raised her hands, wiggling her fingers in silent challenge. She was already edgy, her powers itching and pulsing to be released. If he touched her, she'd scorch him.

"Gorlind, was it?" she said to the stout male.

"Yes, m'lady. Prajna's finest dressmaker," he boasted, adding a shallow bow. "And who might you be, *mala kurva*?"

Little lass he'd called her.

No queen on any throne would be addressed as such. No soon-to-be queen would be, either. He'd seen 'neither hide nor hair of that female.' He knew who he was looking for. It obviously wasn't Eden.

Her synapses started firing, her shrewd intellect puzzling things out. The spokes and cogs of her psyche spun, outputting suppositions, pushing past conjecture and aligning with Gorlind's words and her companions' behaviors.

Her theories were barreling towards one cruel conclusion.

Eden's heart pounded and the oxygen seemed to leave the room. In a way it did—she was inadvertently absorbing it.

"I am Eden, daughter of King Edward of Gwydion," her voice rang true, not betraying the storm raging inside. Her iron grip on her internal tempest was dangerously close to slipping.

"You—you're the King's sieva," he stammered.

"Eden, I beg you," Mariana sniveled, pulling at her arm once more.

Eden remained entrenched in her internal war, refusing to be budged. She couldn't tear her eyes away from the red dress in Gorlind's chubby hands. The lurid silk and tulle swished as he shifted uncomfortably, grating on her tremulous emotions.

"To whom does this dress belong?" she demanded.

His beady eyes darted around. Luka gave a subtle shake of his head. Gorlind's gaze searched for a way out, settling on something beyond the royal guard.

"To-to the future Queen," Gorlind panted.

Eden followed his line of vision to a figure down the hall. Long white hair framing a heart-shaped face. Red pouty lips. A body any male would kill to possess—or, perhaps, in this case, marry.

"Gorlind?" Bianca called, halting when she saw the tense group circled around him.

The future Queen of Prajna had come to meet her dressmaker.

The revelation could not be reconciled with what Eden knew Viktor felt for his mate, with how he treated her, the extent of care he'd shown. The bond could not lie.

*Locked away in his chambers, kept away from the Prajna for her own safety? Or to keep his sieva away from his precious fiancé?* her inner voice taunted, chipping away at Eden's confidence.

Something in the back of her mind told her she needed to pay attention. Eden needed to think rationally, to sort through the evidence logically.

Viktor did not love Bianca, of this she was sure. As she zeroed in on the serpentine pattern of rubies sewn into the bodice of that abominable gown, Eden realized it did not matter.

The truth was in front of her, striking her right in the chest, taking a lethal swipe at her heart.

Eden's blood thundered through her veins. The vampires surely heard it, probably mistaking it for fear of Gorlind's answer.

It wasn't Eden's fear driving her pulse. It was rage. Deep-seated and fierce, white-hot from her magic. If they cut her open her blood would boil to the surface.

She fed on it, welcomed it. It was a far better substitute than the total annihilation of her heart. She could feel her magic eating at the soul-bond, pummeling it in punishment for the betrayal she could not comprehend.

Eden's breaths came faster and faster. Luka's muffled voice started barking orders. She couldn't hear it over the roar of blood pounding in her ears.

Soul-deep pain traveled up and down the bond as she continued the assault, desperately trying to sever it, to break free of the anchor that would surely hold her down and drown her.

Something hot kissed her cheeks, crackling next to her ears. It was familiar, soothing, enveloping her entire body in its warmth. Eden handed her sorrow over to her fury, feeding it, consenting to its control.

"Luka, do something!" Mariana screeched, watching in horror as Eden went up in flames.

A vice clamped around her waist and she felt the familiar compression of traveling through space with a vampire. The accompanying wave of dizziness lasted only a moment as they reappeared under the frigid waves.

Luka had ported them to the bottom of the ocean.

# Chapter 23

*Western Forest of Prajna*

They were moving slowly, sacrificing time for the sake of thoroughness. The group had agreed it was worth the loss of daylight.

Yuri was with Alec and another wolf, a half-mile away, while Kellan and Viktor stayed close to Bran.

It was painstaking work and they hadn't made much progress. Vampires could port, so there was a good chance whomever they were seeking had simply disappeared and gone someplace far away.

Their hope was that they would find a cave or shelter where Agatha had been hiding. If she was with anyone, the dwelling or her things might have a scent they could track.

No one had spoken since they'd started.

As Viktor followed behind Kellan, he pressed on the skin above his heart. It had started with a dull ache a minute ago and was now becoming painful.

He reasoned he might be experiencing some level of uneasiness, hunting one of his own. He rarely felt such emotions, but since he'd met Eden, he had started to feel more and more.

He pictured his little mate in his mind and stumbled, catching himself on the trunk of a tree.

Kellan whipped around. "What is it?"

"Nothing," Viktor lied. He didn't know the answer, but he was struck with the need to check on Eden.

Two howls erupted from the other group and the three of them sprinted towards the sound. They came upon a section of thick thorn bushes growing under the darkened canopy.

Viktor sniffed the air. Agatha's stench was strong here.

"Look," Alec pointed into the brush.

Between a small cluster of trees there was a hovel, fashioned out of branches and tall grasses. Viktor was considering porting into it when agony burst through the soul-bond, powerful enough to bring him to his knees.

Kellan reached for Viktor's shoulder. "What's wrong? Do not lie to me again."

"Eden," Viktor croaked.

Kellan looked at the shack then down to the vampire, torn. Yuri stepped forward and the Vampire King held up his hand.

"No," Viktor ordered. "Stay here, both of you, and find what we need. I have to get to Eden."

247

Kellan held onto Viktor's elbow as the male rose to his feet. "Take Bran with you. He'll be able to scent the bastard, if he's there."

Viktor reached for Bran and ported them both to Castra Nocte.

* * *

*Coastline, Eastern Prajna*

Luka grunted in pain as the boiling water ate away his skin. Eden fought furiously to surface, but he held her under, fearing the air above would fuel the flames.

He wouldn't be able to keep them here for long.

Eden opened her mouth to cry out and her lungs filled with salt water. She thrashed and kicked, panicked by the deadly burn in her chest, but Luka did not let go.

She grabbed at his arms, desperate for oxygen. They felt slippery and ... wrong. She didn't have the capacity to question what it meant.

Her heart started to slow, unable to continue its sprint without a supply of air. The fight inside her bled out into the sea as her mind began to blank.

Compression clamped down on her again and she landed hard. Luka rolled Eden to her side, scraping her face on the rough sand under her cheek. Her lungs resisted the water and she retched onto the beach.

Luka held her in that position until her heaving stopped. He removed his hands and fell to his back beside her.

They both laid there, panting. Eden lifted her eyelids, expecting to see a starry sky. All she could see was mist.

"I would prefer it, my dear, if you not do anything like that again," Luka wheezed.

Eden twisted to look at him and gasped. She pushed herself up to her knees and reached a shaky hand towards his.

"It might be best if you do not touch me right now."

Eden gaped down at Luka's arms, or, rather, of what was left of them. Most of his shirt had been burned away, along with his skin. His hands and forearms looked as though they'd been peeled open, parts of his muscles visible.

Angry red welts where he'd been singed were swollen on his chest and face. Deeper burns coated his lower abdomen. Light pink liquid oozed everywhere.

"Luka, I—I am so sorry."

"Nonsense. You didn't burn me. I grabbed you while you were lit up brighter than the sun. Completely my fault."

"No, I am the one to blame. I lost control of myself. I've never ... I've never lost control," she sniffled.

"I think you were well within your rights."

"No, don't move," Eden scolded through her tears when Luka tried to sit up.

"Didn't you know? We Prajna heal extremely fast and our healer is quite good. This will be completely gone in only," he paused and looked at his injuries, "days."

"Only days he says," she mumbled, wiping her eyes.

"Faster if I get blood."

Eden began rolling up her sleeve and Luka scooted back, like she was on fire again.

"Oh, no, little witch. I'll not be courting the wrath of Viktor just yet."

The fresh wound in Eden's soul continued to seep at the mention of his name. She checked the bond. It was still there, as she knew it would be. Only death could sever it.

"I'm not sure he would care," she countered.

"Then you don't know him very well."

"I'm thinking I don't know him at all."

"Come now," Luka ridiculed, "do not be a bigger fool than he has been."

"But aren't I? A fool? Tell me, Luka, how long has he known he was going to marry Bianca."

"I don't think he will."

"How long?"

Luka's shoulders slumped. "Since the contract was made with Dmitri."

Eden swallowed. "He has been betrothed to her, all this time? Is this common knowledge?"

"He doesn't want her."

"It doesn't matter!" she snapped.

"It does. It matters greatly, Eden."

"He's played me for the fool," she shook her head ruefully. "I won't stay. I cannot stand by and watch him marry another. How could he possibly think I would?"

"How could you possibly think he would let you go?" he groaned as he lifted himself up.

Luka needed blood and he need to deal with the mess they'd left behind outside the throne room. Eden stood with him, holding her hands out like she'd catch him if he fell.

"It's not his choice to make, Luka."

"Fair enough. Best of luck getting home."

"Excuse me?" she squeaked.

"Take a look at your surroundings."

Creases appeared on Eden's forehead. Slowly, she rotated in a circle. She'd assumed he'd taken her to the shore near Castra Nocte. As she spun, all she saw was water. They were on an island, and a tiny one at that.

She couldn't see past the mist surrounding the island, so she had no idea how far from land he'd taken her.

"You'll not leave me here."

"I'll be back. Hopefully with Viktor and you two can have a chat."

"Luka, so help me—"

Her shriek cut off as he ported back to the entryway. He'd assumed Gorlind and the others would have scattered by now, but they were all there.

It seemed they couldn't have left, not with Bianca's neck currently in the jaws of a large wolf, and an enraged Viktor eying them like they were his next meal. *Timing really was everything, wasn't it?*

"So, what did I miss?" he jibed, ducking just in time to miss his brother's fist flying towards his face.

# Chapter 24

"Where is my sieva?!" Viktor roared.

"Calm yourself, Viktor," Luka placated, dodging a second blow. "Your mate is unharmed."

"Where is Eden?" he demanded again.

He needed her. Needed to see with his own eyes she was alright. The pain he'd felt through the bond had been Eden's. She must have been in agony to affect him on a physical level.

"You'll not find out until you're calm. It's your fault for the state she is in, so you'll need to prepare yourself before you speak with her."

"My fault?"

"Your fault. Wedding dress," Luka annunciated slowly, jabbing a charred finger towards Gorlind.

Then he turned to Bianca and pointed. "Fiancé."

Then he moved over near the entry to the throne room where Eden had stood and motioned to the blackened ground.

"Scorch marks, where your little firestarter had the misfortune of putting it all together."

Viktor's claws dug into his palms. Breath refused to come for several heartbeats. Eden hadn't been assaulted, not in the physical sense.

When he'd felt the pain through their bond, he was terrified she'd been attacked. The intensity of it now made sense. He could take physical pain. Her emotional anguish traveling along their link was the one thing strong enough to bring him to his knees.

"Luka, I need to see her," he pleaded.

"This is what will happen if I port you to her right now." Luka displayed his disfigured arms in front of him.

Mariana's fist lifted to her lips.

"Take a minute, Viktor. Think. If you go to her now, I'm not sure we'll get you back alive. I promise you she is someplace safe and there is no possible way she can leave. Trust me."

Viktor's hands went to his hips. "Your arms. Eden did this?"

"Not purposefully. She was a little, ah, shall we say emotional? Yes, apparently when she is very angry she turns into fire."

"She is ... she did not harm herself?" Viktor asked.

"No. It's her own magic. It didn't even singe her clothing."

Viktor's throat cleared. "Good. That is … good."

"Yes, well, for me, not so much."

Bianca whimpered and the wolf growled. Luka had the crazy impulse to free her from the wolf's clutches. He must be losing his sanity.

"I was gone for less than fifteen minutes. So, I'll ask again, Brother, what in the bloody hell did I miss?"

\* \* \*

"Would you like one, wolf?" Viktor asked Bran.

"I could use a drink," he replied.

Viktor poured three shots of whiskey and handed them out. The men clicked glasses and downed the spirits quickly.

He'd had several of the guards escort Bianca to the dungeons. He'd sent Mariana off to the bed with the promise to retrieve her husband as soon as he was able.

"I'm going to go out on a limb here and say Bianca is not a member of Sephtis Kenelm," Luka broke the silence. "Her dresses are cut so low anyone could see if she was marked."

"I would agree with that," Viktor answered.

"Then why is she in the dungeon? Not that I'm opposed to your decision to lock her away. It does make your life easier, after all."

Luka's skin prickled and he cursed the burns upon his flesh. He hadn't realized Eden was powerful enough to boil the ocean.

"Bran?" Viktor prompted.

"When we arrived at the guardhouse, we were told there was an issue outside the throne room. Viktor ported there and I had to be escorted by a guard. As we moved into the hall, I picked up on a scent, one I'd detected only once before. It was the scent we'd caught in the clearing where one of our wolves had been attacked by a demon. Viktor was a little preoccupied with Mariana and that heavyset fellow, so my wolf and I restrained her until told otherwise."

Viktor rubbed his sideburns. "It's circumstantial, but I can't let her loose right now."

"Did you find anything during your search?"

"We did. Yuri, Kellan, and a couple of his wolves are there now, searching where we believe Agatha had been holed up. I need to get back there, but first I need to question Bianca."

"She's not going anywhere. I would suggest prioritizing your sieva."

Viktor's eyes narrowed at his brother. "I thought you said I needed to leave her be for now."

"No, I said you needed to calm yourself. You're calm now."

Luka was correct. Viktor had stuffed his emotions back behind his shields. The future of Prajna now hung in the balance. He wasn't quite ready to share it with Luka, but, depending on Viktor's chat with Bianca, his younger brother would be a big part of it.

"Last I checked, I was still King. I'm going to pay Bianca a visit while you feed. Afterwards, you can take me to Eden."

Viktor rose and Bran did, as well.

"No, stay here," he told the young male. "Someone will bring you a hot meal. I'll come get you before heading back."

"You're sure?" Bran asked. "I'm good at interrogation."

"I'm sure you are, but I prefer to do this alone."

"Understood."

Viktor gave a curt nod and ported into Bianca's cell. She was in a standing position, arms over her head, and chained against wall. Though upright, her legs were spread wide and also secured to the stone.

It was the same position he'd put her in hundreds of times in his feeding room. From the way she pushed her chest out when she saw him, she was thinking the same.

His lip curled and his stomach turned. He'd thought she'd always been agreeable. Now he could see through the façade. Under her suggestive behaviors was nothing but desperation.

Viktor debated coming right out with the accusation of her involvement with the Sephtis Kenelm, just to see how she reacted. Unfortunately, unless she confessed, he had no real proof.

Luckily, there were other ways to get to her.

"Release me from the contract, Bianca."

"This again?" she groaned. "Is this what you meant by drastic measures? Throwing me in a cell? The law is on my side Viktor. Even you—no, especially you, know that. You're magically bound to it. You cannot keep me here indefinitely."

"I'll keep you here as long as necessary."

"Fine. The ceremony won't be planned expertly. It's no bother. At the end of the day, we still end up married."

Viktor approached Bianca, watching her squirm as he moved closer.

"Do you remember the wording of the contract?" he asked.

"Of course I do. It's how I know you can't get out of it."

"On my name, I swore, as the *King* of Prajna, I would wed you and make you Queen, within a century of making the pact."

He tugged on a lock of her hair. It had lost its luster.

"I put the ceremony off until the last possible date. Would you like to know why?"

Bianca held her tongue for once. She already knew why he had never been in a rush to get her to the altar. He'd desired her, but never truly wanted her as anything more than a warm body.

She'd accepted his lack of affection, believing it was better to feel safe than loved.

"I think, deep down, I knew I'd never follow through. I agreed to Dmitri's ridiculous terms only because it had been him asking it of me. I could not deny my friend who had already lost his wife and who was willing to risk his own life for my cause. You were never a part of my decision."

Bianca's face grew pallid. She'd always been so good with her mask, showing Viktor what she thought he wanted to see. Never wanting him to know what she was thinking or feeling, she drove him to distraction with her body. It had always worked, until the witch came into his life.

"You know there are severe consequences for breaking an agreement, Viktor."

Her voice was emotionless. She'd never show a male her fear again.

"I'm well aware that breaking an oath calls forth a curse, one that matches the severity of the promise broken."

A vision of his father's head rolling across the ground popped into his mind. As he'd lowered his sword, when no pain or suffering afflicted Viktor, he knew the penalty wouldn't be physical. It was years before the price had been revealed.

While speaking, he double checked the iron manacles at her wrists, ensuring she could not get loose. Iron was the one thing that could prevent a vampire from porting.

"I presumed I would suffer some crippling punishment if we did not marry. I used to think it meant I would die of some horrid disease or be maimed in an accident, disfigured and unable to put right all my father's wrongs. That was my greatest fear."

"Was?" she croaked, wetting her dry lips.

"Was. As in I no longer think that would be my curse."

Bianca watched him warily. His tone was pleasant—confident, even. Her muscles flexed, bracing for whatever he was about to do to her. A calm Viktor was a dangerous Viktor.

"My curse for failing Dmitri would extract a payment I am no longer willing to pay."

Bianca visibly relaxed. *Silly female*, he thought. A person like Bianca would never understand what he was about to do.

"It was imprudent of me to believe I could hold the throne, fulfill my obligation to Dmitri, and keep Eden."

"Yes, it was," she breathed, shaking with relief, thinking Viktor was choosing to give up Eden.

"Which is why I'll be abdicating the throne. Luka will be crowned King of Prajna in three days' time."

Bianca hissed out a breath, her adrenaline surging, fueled by her panic. She shook her head profusely.

"You cannot! The contract—"

"The contract states that I, as King, will marry you. If I am not King, I can no longer be obligated. Dmitri, unknowingly, gave me an out, as well."

Bianca's body quaked, racked by the sobs tearing from her throat. What would become of her? She could never go back to her village. Never.

"Careful, Bianca, or I might actually think you have a heart."

Her eyes flashed, the glow reflecting on the surface of her tear-stained cheeks. Unable to hold his stare, she dropped her head.

In a way, Viktor felt liberated, like he was shedding the weight of the past. Luka could be a handful, but Viktor had a newfound confidence in his brother.

He took one last look around the cell, unsure if Bianca would ever make it out alive. He found it didn't bother him so much, despite her parentage. Dmitri and the pact were in his past, where they would stay.

All he needed to do now was go and repair the damage to his future.

# Chapter 25

"Where is my mate?" Viktor snarled at his younger brother.

Luka had ported them to the tiny island where he'd left Eden. It was only a half-mile or so offshore, but it was surrounded in mist. No one would have known she was there.

Baffled, Luka shrugged.

"This is where I left her. When she lit herself on fire, I latched on and ported straight to the ocean. Once the fight in her tapered off, and I was sure the flames were out, I brought her here."

"And left her. Alone." Viktor's tone was accusatory.

"You would prefer I ported her back to the castle? Maybe to finish the little chat she was having with the dressmaker or to have tea with Bianca?"

Viktor grumbled deep in his throat.

Luka rolled his eyes. "If she'd been with me when I landed next to you, it would have been you who needed saving. I think you're in love with the most savage female I've ever met. She's terrifying."

Viktor snorted. "Yes, well, I'm not out of the woods yet."

"Why aren't you panicking?" Luka asked him suspiciously.

"I don't really think she'll try to kill me, Brother."

"No, why aren't you panicking that she's not here?"

"I'd feel it through the bond if she was being harmed. Wherever she is, she's not hurt."

By his assessment, Eden was no longer grieving. It bothered him. He'd always been able to glean something of her feelings through the bond. When he checked it once he realized she wasn't here, he could get a sense of her physical well-being, but her emotions were difficult to figure out.

She'd somehow managed to block him. Either that, or she'd anaesthetized herself. It was something Viktor had done towards the end of Nikolai's reign. Feeling too much had been debilitating, so he'd learned to lock that part of him away.

He'd gotten so good at it, he hadn't felt much of anything until the day he found Eden eavesdropping at the door of Theron's study. She'd managed to get a death grip around Viktor's heart and he'd die before he allowed her to let it go.

Viktor wished he could go back in time and change the decisions he'd made. If he'd only been a better brother to Luka, he would have trusted him when he originally thought the way out of the contract was to give up the throne.

His sense of self-importance and drive to pay for the sins of his father had clouded his judgement. He had duped himself, thinking he could fulfill every obligation.

Eden was right to be upset with him. If he could only find his little witch and tell her as much, his life might turn out okay.

"Well, would you look at that," Luka spoke, his voice filled with awe.

Viktor looked where Luka was pointing. Some distance away was a break in the ocean. It looked like a small hole was cutting through the shallows, towards the beach.

"It seems there's more to my mate than meets the eye," Viktor remarked.

"Oh, definitely," Luka agreed. "Should we go get her?"

"No. If we startle her she'll probably lose her hold on ... whatever she's doing to part the water."

"True. Race you to the shore," Luka challenged, porting away.

"Kings do not race to the shore."

Viktor's words dissolved as they were carried off by the wind. He'd yet to inform Luka what he had planned. First, he'd deal with Eden. Then, he'd tell Luka he was about to hand him the crown. He only prayed Luka would not refuse.

\* \* \*

Eden nearly wept with joy as the sand started to slope upwards. She was exhausted after expending so much energy, first with the fire and now with her power over water. Holding the ocean apart was tough.

As she trudged up and onto the beach, she could see the outline of two large bodies standing in front of the dunes. One was smiling, one was fixed on her with an intensity she could feel down to her bones.

Eden let the parted waters close behind her. Her fingers itched, but she didn't know if she had enough power to call forth a single flame. An hour ago, she would have gladly set Viktor on fire. Now, she wasn't sure he was worth the effort.

"Luka," she bobbed her head in deference, noticing his arms were already healing. He must have gotten blood. She angled slightly towards Viktor and curtsied.

"Your majesty," she greeted, her cold eyes turning down as she genuflected on unsteady legs.

Viktor nearly reached for Eden. She was close to toppling over. Her body language warned him to stay away.

Her address rankled him. His Eden was warm, loving. He wanted that back. He may have put her in this position, but he would once again have what he wanted from her.

"Since when do you address me so formally?"

"I've long been remiss in my duties as a *visiting* dignitary. I'm merely rectifying my mistake."

Viktor recoiled at Eden's implication her stay in Prajna was temporary. She was no visitor here. He reviled her distant manner.

"Leave us, Luka. I need to speak to my sieva alone."

"Are you sure that's a good idea?" Luka asked, looking between the two.

"Go. I'll find you later."

Luka's questioning eyes found Eden's. She gave no indication she was about to pounce, so he ported back to Castra Nocte.

"You're soaked," Viktor observed. Eden's multi-colored hair was darkened from being wet. Her dress clung to her curves, tempting him to tear it off her body.

"Yes, Luka thought to take me on an evening swim."

Viktor held out his hand. "Come, I'll take you to our chambers and you can have a warm bath. Then we'll talk."

"No, thank you."

"Eden, be reasonable."

A fissure cracked in her mental shields. A small flame tried to sputter from her right hand and she snuffed it out immediately, before Viktor could see it. She pushed everything out, focusing on remaining calm.

"Considering what I've been through today, I'd say I'm acting quite reasonably."

Eden's voice was too detached. He'd expected tears, anger, some sign she was affected. Her apathy scared him. It clouded his judgement and he poked at her, needing a reaction.

"No, you're acting cold. You've never been cold with me."

"You're right. I haven't. It was unwise of me to become so enamored, counting every look, every touch, wanting them so badly I would give you anything you wanted just to have a piece of you. I'll never make that mistake again."

Viktor's chest rumbled and he took a step towards her. Eden stepped backwards.

"Keep your distance, Viktor. You are, after all, exceptionally good at it."

"I have never hidden my feelings for you, Eden. I may not have said the words, but our souls are bonded. You can feel my affections for you."

"Yes, how inconvenient that must be for your wife," Eden mocked.

"I'm not married. I have no intention of marrying her."

"Do not lie to me!" Eden's pretense of calm withered and died before him. She could only take so much.

"I will not be misled by you again, Viktor. I saw, with my very own eyes, one very frantic dressmaker trying to get in the final fitting with the future Queen for the wedding ceremony in *two* weeks. How much longer had you planned to hide the truth from me? Or was I to live eternity in your room, locked away like some dirty little secret?"

Her voice shook. She wrapped her arms around herself, needing warmth and comfort.

Viktor ported directly in front of Eden, grasping her arms, afraid she was about to collapse. Then he ported them up to their rooms and held on until she was steady.

Eden jerked out of his hold and moved to the other side of the large chair, putting the obstacle between them when she really required a mountain of distance.

"I was wrong, Eden. I should have told you. I was trying to find a way out of it. Finally, I believe I have."

"I do not care."

Viktor blanched. "Did you not hear me? I think I've found a way out of that damned contract. I'll not have to marry Bianca."

"Congratulations. It changes nothing."

"What do you mean? It changes everything!" he yelled.

"Maybe for you. For me, it does not matter."

Viktor swung his giant arm, launching the chair between them across the room. It crashed against stone, falling to its side in pieces. He stalked towards his mate.

"You love me," he growled, backing Eden up against the wall.

She didn't bother denying it. He was right. Eden did love him. Her eyes burned as they filled with the tears she did not want to shed in front of him.

His large hands grabbed either side of her neck, holding her jaw up so she could not turn away.

"You are my sieva. *Mine*. You are the most important thing in my world."

"Apparently, not important enough," she whispered, a lone tear escaping down her cheek.

Viktor's insides twisted. His words weren't getting through to her. He blasted as much love and adoration as he could muster through their bond.

Eden whimpered, her legs finally giving out from her exertions. She hated she was so weak in this moment.

Viktor grabbed her around the waist and ported them to the bed. His mouth crashed into hers in a punishing kiss as he nudged her legs apart with his hips.

Though her legs willingly fell open to cradle his body, Eden did not kiss him back. She held very still, her mind warring with her body. Could she give herself to him after what he'd done?

Viktor's emotions continuously crashed through the bond, besieging her fragile heart. She felt his love, felt it in her soul. Her body overheated, stimulated by his soul's cry for hers, as well as his frenzied movements.

It was the touch of his soul, so pure in its devotion, that swayed her to return his kiss. It might be the last time she would ever feel anything so rapturous.

Right or wrong, Eden wasn't ready to let it go.

Her hands fisted in his hair as she held his head in place. She boldly stroked his tongue with her own. Eden felt out of control. Wild. Angry.

He'd hurt her with his lie of omission. It didn't change the fact she needed him like she needed the air to breath. He ground his hips into hers and all she could think about was feeling him inside her, even if it was only one last time.

Viktor could smell his mate's slick desire. Eden's little moans against his mouth made him feel desperate.

"Tell me you want this, that you want me," he growled, needing to know she wanted to be taken.

"I want you," she cried.

His claws slashed away her dress. His fangs descended and he was tempted to strike her neck, to feed while he took his sieva. He refrained, worried he'd weaken her further after her exhaustive trek across the ocean floor.

Viktor tore open the front of his pants tearing just enough to expose his hard length. He rubbed the crown up and down her folds, coating himself before plunging inside.

Eden cried out, her fingers digging into his back. Viktor took advantage of her parted lips and slipped his tongue inside. He groaned into her mouth.

He loved her. He loved her so godsdamned much. Their love vibrated back and forth, across the bond. Overcome, he was incapable of halting his release.

Viktor reached between their bodies and pressed his thumb on her hardened nub, catapulting Eden into her own climax.

Eden's shouts of pleasure echoed off the stone walls. Her core spasmed, tightening around him. Viktor continued to spill against her womb as he called out her name.

They held tight to one another, chests heaving and skin damp with sweat. Viktor withdrew, but remained on top of her with his face buried in her neck. When their breathing evened out, he ported them to the bathing chamber.

After Viktor opened the faucet, he set Eden on the side of the bathing pool. He removed her boots and what threads of fabric remained attached to her body. Then he removed his own.

It reminded him of their first day together when she'd willingly tied her soul to his. She'd never questioned it, putting her blind faith in a male who would later wound her heart. It was the only thing her father had asked him not to do.

He scrubbed his face with both palms, ashamed he hadn't been able to fulfill that request. He eyed her over his fingertips.

"Can you warm it or should I ..." Viktor nodded towards the heating rocks.

"I can do it," she answered quietly.

Eden lowered her hands into the cool water and pushed out enough energy to heat the water.

"I assume this is far less taxing than parting an ocean," he tested, trying at humor to lighten the mood.

She nodded, but she did not meet his eyes. He scratched across his chest, the tightness becoming unbearable. Viktor didn't know how to bridge the gap growing between them.

He walked down the steps into the bathing pool and moved to the edge where Eden was sitting. He reached for her. When she didn't protest, he pulled her into the water.

Viktor sat on one of the steps, resting his back against the stone and holding Eden sideways on his lap. He pulled her against him and let his hands drift over her skin.

Eden tucked her head under Viktor's chin. She was confused. She was hurt. She was also close to passing out.

"I have a few things I need to say, Eden. First, I realize now how poorly I have handled everything. I should have been forthcoming and I wasn't. For that I apologize."

Her eyes stung and she blinked hard.

"More than that, when we first met, I made the monumental mistake of thinking I could bond to my sieva *and* fulfill my contract with Dmitri by marrying his daughter."

Eden stopped breathing. Her fingers twitched.

"Hold off on burning me until I've finished, *mala vestica*," he requested.

Eden huffed at his second lame attempt at a joke.

"I never wanted to marry her, nor did I believe I would ever find my sieva. I put the ceremony off as long as possible. It's been looming over me for a long time. Then, one night, five years ago, my cicatrice awoke. It was a complication I didn't need."

"I'll bet."

Viktor ignored her biting tone and continued. "Then I found you and all I wanted was to spend every second with you. I'd never imagined the soul-bond would be so intense. I was consumed and I nearly forgot why it was a complication because I was so damned happy. Then Bianca returned and I wrestled with what to do. Both Yuri and Luka have been trying to help me find an out. I even went to Bianca and demanded she release me. Dmitri gave her an out. If she didn't want me, she didn't have to marry me."

Eden sighed. "Let me guess, she still wants you, even after soul-bonding to me."

"Unfortunately."

"So you didn't find a way out," Eden griped, trying to sit up and put a little distance between them. Viktor held her in place.

"No, I did, but I'll get to that in a minute. The night I took you to the lagoons, I knew. I knew beyond all doubt that whether or not I found a way out, I wasn't going to marry her. How could I when I was so in love with you?"

Eden's heart banged against her ribs. It was the first time he'd declared his love aloud. The bittersweet moment affected her, but she couldn't bring herself to return the sentiment.

"You should have told me the entire truth of that contract, Viktor."

He sighed, unable to deny it. Eden was right.

"Yes, I should have. My only excuse was I didn't want to hurt you. In the beginning, I was sorely delusional. Once I knew I loved you and you felt the same, I couldn't bring myself to do it. I'd planned to figure a way out and tell you after the fact. The truth had to come out eventually, especially if I violated the terms."

"I thought breaking a magical oath was virtually impossible."

"It is. When you break one, you suffer greatly. It's thought the magic that enforces the oath creates a curse of equal weight."

"You were willing to curse yourself?" she asked incredulously, her voice rising an octave.

"I was. I—"

A loud bang came from the door. Viktor spun and placed Eden behind him.

"Hate to interrupt, Brother, but you need to come quickly," Luka's muffled voice carried into the bathroom.

Laughter erupted and Eden rolled her eyes at Luka's immaturity. Viktor's mouth quirked. His brother was going to be the worst king the kingdom had ever known. *Well, perhaps not as bad as Nikolai.*

Eden's tentative hands fell on his hips and he realized he didn't really care. Luka gave a damn about the fate of Prajna. It would have to be enough.

He twisted in Eden's grasp and hugged her close. "I have to go. I left Kellan and the others in the woods. I need to get back."

"I understand."

"Please don't ... leave."

Eden craned her neck to see his worried face studying hers. *Had he meant don't leave the chambers or don't leave him?*

"I don't really have any place to go."

"We'll talk more when I return. I swear it. Please be here when I come back."

"Okay."

His shoulders lowered. He hadn't realized how tensely he'd been holding himself. Viktor planted a chaste kiss on his mate's lips and hauled himself out of the bath.

# Chapter 26

Viktor dressed hurriedly before flinging the door open. His brother was leaning back against the wall, arms and legs crossed.

"Did I, in fact, interrupt something?" Luka asked hopefully.

"What is the emergency?"

"Ever the responsible ruler," Luka sighed. "Yuri came back. Said it was imperative he speak with you at once."

"Where is he?"

Luka pushed away from the wall, his lips flattening into an uncharacteristic show of seriousness.

"War room."

Viktor's eyebrows drew close. They hadn't used the war room in years.

"It's bad, Viktor."

"He already told you?"

"I refused to allow anyone near you until he confided. I wasn't about to add further strain on you until you'd smoothed things over with Eden."

Viktor was seeing his brother in a whole new light. More and more, Luka was showing he was not as irresponsible or uncaring as Viktor had once believed.

"Thank you."

"It was nothing. Come, let's go play warrior," Luka winked and blinked out of existence.

Viktor almost rolled his eyes as he ported after him. *Kings do not wink. Or roll their eyes*, he mused.

He'd half-expected the room to be filled with battle-ready Prajna, but only Luka and Yuri were present. Luka was standing behind his old seat, hands clutching the back.

Yuri was pacing and spun towards Viktor mid step.

"Finally," he blew out in a huff.

"Tell me."

"You need to come with me, back to the shelter. Put some guards on Eden. Luka should probably stay with her, in your quarters."

Bianca had been the only person to dare going near his living space. Only one of the Sephtis Kenelm would risk venturing close. If this was Yuri's fear, Viktor wasn't inclined to leave Castra Nocte.

"What did you find?" Viktor demanded.

Yuri hesitated.

"Tell him," Luka snapped.

"We picked up a scent. Alec said it was the same one they found during Edward's attack."

Yuri's eyes had fallen onto the table.

"You know whose scent it was," Viktor assessed.

Yuri's chest rose and fell as he nodded slowly.

"Whose scent, Yuri?"

The male's gaze lifted, meeting his King's stare. A shaking hand pointed to the seat across from Luka's.

"'twas a ghost's."

\* \* \*

Eden had just poured herself a cup of tea when someone knocked softly on the door.

"Yes?" she called, not wanting to open it. A vampire meaning harm could have gotten to her easily. A soft knock was likely another servant bringing something Viktor had ordered for her, like the tea.

"Do you have time to tend to my wounds, dear lady?"

Eden tittered at Luka's ridiculousness. Despite his absurd behaviors, he was growing on her. Luka ribbed her as an older brother might. Irrationally, she liked it.

"If they're that bad, why bother knocking?"

"I was trying to give you time to cover yourself," the voice spoke from directly behind her.

Eden yelped and sparks shot from her fingertips.

Luka laughed, tempting Eden to throw something at his head. Seeing his arms wrapped in gauze saved him from further damage.

"Why would you think I wouldn't be clothed? Nevermind, I don't want to know."

Eden picked up the kettle. "Tea?"

"I would love to have tea with my future sister."

Eden nearly dropped the teapot. She had to use both hands to finish the pour.

"Do not make such jokes, Luka. I cannot ..." her throat constricted.

"Here," Luka reached for the kettle and set it on the table. He pulled Eden into his arms and swayed back and forth, as his mother used to do when he was troubled.

"I didn't say it in jest, Eden. Someday, it will be official."

Eden pulled away and sat down in the chair that someone had brought to replace the one Viktor destroyed. Luka took his mother's old wingback.

"He'll be cursed if he breaks the oath, Luka."

"He's not going to break it."

"Then he lied to me?"

"No, not if he told you he wasn't going to go through with the wedding."

Eden rubbed her temples. She could sometimes stave off a migraine, but this one was coming on strong.

"Perhaps it would be best if I go back to Gwydion or to Sanctus Femina," she thought aloud.

"You cannot."

"I don't know if I can stay."

Luka slapped his hand on the table. "You must stay. He is yours. You are his. Your souls are bound, Eden. There is no end to this for either of you. Do not waste this gift, one others would kill to have."

He ran his fingers through his hair. "You have no idea what he's done, what he's giving up in order to be with you in the way he wants."

"We didn't have time to discuss much. I promised to stay and hear him out. That's all I can promise right now."

Luka dropped to his knees before her. He took both her hands in his, his eyes beseeching.

"He's renounced the throne Eden. The contract with Dmitri was that, as *King*, he would make her the Queen. If he is not on the throne, the contract is null. He shared this with Yuri and I just before he left."

Eden had to force air in and out as her heart felt like it had stopped. He couldn't possibly, not after all he'd done to take control from Nikolai.

"No," she whispered.

"Yes. He's already set it in motion."

"Who will replace him?"

Luka let go of her hands and dropped the weight of his haunches onto his calves and heels, sagging his posture. It was the pose of a child.

His eyes glassed over, the regret obvious.

"I tried to tell him no. I'm not the one who it should be. Legally, yes, but in reality?" he huffed. "I'm no king."

Eden wanted to console him. Luka lacked confidence in his worth.

"When he told me it was the way out of the oath, I agreed. For the both of you, I agreed."

"Luka," she signed.

"Fight for him, Eden. He'll fight for you. He *is* fighting for you. His road has been a hard one and I know he made the gravest of errors where Bianca is concerned and it wounded you deeply. But if you love him, you need to fight for him. Very few ever have."

"Fought for him?"

The corners of his mouth turned down. "Loved him."

He shifted backwards and rested his spine against his mother's chair. "We only ever had our mother."

"You had each other."

"For a time," he shrugged.

"He had Yuri. Dmitri."

Luka hissed and Eden recoiled. His eyes were a little wild. His jaw ticked.

"I'm sorry," he bit out.

"It's okay."

"No, you don't understand the mess it's all become."

"All what?"

Luka ported to the small serving cart where Viktor kept his spirits. He poured three fingers of whiskey, downed it, and did it once more. Eden thought his mannerisms were almost identical to Viktor's.

"Luka?" her concerned voice grabbed his attention.

He swallowed the liquor and slammed his glass on the cart's surface.

"It seems our beloved Dmitri was a crafty one."

Eden's brow lifted. While finishing her bath, after Viktor left, she'd been mulling over the oath Dmitri had gotten from Viktor. She found it unusual a vampire, one who had found his own sieva, would complicate his daughter's chances of finding her own.

Dmitri asking Viktor to take care of Bianca made sense. It was the condition of matrimony that did not, not when the Prajna were a faction who had fated mates.

She didn't know the male, so he could have been shallow enough to simply want to make his daughter a queen for the title alone.

"Your tone implies you're aggravated with Dmitri. I thought he was a friend."

"So did I."

Luka looked down at his empty tumbler, contemplating filling it up again.

"The pact was made a hundred years ago, so I'm guessing something new has come to light."

"More like come to life," he mumbled, tipping another serving of spirits into his glass.

Eden's fingers dug into the fabric of the chair. Her skin tingled and her posture stiffened.

"What are you saying, Luka?"

"I am saying, dear Sister-to-be, it seems the bastard is not dead, after all."

Luka held his glass up in Eden's direction. Her pupils dilated, nearly hiding the greens of her irises. Her barely visible shock was a fraction of what Viktor's had been— and he was the most self-contained being Luka had ever known.

"Cheers," he toasted and knocked the drink back summarily.

Eden gave Luka enough time for the whiskey to settle his nerves. His world had shifted drastically this day, much as hers had. She needed more information to fully comprehend Luka's distress, aside from his hesitancy to ascend to the throne.

When his jaw finally slackened, Eden spoke. "I suggest, Luka, you start from the beginning."

# Chapter 27

*Western Forest of Prajna*

Viktor and Yuri landed silently outside the thicket surrounding the hovel. He'd left Luka in charge and decided to leave Bran behind as extra protection for Eden. The wolf knew both Bianca and Dmitri's scents, and he could alert the castle guards if there was trouble from the enemy.

Kellan was sitting, peeling an apple with his claws. The Wolf King's head tilted when he heard the newcomers.

"Where are the others?" Viktor asked, striding towards the wolf.

"Once their wolves picked up the scent, they got antsy. I let them go out to scout. Though, I'm guessing the vampire is long gone by now."

Viktor's eyes glowed bright at the mention of *the vampire*. A tiny part of him still clung to the idea Yuri could have been mistaken.

"Viktor, you should go inside. See for yourself," Yuri spoke softly.

Viktor's head swung to the shelter. It was small. Primitive. It reminded him of the huts he and Luka used to build when they were children—the ones Dmitri had taught them to make.

Small logs and branches were held together by the strong, tall grasses that grew on the edges of the forest. Dried mud had been haphazardly packed into the crevices to keep out the elements.

The thatched roof was sagging, it's weight too much for the branches. It wasn't a shelter meant to be used for long. It was a child's hideout.

He had been too distracted when they found it to make the connection.

Kellan's large hand fell upon Viktor's shoulder.

"Perhaps one of us should come with you," the wolf suggested. He knew well the turbulent feelings incited by the deception of someone once trusted.

"No. I'll go alone."

"Very well." Kellan released Viktor's shoulder and the vampire ported into the center of the thicket.

Viktor would have landed inside, but he was being overly cautious. Dmitri was a master planner. He would know Viktor would eventually come for him if he ever found out.

Viktor pushed open the small door. It was nothing more than kindling and twigs woven together. It fell to the ground having been pushed one too many times.

Viktor stepped forward carefully, alert to everything around him. The roof was a foot shorter than his nearly seven-foot height. The doorway was even smaller. He had to duck to get inside and remain hunched to walk around.

The single-room shelter was no more than eight feet across. The contents sparse. A pallet was on the opposite side from Viktor, made up of several blankets.

The dirt floor was littered with dried leaves and herbs. In the center of the room was a small firepit with an iron pot sitting atop the raised stones. Medicinal bottles and flasks were scattered around the edges.

Agatha had been a healer. She may have been making medicines—or poisons. Viktor picked up one of the small decanters and scented it.

The distinct scent of hellebore emanated from within. Hellebore was a plant poison especially dangerous for elementals to ingest, the same one used to poison Eden's sister.

Viktor's claws flexed as his hand tightened around the container. He smashed the bottle on the ground and continued his inspection.

A large leather bag sat to the right of the door. He squatted down and pulled the flap open. More bottles were inside, along with some pouches of what looked like dried roots and other plants he did not recognize.

The odors of Agatha's concoctions were overpowering. He'd expected to be overcome by the vampire's scent. Thus far, he hadn't picked up on it.

He closed the flap and turned back to room. There was nothing else inside.

Frustrated, Viktor walked the perimeter of the small space, inhaling deeply. A foot from the pallet, his steps faltered.

Viktor crouched closer to the makeshift bed, the familiar aroma of dark spices and soot from a pipe flooded his olfactory system. He lifted one of the blankets to his nose.

*Dmitri.* He'd been here not long ago. A wrenching pain, the one Viktor had been holding back with all his might, abruptly tore through him, soiling every memory he had of his former friend.

His mental shields came slamming down, crushing the heartsick sorrow over Dmitri's treachery, over Viktor's trusted ally, who had really been his enemy.

Hindsight made things very clear. Dmitri was likely already a part of the Sephtis Kenelm when he'd asked Viktor to take Bianca into his protection and ultimately make her his wife. He was setting the stage so Viktor's sieva would never sit on the throne.

He could still picture Dmitri's pinched face, his eyes darting about without looking directly at his King. Viktor had mistaken his comrade's worry and urgent manner for concern over Bianca's welfare.

Soon after the regretful agreement was made, Dmitri faked his own death. They'd never found his body and so he'd been presumed dead. The accceptance of Dmitri's murder had only been reinforced after Nikolai taunted Viktor that Dmitri was lost to him.

Looking back, Viktor wondered if his father knew what Dmitri was up to. It would be just like the scoundrel to know and do nothing about it.

Viktor shook himself out of his baneful recollections. There was nothing to be done for the past. His only choice was to move forward.

He lifted each of the blankets, ensuring it was only Dmitri's and Agatha's stink he smelled. Bianca's scent had been found near the place where Isla had been attacked by the demon. If he had evidence she'd been here, he'd sign her death warrant.

When he got to the last blanket, and no one else's essence was evident, aside from Yuri and the wolves, he threw it aside in frustration. A slight thud sounded near his foot.

Viktor crouched low to look at what had fallen.

It was a flask. Damaged and centuries old. The once-shiny surface had dulled with the passage of time. Several deep scratches blemished the dark silver.

The Cojocaru family crest remained intact, its red and gold shield standing out against the darkened metal. Viktor knew this flask. He had, in fact, drank from it many a time, including the night he'd pledged an unwise oath to his friend with two faces.

Cojocaru was Dmitri's surname. His grandfather had fashioned the flask long ago and left it to his only grandson.

Viktor picked it up, denying himself the satisfaction of crushing the offending artifact. Dmitri had kept it with him at all times. He would not have left it behind, not unless he'd escaped in a hurry.

The question was, to where would the traitor flee?

\* \* \*

*Castra Nocte*

Eden sat quietly, patiently listening to Luka's tale. As he spoke, her heart ached for both Luka and Viktor. She knew there were very few people either of them had ever trusted. This would be a hard blow to them both.

Evidently, inside the shelter where they'd tracked Agatha, Yuri and Kellan had found Dmitri's scent on an item belonging to the vampire.

Technically, they'd never found his body back when Dmitri was allegedly aiding Viktor's coup. There was no way his scent held strong for a century. The shelter had only been thrown together in recent weeks. The only way his scent could have lingered inside was if he'd actually been there.

The marriage contract now made more sense to Eden. Sephtis Kenelm feared a single faction gaining too much power. The agreement would have ensured a queen of vampire origin would reign.

Complicating matters further, Luka informed Eden one of the wolves, Bran, had recognized Bianca's scent as one they'd found when hunting the demon, Bogdan. At some point, she'd been in the same location as he and the she-wolf who had poisoned Nora.

When he finished speaking, he offered Eden a small nip of whiskey. She took the tumbler from him and sipped it slowly. It tasted terrible, but the warm burn sliding down her throat was a welcome distraction.

"She's not a member," Eden affirmed, setting her unfinished drink down.

Luka immediately picked it up and dumped it into his own glass. She made a note to address his drinking another time, when he wasn't so agitated.

"Her attire is revealing enough to where everyone can clearly see her chest," she added. "There's no marking over her heart."

"Yes, but her father is probably the fourth member. He could have involved her."

"After all the strings he'd manipulated, it would have been risky to reveal himself, even to her."

"Probably."

"Still, it seems awfully coincidental."

"Undeniably."

"She'll need to be questioned."

"Certainly."

"Can you speak in longer than one-word sentences?" she complained.

"Yes," Luka smirked.

Eden stared at the last of her drink flowing into Luka's mouth. She puckered her lips as she waited for the alcohol's razing path to reach his stomach.

"Do you even want to be king?" she asked.

"No."

"Are you really going to accept the throne?"

"I don't see how I can refuse."

"But you can."

"Eden, I would prefer to take a position I never wanted instead of watching you and Viktor crumble under the weight of his stupidity. He won't show it, but he's a desperate male. You've brought him back to life and he'll not give that up. Not even for the throne of Prajna."

A small tear in her soul stitched itself back together. It didn't repair all the damage, but it was a start.

Luka set his glass down. "He's under a tremendous amount of stress, Eden. He's broken up over the pain he's caused you. His past is coming back to haunt him in the absolute worst of ways. He'll not rest until he's figured out how to undo everything Dmitri has done, that includes making you safe, happy, and whole."

"It also means finding Dmitri."

"Too right."

"We could help."

Luka's eyes widened. "Really? You think I'm going to take you out into the forest to hunt a dead man?"

"No. I was thinking more along the lines of his daughter. Has anyone asked her where her father is?"

"No. Viktor didn't want to show his hand. Though, he did give her the parting gift of knowing he was abdicating. It went over splendidly."

The skin on Luka's palm itched as his sarcastic quip leapt off his tongue before he could stop it. He would never voice it, but he felt a little sorry for Bianca. He knew what it was like to be treated as a pariah among the Prajna.

Regrettably, if he was crowned King soon, he'd need to maintain a level of distain towards the female in case he had to remove her head.

Eden didn't like the cruelty of Luka's comment. She didn't chastise him, though. On some level, she knew his jaded remarks were how he coped.

"I can see the spokes in your mind spinning, Eden. What are you thinking?"

"I'm thinking we help Viktor on two fronts without putting me in any danger."

"Torture Bianca?" he threw out nonchalantly, trying to get back to the comfort of his dark humor.

"What? No," she sputtered.

"Fine. I'm listening."

"First, we simply ask Bianca about her father and see what she has to say. Bran is still here. He can come, too, and scent any deceit in her response."

"Then we torture Bianca?"

"That is a firm no, Luka."

"Well, that's disappointing."

"Can you please be serious? If only for a few minutes?"

"Very well. Your second proposition?"

"Since you do not want to be King, and the only reason Viktor is even considering stepping down is for me, we need to help him keep his position."

"And how do we do that?"

"Easy. We find Bianca's sieva."

Eden's eyes dropped to Luka's left hand as it twitched. He probably wasn't aware he'd been scratching it off and on since he entered the chamber.

The skin on Luka's palm warmed and he closed his fingers into a tight fist, shielding it from Eden's attention. His cicatrice no longer looked like the lightning bolt it had been.

He vividly remembered its original shape. The memory of the day his father had mutilated the skin was one he tried to keep buried; but it kept emerging more and more often lately.

He'd rationalized it was because he'd placed too much hope in his brother's soul-bonding, that it would be the beginning of the end of the curse. Unfortunately, Eden had been bonded to Viktor for weeks and Luka hadn't heard of any sievas finding one another. It was news that would have been reported immediately.

However, if Bianca found her sieva, and their cicatrices awoke, she would want her mate. The powerful pull of the magic of mates would be too great for her to resist. She wouldn't want Viktor.

The problem was, her sieva could be anyone, even someone who had yet to be born. Historically, most female mates were born after their males, but the opposite had been known to happen from time to time.

"It might not be possible," he told her.

"But it's not *im*possible."

Luka ran his tongue over his teeth as he eyed his brother's mate. Viktor had said she was smart. Luka knew she could be ruthless. The combined attributes would make a queen capable of handling the Kingdom of Prajna.

"Alright," he agreed and she jumped up, nodding enthusiastically.

"First things first, Eden. Bran and I will both escort you to Bianca and we will both stay with you the entire time. You are never alone or out of our sight, understood?"

"Understood."

"Second, I have no idea how long it will take to find her mate. No sievas have been found since you and Viktor, and before that it had been a century. Do not be too disappointed if we cannot find her match before the deadline."

"I understand, Luka. I am not naïve. I've thought it over, attempting to put together everything, including how I even ended up here. My sister, before she left for the North, gave me a portent. She'd said to search my truth in the East. It cannot be mere coincidence that, when I told my father we needed to go East and we ended up at the temple, Viktor just so happened to arrive while I was there. Our cicatrices are a perfect match. That is not coincidence. That is Fate."

"Fate, huh? So you plan to stay?"

"I—"

"Marry him?"

Eden flung her hands up in exasperation. "Stop."

"I'm merely making an inquiry."

"He hasn't asked and I am in no way over what he did. It's beside the point. What I'm trying to say is I am hopeful because Fate has brought me here for a reason."

"And what reason is that?"

She crinkled her button nose. Luka would tell her how young it made her look, but she'd probably set him on fire.

"I don't know, but I hope it's to help stop whatever curse has settled upon the kingdom."

"And then we can torture Bianca?"

Eden barked a startled laugh. He was unlike anyone she'd ever met.

"You're impossible."

"I'm also agreeing with you. Take it while you can."

Luka held out his arm. "Let's go visit the dungeons. I've been negligent in my tour duties."

# Chapter 28

Luka led Eden and Bran down through the lower levels of Castra Nocte. As they approached the door into the dungeons, he turned and placed both hands on Eden's shoulders.

Mismatched eyes met his without the slightest hint of emotion. No trepidation. No irritation. Nothing. She could be so similar to Viktor in her reticence it was frightening.

Luka wasn't sure what she would feel, confronting Viktor's former dalliance, one he was contracted to wed. If he was in her position, he'd have come armed to the teeth. Then again, he'd seen firsthand she was her own lethal weapon.

"Do not get too close to her, Eden."

"I know."

"Bran?" he said.

"Yes, Sir?"

"Stay alert."

"Absolutely."

Luka nodded curtly and motioned for the guard to allow them inside. The heavy door squeaked, the uncomfortable sound echoing as it swung open.

Bran angled his head. "Are we under water, by chance?"

"No, we're not that far down," Luka answered. "Why do you ask?"

"I thought I could hear water."

"The ocean is close. There are caves and tunnels near where the tides bring in seawater, but we're not under it."

"That's probably what I'm hearing."

Luka strained to listen, too. He was on edge bringing Eden down here and would not discount any potential peril.

To his left, near where Eden was standing, he thought he heard a faint swooshing. It did sound like water moving behind the rock. Water was powerful and could easily carve out paths in the stone.

He would need to bring it up with Viktor later. The integrity of Castra Nocte's foundation may require an inspection. At the moment, the sound wasn't a threat and that was what mattered.

Luka continued leading them deeper into the dungeons. Eden's head swiveled, mentally recording what she saw.

The passage was lined with cells carved into the rock. Each cell looked more like a cave with steel bars covering the mouth. They walked the length of the corridor to the last cell on the left.

"Open it, Davon."

The guard on duty unlocked the latticed gate and stepped aside. The trio entered, the males keeping Eden between and slightly behind them.

"Leave us," Luka dismissed the guard.

Davon paused at the Prince's order.

"I'll call for you when we're finished," Luka assured him.

"As you wish, Sire." Davon bowed and left the cell.

Bianca straightened as much as she could in her restraints. Viktor had never lifted the vow he'd made to Bianca about treating his sieva with nothing but respect. It was senseless of her to think he ever would.

The female Prajna remained silent, observing her visitors warily. She picked up a slight swooshing sound and her eyes widened.

"Hello, little dove. I trust your accommodations are acceptable?"

Eden put her hand on Luka's elbow. There was no sense in being callous, not when they needed answers.

Bianca's lips pressed into a thin line.

"Hello, Bianca. I am Eden—"

"I know who you are," Bianca rasped. The magic of the oath to be respectful toward Eden pressured her to check her tone.

It didn't help that her throat was dry. She hadn't fed enough this week and it was starting to get to her. She'd asked the guards for blood and they'd laughed at her.

"Yes. I'm sure this all is a shock. Goddess knows it was for me."

"Why are you here?" Bianca questioned.

"We need to ask you something. This is Bran," Eden gestured with her hand towards the wolf.

"We've met," the female deadpanned.

Luka's lips twitched. He almost liked Dungeon Bianca. She'd dropped her sex kitten disguise for once. He scratched at his palm again. The scar had been itching furiously since Eden had burned him.

"He can smell a lie, so I would appreciate your honesty," Eden said diplomatically.

"Or what?"

"Pardon?"

"If wolf-boy smells a lie. What will you do?"

Luka opened his mouth to offer his suggestion of torture, but was cut off by Eden's elbow to his ribs.

"You'll find out if you are untruthful," Eden spoke over Bran's mumblings over being called a boy.

"Very well. What is your question?"

"Where is your father?"

"As far as I know, long dead."

Eden looked at Bran.

"Truth," he confirmed.

"As far as you know?" Eden thought aloud, considering her wording. She needed to reword her inquiry.

"Is there any reason you might think he is still alive, other than the fact they never found his body?"

Bianca looked away, her hesitancy speaking volumes.

Eden took a step forward and Luka did the same, blocking her with his arm. The swooshing sound was a little louder now—and it wasn't coming from the wall.

His attention left Bianca and he peered down at Eden. His eyes widened. *Holy Mother of Imperium!* his brain screamed. It had been so long, he hadn't recognized the sound for what it was.

"Eden, I think we should return to your chambers," he suggested in a low voice.

"What? No. We've just arrived," she hissed. "Bianca, answer the question."

Bianca moistened her lips. She didn't think Eden had it in her to have anyone tortured, but the witch would know if she lied. In turn, Viktor would know Bianca lied, and he would likely torture her himself.

There was no reason to be untruthful. Maybe if her father was still alive he could get her out of this mess.

"Just one," Bianca finally admitted.

Luka's chin lifted back to the white-haired vixen. His fist clenched and his claws slowly extended. Even chained against the cell wall, she was a vision.

"When Viktor sent me around Prajna, to visit the people, it was ... difficult," Bianca acknowledged. She'd pretended it was a task beneath her station, but really, it had rattled her.

"I didn't know how to comfort them. I couldn't help them. I did not understand why he'd subject me to their misery. I'm not exactly known for being nurturing."

Luka snorted and Eden slapped at his arm.

"One day, in the town of Mosnik, I watched a female collapse in sobs after telling me she'd lost every child she'd ever carried. I was stunned. I quickly felt very foolish. I had thought no live births meant no one got pregnant," Bianca shook her head sadly.

She met Luka's hard stare, which softened at the way Bianca's mouth turned down. He could tell she pretended to not be affected. She'd always been so cold when she wasn't using her sexuality to get what she wanted. It was all an act. Those villagers *had* affected her. Greatly.

The two of them were more alike than either of them realized. Luka didn't know what to make of his silent discovery. He only knew he wanted to unravel the tangled mess chained before him.

"I needed a break," Bianca continued, "so I took a walk. I didn't go far. A little ways into the woods I stopped. I picked up a faint scent. It reminded me of my father, so I tracked it."

"Where did it lead you? To Dmitri?" Eden asked.

Bianca shook her head, her eyes filling. "No," she whispered. "That is not what I found."

Eden's hand ran along her collarbone, pondering Bianca's reaction. They knew it had been Bianca's scent in the clearing where they found Isla.

"Where is Mosnik?" she asked.

"Close to the border of Burghard." It was Bran who answered this time.

"What did you see, Bianca?"

The female took a shuddering breath. Her face drew tight. She'd swore she'd never speak of it, never think of it. She'd done what she could to fix it and then she'd fled.

"A demon. He was," she swallowed, "he was with a she-wolf. He was hurting her. He was forcing her to … do things and she was begging him to stop."

Eden's skin felt too tight. Any female would feel disgusted and angry over witnessing what Bogdan had done. She didn't know the details, but she didn't need to.

Eden could guess why Bianca would have had such a visceral reaction, especially with all the unwanted attention the female vampire had been getting before she came to Castra Nocte.

The demon deserved a slow, painful death. Too bad Kellan had already killed him shortly after he'd been caught.

"I could not leave her to that. No one deserves to be violated in such ways," Bianca hissed vehemently.

"What did you do?" Luka leaned towards her, his left hand slightly reaching to comfort her.

"I stepped out of the woods and he ran off, leaving the female. She was talking gibberish. Bloodied. Battered. Her eyes were swelling shut. Without thinking, I told her to open them and commanded her to forget. I could hear wolves coming in the distance and, since I had crossed the border out of Prajna without permission, I ported back to Mosnik."

"You hypnotized her so she wouldn't remember what he'd done," Bran asserted. "That's why Isla couldn't remember," he said to Eden.

"Isla?" Bianca asked. "She lived?"

"Aye."

Bianca sagged in relief. Luka's palm started to tingle, almost to the point of burning. It should be healing, not getting worse.

Small shards of silver light above Bianca's head captured Eden's attention. The female's hands had fisted tightly earlier in her cuffs, now they were relaxing as the weight of her emotional burden started to lift.

"Luka," Eden gasped. "Her hand."

Luka's breaths were shallow. He felt like he'd been punched in the gut. He kept his palm down, terrified of looking at it.

On unsteady legs, he approached Bianca. She shrank back as much as she could.

"Open your hand."

"No." Bianca made a fist.

"No?" he lowered his eyes down to hers. She was terrified.

"I'm not going to hurt you, dove, I just want to look at your palm."

"It's been itching all week. Today, it started hurting."

"You understand what it means?" he asked smoothly, keeping his voice steady.

"I—I don't want it. I don't know who ... I won't leave Castra Nocte. It is safe here. I won't leave."

Eden stepped backwards, closer to Bran. She felt like an intruder watching Bianca fall apart.

"Open your palm, Bianca." He'd used her name, said it with his powers to sooth her.

Bianca opened her hand and Luka's world tilted on its axis. He took several deep breaths, slowing his speeding pulse.

Her worried eyes searched his. He was speechless. He could feel the pull of the cicatrice. Luka was dumbfounded. He'd known Bianca for a long time, never had he felt anything for her aside from physical attraction.

Theron was right. The leader had found his sieva, and so now would others. It had taken weeks, but that was probably because Eden was now—

His hand started to reach for Bianca's and he flung it back down to his side. There would be no soul-bonding in the dungeon.

"Luka?" Eden spoke. "Is it ...?

"Incredibly coincidental? I'd say yes," a male's voice came from behind Eden.

She started to spin away but quick as a flash he had her pulled to his body, his claws embedded deeply in the skin over her heart. Eden held herself very still.

Luka had jumped in front of Bianca to shield her from the threat and Bran was moving slowly along the edge of the cell, unwilling to pounce and risk harm to Eden.

Luka's angry eyes darted to Bran. "I thought you knew his scent, wolf."

"He's not giving off any scent," Bran complained, raking his eyes over the disheveled male holding Eden captive.

Dmitri slanted his head, grinning. A lock of dark hair fell over one manic eye. His dirty hands flexed and more blood pulled around the punctures in Eden's chest. Bran wanted to lunge but the vampire's claws were too close to her heart.

"Ah, yes. Caught on to that, did you? Of course you did, you are wolf, your noses are virtually faultless," Dmitri praised Bran, as if he'd done something remarkable.

"Agatha and I had been experimenting with some medicines. Smart little wolf found something to mask any scent."

"Father?" Bianca's strangled voice creaked.

"Hello, darling. Sorry, this visit must be short. But do not fret, your sieva here will make sure Viktor does not harm you."

"I haven't seen you in a century and that's the first thing you choose to say to me?" she seethed.

Dmitri's chin jutted with indignation. "I set you up to be a queen. From what I've seen, you still might be, if Luka takes the throne. Thanking me would be a more appropriate response, I think."

Bianca's face hardened. Her father had always been doting and kind. His soft tone always reserved for only her and her mother. This was not the male she remembered. This was a male coming unhinged.

"What makes you think I would take the throne?" Luka asked, wanting Dmitri's attention off of Bianca.

"You're the only heir. Once Viktor is dead, it goes to you."

Luka's eyes darted to Eden's stomach. Dmitri noticed and chuckled, digging his claws in deeper.

"This heir doesn't have long to live."

"Wh-what heir?" Eden stuttered over the pain burning above her breast.

Dmitri's free hand went to her lower abdomen, his fingers pressing firmly into her belly. "The one growing inside your cursed womb, witch."

Her logic wanted to protest, thinking it was too soon. Sadly, she didn't know anything about the gestation period of vampire offspring. Luka's nervous eyes bore into hers, and the truth of Dmitri's words rang through her ears.

"Father, no," Bianca pleaded. Dmitri didn't acknowledge her.

Eden's entire body locked up. Instinctually, her soul tugged at the bond she had with Viktor. She fought to tamp it down. Dmitri had his talons precariously close to her heart and the others were too close to her child.

Her *child*.

The last thing she needed was for Viktor to port nearby and startle Dmitri, causing him to flinch or tear her flesh to shreds.

She needed to think. Eden could burn him, but it wouldn't be fast enough to kill him. Neither would stopping his pulse. If it was only her life at stake, she wouldn't hesitate to do something.

Bran crouched ever so slowing, like an animal preparing to attack. Eden subtly shook her head. She'd have to free herself, or get Dmitri distracted.

"Ah, ah, wolf," Dmitri reprimanded. "I wouldn't if I was you."

"What are you waiting for, Dmitri?" Eden goaded.

"Your mate. Why don't you give a tug on that bond so we can get on with things?"

Eden's heart hardened at his words. It helped ignite her anger, drowning out her fear. She was furious on Viktor's behalf, irate one of the few people he'd ever considered a friend would harm him. He might end her life, but she'd never allow him to end Viktor's.

"No," she replied resolutely.

"You're not really in a position to refuse me. Alert your mate. Now," he growled.

"I said no," she repeated.

"I will kill you right here, female! Call for him!" Dmitri's voice boomed with his frustration.

His irritation had gotten the better of him. Eden could faintly here the guards moving down the corridor. She was running out of time.

"Damnit," Dmitri cursed.

His spiteful gleam fell one last time on Luka.

"Tell your brother he can see his sieva again. In the Netherworld."

Compression closed in on Eden as Dmitri ported them away.

# Chapter 29

Viktor landed on the balcony outside his chambers. Yuri arrived a second later. They'd left Kellan and his wolves to continue searching after deciding to return to Castra Nocte and confront Bianca. First, he needed to check on Eden, if only to see her for a moment.

Entering through the glass doors, he immediately knew no one was inside. His senses heightened and he felt for the soul-bond, making sure his mate was alright.

He could feel traces of worry. He'd felt hints of her distress since Luka had left her on that tiny island, but nothing close to the agony which had seared through the bond when she'd found out about the betrothal.

"She's not here," Viktor informed Yuri who was entering the bed chamber. His teeth gnashed, uneasy Luka had allowed her to vacate the safety of these quarters.

"We can assume she's with Luka. Did you tell Eden not to leave?"

Viktor's lungs constricted, imagining Eden attempting to leave him. He didn't really believe she'd try, not after she'd agreed to be here when he returned.

Luka wouldn't have taken her far, even if she'd asked. No, she was still in Castra Nocte.

He should have asked her to stay in his chambers and set guards on the balcony, as well as outside the door instead of only Luka and Bran. Sadly, Luka and Bran had been the only two he trusted right now with his mate. Who knew what tricks Dmitri was using, possibly compromising Viktor's men.

Viktor couldn't imagine Dmitri himself coming for Eden in their chambers, not with the threat he'd made to unwelcomed guests so long ago. He hoped his own arrogance hadn't clouded his judgement.

"She agreed to be here when I returned," Viktor answered.

Yuri looked around the room, checking for evidence of a struggle. His gaze fell upon the empty bottle of whiskey and two tumblers.

"There's no sign of foul play," he commented.

"No, I'm guessing Luka escorted her somewhere inside the castle."

Yuri picked up the empty bottle and held it aloft. Viktor's brows knitted together. Eden wouldn't have finished the bottle. She could barely finish a glass of wine.

"Let us ponder for a moment, where your sieva would go, hours after discovering what you had been hiding, and a short time after consuming at least a dram of hard liquor."

"Aside from back to her father?" Viktor grunted.

"Aside from that, yes."

Viktor's face tilted up towards the ceiling, thinking. She had no need to go anywhere. Food and drink had been brought up. She had company. Granted, it was Luka, but she didn't seem to mind him.

What would spur Eden to leave the safety of her chambers? After imbibing? After setting herself afire in a moment of tremendous emotional upheaval?

He considered what he would do if in her shoes.

"She wouldn't," Viktor groaned.

"Oh, I think she did."

"Luka wouldn't allow it."

"Have you met your brother? He'd pay good coin to watch your mate confront your ex-lover."

Viktor pinched the bridge of his nose.

"Viktor, we're going to question Bianca anyway. Let us go to the dungeon first and perhaps we'll come across your mate. You can send guards to look for them if they're not there—or go yourself if you feel the need."

"You're right."

"I know."

"You sound like Luka."

"And you, Sire, are cruel to say such things aloud."

"That I am, Yuri. That I am."

Viktor's voice was too melancholy for Yuri's liking. He patted his friend on the back.

"Come, my King. Let me help you salvage ... things."

Viktor snorted. He needed all the help he could get.

They ported to the large door leading into the dungeon. It was standing wide open. Guards were running about while Luka barked orders from down the corridor. Viktor's hackles immediately rose and his claws extended.

"Don't jump to conclusions, Viktor," Yuri said, crouched and alert, coming up beside him.

Viktor held still, analyzing the movements. The guards were running off to do Luka's bidding, not engaged in a fight.

"The threat isn't here," he calculated.

Sure of his assessment, he took off towards his brother. Luka was standing at the opening of Bianca's cell.

He did a double take when he saw Viktor and Yuri approach. Luka's posture folded ever so slightly, like it did whenever he was reprimanded as a child.

Movement drew the King's attention to inside the cell. Bran was pacing agitatedly. Bianca was sitting on the cot in the corner, no longer shackled. Eden was nowhere in sight.

"Viktor," Luka exhaled.

"Where is she?"

"Dmitri," Luka seethed. "He took her."

One second Luka was staring into his brother's face, the next he was staring at the ceiling, pain exploding across his jaw. Grunts and curses to his left had him lifting his head.

Yuri and Bran each had a hold of one of Viktor's arms. Luka hurried to sit up, in case his brother got loose. Warm hands gained hold under his arms, helping to lift him to his feet. Bianca.

"Best if we do as little touching as possible right now, dove. A bit of a crisis happening. Mind staying over by the cot so Viktor doesn't kill you?"

Once Luka was standing, Bianca backed away, returning to her previous spot in the corner. Raptly, she watched his hand wipe the trickle of blood from the corner of his mouth.

Luka turned back to his brother despite his cicatrice screaming at him to pick up his sieva and port away. He couldn't abandon Viktor, no matter how many times his brother drew blood.

"I told you to protect her! To stay as close as possible. How did he get to her? How, damn it?!"

"He masked his scent. We didn't know he was here until he was close enough to grab Eden," Bran's voice rang out with regret. "He said Agatha figured out how."

This time, Yuri swore. Masking scents would be a huge obstacle in their search.

"Let him go," Luka told the males still holding onto Viktor. He didn't know why they bothered. The enormous brute could get free if he truly wanted.

Viktor jerked his arms out of their grasps, but refrained from attacking Luka again. He needed his wits about him.

"How long ago?"

"Eleven minutes," Bianca's quiet voice answered from the shadows.

"You will not address me," Viktor warned. "I've no use for conniving traitors or their daughters."

Luka stepped menacingly towards his brother, his cold gaze sharpening as he did. "Watch how you speak to her, Viktor. This is neither the time nor the place. I suggest you focus on finding Eden."

"You stand up for her? What is wrong with you?"

Luka lifted his left hand and held his palm in front of Viktor's face. The faint silver glow reflected in the King's eyes. His pupils grew small.

Viktor's head swiveled towards the female vampire. Reluctantly, Bianca lifted her palm. Viktor didn't have to ask again. He knew what was wrong with Luka.

"I propose," Yuri's deep voice interrupted, "we shelve this for now and go after Eden."

"Indeed," Viktor groused and Luka dropped his arm. "Now, I suggest you start from the beginning, Brother, and be quick about it."

Luka couldn't help the twitch of his lips. Eden had said the same thing to him, almost verbatim. She really was the perfect match for Viktor. Sobering, Luka relayed what had happened as succinctly as he could.

Viktor's fury compounded with each passing word out of Luka's mouth. He'd made the mistake of believing Dmitri would not be brave enough to sneak into the castle.

Dmitri had been an advisor only. He wasn't a warrior. Any one of the castle guards could have easily subdued him, if they'd gotten their hands on him. It was one of the reasons why Viktor had so readily believed his father had offed him.

He tried not to blame Luka. The male had, after all, just found out Bianca was his mate. Anyone would have been distracted by the influence of the cicatrice. Viktor didn't know how his brother was reacting internally and it wasn't the time to ask.

"... then he said you could see her again in the Netherworld," Luka finished.

"Netherworld? You're sure?"

"I'm sure."

"Then I think I know where he is."

Four stunned faces blinked at him.

"Where?" Luka demanded.

"Diavol Crest."

Yuri scratched at his short beard. "Why would he go there?"

"After Father—Nikolai—killed Dmitri's sieva, that's where he went to spread her ashes. The eddy below the ridge is extremely powerful. He told me, had he been a braver male, he would have thrown himself into the vortex so he could see her again in the Netherworld. I made him promise to never speak such nonsense again."

Only, now Viktor was soul-bonded himself, he knew it wasn't nonsense. It was the result of the crushing grief over losing a mate. It might have been enough to twist Dmitri into something he might not have been otherwise.

Bianca sniffed. Her claws had come out and were digging into her palms. Luka wanted to pull her hands into his and had to fight to keep them at his sides.

Viktor didn't allow himself to pity Bianca. That was a situation he would have to sort out later. For now, he needed to use her.

"You cannot go alone," Luka warned his brother.

Viktor's eyes narrowed, looking to Bianca. "I do not intend to."

* * *

"What are you waiting for?" Eden grunted.

The moon came out from behind the darkened clouds and she could see Dmitri had ported them to a high cliff above the ocean. The wind whipped her hair across her face so hard it stung.

"Are you really so eager to die, female?"

"Not particularly."

Eden knew he was waiting for Viktor to come after them. She'd had to use her magic to control her pulse, fearful Viktor would be able to pick up on her distress. She would not allow Dmitri to harm him.

Now that they were away from the castle and alone, she needed to figure out how to get some distance between them. A few inches and she could blast him with enough force to prevent him from reaching her again. Her fingers were crawling with power, waiting for the right moment to strike.

Inopportunely, Dmitri still had one arm wrapped around her front and his claws had yet to retract. He hadn't punctured her breastbone, but he could do so easily if she tried burning him.

At least his left hand had removed itself from her abdomen. She wouldn't have believed his proclamation if not for Luka's panicked glance at her stomach. That swooshing sound he'd heard had not been water. It must have been the babe's tiny heart pumping blood.

Dmitri drug her close to the edge. A small jolt of fear accompanied the adrenaline her body started to release. She could swim. She could even part the water. She could not, however, survive a two-hundred-foot drop.

If he'd only release his talons, she could use her power. Maybe even use the wind to send him off the cliff. *Would a vampire survive it?* No, it would be best to use flames.

"Why are you doing this, Dmitri? Viktor loved you."

The band around her chest tautened and she whimpered. She'd struck a nerve.

"It has nothing to do with Viktor," Dmitri censured. "A witch on any throne outside of Gwydion cannot be allowed. No faction can have an outsider reigning over its people. It upsets the balance of power."

"You made that contract with Viktor a century ago. You couldn't have known an elemental was to become his mate."

"It was more than a guess. Did your father teach you nothing of portents?"

He spun them so his back was to the ocean. His focus on the space between the cliff and the tree line. Searching. Waiting.

"My mother never predicted I'd be in Prajna. She arranged for me to go to the Northland. Besides, she hadn't even been born yet when you tricked Viktor into doing what you wanted."

Dmitri huffed. "Stupid girl. Your mother wasn't the only seer in Imperium. My wife had visions. Not as strong or as frequent, but she dreamt of Viktor mating with someone who was not vampire. It could not be allowed."

"He was willing to give up the throne. If you'd just left well enough alone, even after all you've done, Luka would have taken his place and Bianca would be Queen."

"Oh, she'll still be Queen."

"When Viktor told me you asked him to take care of her, I'd thought you an honorable male."

Eden blew out a humorless laugh. "How mistaken I was."

"Despite what you might believe, I did make arrangements for Bianca for her benefit. I love my daughter."

"She does not believe it. Did you see her face when you appeared? When she realized what you'd done? Horror. Disgust. *Shame.*"

Dmitri laughed. "Bianca is resilient. Nothing gets to her. She was raised to be so. She'll get over it."

"I don't think you know your daughter as well as you think you do."

"Hush. I grow tired of this conversation."

Eden altered her stance, testing his hold. He flexed and she stilled. She might not be able to break his embrace. Her mind started flipping through her last-resort options. None of them were good, but if she was going to die, she intended to take him with her.

Eden's back arched slightly. Viktor was pulling at their bond. He was upset. She hastily tried to send calming vibes. Though she was hurt by his lie of omission, she still loved him. She didn't want to die without him having that assurance. He would need it after she was gone.

None of this was fair. Or just. Viktor made mistakes, but he did not deserve Dmitri's dastardly actions.

The longer they stood there, the more time Viktor had to find them. She would not allow Dmitri to take her mate's life on top of hers and their child's. Her heart split wide open. Could she really do this, knowing both she and the babe would perish?

It would be worse if Dmitri killed her in front of Viktor. Maybe if she took the traitor out, she could save Viktor from the pain of having to watch.

Closing her eyes, she leaned back into Dmitri, adjusting her feet to push off from the rocks. She called her magic, readying it to cover them both in a sudden roaring blaze.

It was the only way to prevent him from porting when she pushed them both over the cliff. She prayed his pain and shock would be enough to keep him attached to her as they fell.

*One*, she counted in her head, gathering her courage.

*Two.*

*Three*—

"Eden, no!" Viktor roared across the cliff, some twenty feet away from his sieva.

Her eyes popped open, flooding with tears. She cried out at the sight of her mate, both elated and frustrated he'd come for her.

Viktor didn't move a muscle. He kept his captive's body close, his hand around her throat. Bianca, to her credit, allowed her body to shake with fear.

"Viktor," Dmitri snarled. "Let Bianca go."

"Of course. As soon as you let Eden go."

Dmitri's hot breath came out hard against the side of Eden's head. His body hummed with agitation, vibrating slightly against her back. Eden kept her power swirling in her hands, ready to be released.

The group remained locked in a standoff. Viktor allowed his claws to break Bianca's skin. Her blood oozed between his fingers. Luka would be furious with Viktor, but it had to look real.

"F-father?" Bianca sobbed, a lifetime of dramatics culminating into a perfect performance.

"Don't do it, Viktor. You'll only curse yourself if you take my daughter's life."

"I'm willing to risk it, Deceiver. If Eden dies, so will your daughter."

Viktor was tempted to swear it upon his name, to seal it with magic and force Dmitri's hand. He'd sworn to Luka, before they'd left the dungeon, he wouldn't do anything quite so drastic.

Dmitri stiffened. Torn. Viktor was The Heartless King of Prajna. He did not make empty threats. His internal conflict forced him to hesitate.

His mission or his daughter? If he could just get Bianca free, he could continue his mission.

"What are you proposing?" he asked.

"A trade," Viktor replied.

"You know it won't end here."

"I know."

"Very well. We'll release them at the same time. You take Eden back to Castra Nocte, and I will take Bianca away."

Viktor almost believed the male meant what he said. Almost.

Dmitri withdrew his talons from Eden's chest. The fabric of her shirt was saturated in dark red liquid. Viktor strangled the rage building behind his stoic pretense.

"Walk towards your mate, witch." Dmitri pushed her in Viktor's direction. "Bianca, come."

Eden stumbled forward, keeping Viktor in her sights. As she walked, she considered turning around and blasting Dmitri with power. Only the fact Viktor wouldn't have come without a strategy stopped her. Nor would he want her involved in taking Dmitri's life. Viktor had earned that right.

She didn't know what he planned and she did not want to further traumatize Bianca. If Eden had more time, she could have made a better decision.

Bianca's forlorn face didn't so much as peek at Eden. Surely the female wasn't going to willingly port away with Dmitri. Luka wouldn't stand for it.

They passed, shoulders only inches apart. Eden was two steps past Bianca when she felt two hands on her waist. From behind.

"Say hello to your mother," Dmitri hissed and used his vampiric strength to throw her over the cliff.

Viktor watched in horror as Eden's body flew through the air and disappeared from sight. He sprinted to the edge, searching.

Dmitri's hand shot out to grab Viktor. It never reached its target. An iron manacle clamped around his wrist just as Viktor disappeared.

Dmitri's head jerked up and he was staring into the bright green eyes of his daughter's sieva.

"Miss me?" Luka taunted.

Dmitri tried to port but the iron prevented it. Luka had a hold of the chain attached to the handcuff. Dmitri jerked, trying to free it so he could at least flee on foot.

Luka's grip was true and Dmitri couldn't get the chain from the Prince's grasp. Alarm erupted through his body. This could not be the end.

He could not be taken. He was the last of the Sephtis Kenelm. He had yet to replace the others. It could not end like this.

With his free hand, Dmitri reached down and pulled the knife from his boot.

"Luka!" Bianca shouted in warning, erringly drawing his attention away from her father.

Dmitri struck, his blade sinking deep into Luka's chest. Luka fell to his knees and his hold on the chain loosened. Dmitri pulled away, his sole concern to ensure the death of either Viktor or Eden.

*Or both,* he hoped.

# Chapter 30

Eden's weightless body plummeted towards the swirling dark water below. Her stomach rose to her throat and she struggled to remain calm.

The full moon was bright enough to hint at how far she'd fallen. She could hear the roiling eddy's powerful clashes against the rocks.

Facing the sky, she used her magic to call to the air and wind, desperate to slow her fall. Earlier, she'd been able to part the sea and walk through it. Now, she feared she didn't have enough energy left to both break her fall and fight the whirlpool.

Drops of ocean spray landed on her exposed neck and hands. She yelped, knowing she was dangerously close to her death.

Her momentum had decelerated. She hoped it was enough. Eden closed her eyes, preparing for the worst. Suddenly, her body jolted and compressed.

She waited for the painful fingers of frigid water, for the burn from the lack of oxygen. Instead she felt ... warmth and two giant arms crushing her tight.

"Open your eyes, love."

Eden's lungs expelled all the air she'd been holding in. Her body racked with soundless sobs at the realization she was safe in Viktor's unrelenting embrace. She could have been killed, both she and their child.

She clung to Viktor, shaken. They were safe, all three of them. Safe in their chambers, away from Dmitri. The impression of his name in her consciousness terminated her temporary respite.

Viktor's lips landed on Eden's forehead, then her temple, then her mouth. Abrupt and unyielding. His heart had stopped when he'd watched her go over the cliff.

He wanted to taste her tongue, to strip her bare and devote hours to loving her in their bed. He wanted to hold her, to convey what she meant to him. Viktor needed to atone for what he'd done to his mate.

It would have to wait. He had to eradicate the menace who had dared to put his hands on Eden. He lowered her until her feet landed on the floor.

"I have to go back," he told her.

"I know. Don't go alone. Take Bran or Yuri, and a dozen guards—or more."

"I'll be okay, *moj vestica.*"

Eden caressed his jaw. "I need you to come back to us, safe and preferably in one piece. Please don't go alone."

"If it will make you feel better, I'll grab the wolf on my way. I'll send Yuri up here to stay with you until I return. Do not leave these quarters, Eden."

"I won't."

Viktor planted one last searing kiss upon his mate's lips and then ported away.

\* \* \*

Ignoring his daughter's shout as she ran to her mate, Dmitri moved to the edge of the cliff. There was no sign of either Viktor or Eden. With any luck, her body had hit the water and Viktor went in after her.

Though, he doubted the King had perished. Viktor could have gotten her in time by porting to her in the air.

Dmitri held up his arm. He needed to get the shackle off so he could get himself to safety and come up with a new plan.

He turned back towards Luka, thinking he would search him for the key. Bianca stood in his way.

She took in the sight of her beloved father. She'd always been so proud of his sacrifice, so confident in his love for her. He'd gone to great lengths to ensure she was well off after he'd disappeared.

Bianca bit back the devastating disappointment of discovering not only was he a traitor to the crown, he'd used her as a pawn to suit his own purpose. She was done being used.

"Bianca, come, port me away from here."

She leered at his hand, at the cicatrice that matched her mother's. Her grip on the sword against her thigh tightened. Her father hadn't even noticed she'd taken it from Luka's scabbard.

Luka groaned incoherently from behind her. She would not let her father near him again.

"Did my mother know?"

Dmitri dropped his hand. He hadn't much time, but his only child appeared reluctant to reach for him. Bianca was determined to have answers and he couldn't blame her.

"Did she know what?"

"That you were going to betray Viktor."

He exhaled heavily. "She knew Viktor's mate was not vampire. She'd dreamt it."

"Answer my question."

"She found out, yes. It is difficult to keep the mark hidden when it is so boldly scripted across one's chest."

Her eyes flicked to the area over his heart.

"How did you get the mark?"

"That is not for anyone to know, Bianca."

"Not even me?"

"Not even you."

Her indignation intensified. The more she studied him, the more she realized she didn't know him at all.

"If that is all, Bianca, let us leave. Someone will be coming."

"One more question and then you can depart. Why did Nikolai kill my mother? You never gave me a reason and I was too young to know to ask."

It wasn't lost on him that she'd said *you* and not *we* could depart. She wasn't going to come with him. He should have known he'd have no sway over her, not when her sieva was lying on his back with a knife stuck between his ribs.

"I don't know."

"Lie."

Dmitri's head jerked to the right. Standing beside a very alive Viktor was the young wolf from the dungeon. The damned animal could smell a lie.

"You don't look surprised to see me," Viktor's smooth voice purred. It was the voice he used when dealing with deplorables at court.

"That's because I'm not."

"Answer her, Dmitri," Luka grated through gritted teeth. "Give her some truth after your litany of lies. You owe her that much."

Viktor surveyed his brother a moment. Luka was very still, but he was breathing and he was capable of speech. These were positive signs.

"Well?" Bianca prompted, moving a step closer.

Viktor and Bran inched towards Dmitri, as well. They had him pinned, his back to the edge of the cliff. There was nowhere to go but down.

"Eliza went to Nikolai and told him what she'd seen in her dreams. I told her to keep quiet, but she didn't listen. Nikolai didn't want Viktor to ever know his sieva was not Prajna. He killed her for it. When he confronted me, I already had this," he pulled his shirt aside to reveal the swirling black ink upon his skin.

"He knew we were of the same mind, despite what he'd done to Eliza. Nikolai was almost joyous over it. He extracted an oath from me never to act against him and allowed me to escape."

Viktor's nostrils flared. His father had known his true mate was not of their faction? The tyrant had meant to withhold the truth from his own son—had meant for Viktor to never find Eden.

Bianca glanced at Bran.

"Truth," the wolf pronounced with a low growl in his chest. He was disgusted on Viktor's behalf. It was not right what his father did. Matehood was what made life worth living.

Bianca's perfect eyebrows slanted. Dmitri swore he could feel his daughter's suspicion. "What? You thought *I* had something to do with your mother's death?"

"Apparently, I know nothing of what you did or did not do. Everything I thought I knew of your existence was a lie."

"Bianca—"

329

"I wish you had actually been killed as I believed."

Dmitri flinched. Her declaration had been devoid of feeling. She'd stated it matter of fact, masking her emotions as he'd taught her to do when she was very young.

He'd never intended for her to suffer. He thought he'd left her in the best position possible. She was cool and calculating, unencumbered by the emotions plaguing others. She would be a great queen.

Viktor and Bran drifted nearer. Dmitri needed to escape. He was no match for Viktor or the wolf, especially now he was unarmed.

He stepped towards Bianca. Moonlight caught on the steel of the blade she lifted between them. She gripped it expertly, as though she'd done it a thousand times.

Bianca's posture was relaxed, her hold on Luka's weapon steady. Years of living in a perpetual state of numbness saved her from any show of wavering.

"Bianca, move away from him," Luka begged, holding one hand over his wound and the other out to his mate.

"Listen to your sieva," Dmitri ordered, braving another step towards her and away from the men closing in.

Viktor considered porting Dmitri straight to the dungeons. Their original plan had been to capture and question him.

Having seen his mate get thrown from the top of Diavol Crest, the only thing that would satisfy his thirst for revenge would be watching Dmitri's head fall away from his body.

"Bianca," Viktor soothed, trying to make sure she did nothing to endanger herself. It would crush Luka if she was harmed. "Give me the sword."

"No."

She lunged at her father, swinging the length of steel in a wide arc. She was aiming for his neck.

Dmitri's eyes widened and he propelled himself backwards, narrowly missing the tip of the sharp blade. Instinctually, he tried to port.

With the iron cuff still attached, it did no good. Too late, he realized his mistake as he tumbled over the rocky cliff.

Viktor, Bran, and Bianca ran to the edge. They watched Dmitri's descent until he splashed into the black vortex below.

Bianca hissed in frustration. She wound back, about to throw the sword after her father when Luka's weakened voice stopped her.

"I would appreciate," he panted, "if you did not lose my favorite weapon."

The metal clinked against the rock as she dropped it and ran to him. The bleeding seemed to have slowed, but his skin had become ashen.

She reached for the hand Luka had clutching the knife. Viktor grabbed her wrist.

"Don't touch his hand, Bianca."

Her eyes flashed and her palm tingled, protesting. Luka needed her. Their souls were pushing them together.

"Let me get him help first. At the very least, the knife needs to come out before ..."

He let the rest linger, not wanting to think about his brother binding his soul to Bianca. She may have finally shown some of her true colors, but he was still wary.

At least she hadn't been conspiring with Dmitri. Viktor honestly did not know what he would have done to Luka's mate if she had been in cahoots with her father.

Viktor knelt beside Luka and lifted him into his arms. Luka ground his teeth with the movement.

"Bianca, port with Bran to the infirmary."

"If it's all the same," Bran interjected, "I'd like to stay here, make sure he doesn't come out of the water."

Viktor didn't think Dmitri would be strong enough to survive the whirlpool, but it would be wise to make sure.

"Thank you. I'll send others along shortly to help you. We'll need to check the banks, as well. Bianca, we'll see you in a moment."

Viktor ported Luka to the rarely-used infirmary. It was empty, aside from one guard on duty. The startled male jumped when the King appeared carrying the very bloody Prince.

"Go get the healer," Viktor barked.

"Right away, Sire."

Bianca landed and strode to the nearest bed, turning down the sheet. She rolled up her sleeves and grabbed a basin and some rags from the shelving beside the bed.

"What are you doing?" Viktor asked.

"Helping."

Luka coughed out a laugh in between grunts of agony when Viktor placed him on the bed.

"Viktor, have you met Bianca?"

Viktor stared, dumbfounded, at Luka's mate. She was determined to assist, something he'd never seen from her. Even her movements were different. Expedient. Not a hint of seduction in her actions.

"I'm starting to believe I haven't," Viktor replied.

Bianca ignored her mate's strained chuckle and continued prepping supplies. She kept her head low to hide her reddened cheeks.

# Chapter 31

Viktor ported to his balcony. Afraid of startling Yuri or Eden, he opened the glass doors slowly giving them time to hear and see it was him.

Eden crashed into his body before he crossed the threshold. His arms automatically encircled her. Gently, he walked her backwards so he could shut the doors.

"I'm happy to see you, as well, little mate."

Eden grinned against his shirt. Her hands flattened against his front. The fabric was damp. She pulled back and saw the crimson stains smeared across his abdomen and arms.

"What happened?"

"It's not mine."

"Is it ... Dmitri's?"

"Unfortunately, no."

Yuri leaned forward in his seat. "He lives?"

"I don't think so."

Yuri started to rise and Viktor held up a hand. "No, stay seated." He guided Eden to the wingback chair, sat, then pulled her onto his lap.

She snuggled under his chin, uncaring she was getting blood on her own clothing. She just needed to be close to him for a minute.

Stroking his sieva's hair, he told them what had happened when he returned to the cliff. By the time he finished, Yuri's mouth hung open, speechless. It was almost comical.

"Luka will be alright?" Eden asked.

"He'll mend. As for being alright? I'm not sure. He's about to soul-bond with Bianca," Viktor replied.

"Yes, rather unlucky," Yuri added.

"I think you're both wrong. There's more to her than either of you know," Eden dissented.

"Such as?" Yuri prompted.

"Such as the fact she came across that she-wolf—what was her name? Isla. Yes, Isla, the one involved with the demon Bogdan. He'd beaten her, was doing terrible things to her and Bianca scared him off. She was so upset she erased Isla's memory of it."

Yuri scratched at his beard as he did so often when thinking. "She told you this?"

"She did. In front of Bran, if you're wondering why I believed her."

"What was she doing across the border?" Viktor asked.

"She thought she'd picked up her father's scent, when she was out visiting the villages and towns. She followed it and it took her into Burghard. She didn't know he was alive, Viktor. You cannot punish her for colluding with him."

"I know."

"I know my knowledge of her is limited, but I think you should sit and talk with her. Maybe, now that she's found her sieva, she'll feel comfortable dropping the persona she's been displaying for so long."

Viktor kissed her nose. "You may be right, my love."

Eden smiled shyly at his endearment. It was the second him he'd done it. She'd never tell him, but she also liked when he called her little witch.

Yuri stood. "I best get back to my wife. Do you need anything before I go, Viktor?"

"Could you send word to Kellan? Theron will need to be informed, as well.

"I'll drop in on the Wolf King now so he can get home to his mate. I will visit Theron in the morning, if that is acceptable."

"Yes, thank you."

"Anything for you, my friend. You, too, Eden. I hope you know that."

"I do. Thank you."

Yuri bowed and then exited through the door. As he walked, he wondered how long it would be before Viktor heard the sound that would change his life once more.

Yuri hadn't said anything to Eden about it, unsure if she was aware.

Both Eden and Viktor watched him go, staring at the door long after it had shut. The fire crackled and a whisper of something whooshed in the background. It was almost like horses galloping in the distance, but was too faint for him to decipher.

"Viktor?" Eden's voice distracted him from his listening.

"Yes?"

"I—I need to tell you something."

He looked down at his sieva, noticing the red on her hands and shirt. He grimaced.

"Can you tell me in the bath? I don't mind the blood on me, but I detest anything foul touching your beautiful skin."

"Oh," she lowered her head, peering down at her now dirtied clothing. "Of course."

Viktor rose, keeping Eden in his arms and carried her into the bathing chamber. Together, they prepared the water.

He removed his clothing, throwing anything tainted into the fire under the heating stones. Eden kept her back to him as she undressed. She wasn't showing in the slightest so she wasn't sure what she thought she was hiding.

Once she was nude, she lowered herself to the ledge, dipping her legs into the heated water. Eden crossed her arms across her belly, protectively.

Viktor felt uneasiness rush across their bond. He twisted to check on Eden. She was sitting on the side of the bathing pool, her shoulders slumped and head bowed.

He lowered himself into the pool and walked to the side where she was seated. Slowly, spread her knees apart with his hands and stepped into the space. She didn't lift her face.

Viktor gently hauled her into his arms and pulled her close. Her legs wrapped around his hips and he backed them away from the edge. Her arms tightened around his neck.

Eden wasn't the sort to hide from him or shy away from speaking frankly. Something was bothering his mate, something besides his unwise actions.

"Hold your breath, *mala vestica*."

Holding her to him, he dropped below the surface and immediately popped back up, as he'd done not that long ago when she'd vexed him for the first time.

"What was that for?" Eden sputtered and wiped the water from her face.

"That was for being afraid to speak to me. I didn't like it."

One side of Eden's mouth quirked. "I'm not afraid to speak to you."

"Then why did you go from clinging to me one moment, then avoiding me the next?"

"I have to tell you something."

"You think I won't like what you have to say. Is that it?"

"Yes," she whispered.

If he didn't react well, she didn't know what she'd do. This day had been the most difficult of her life. This should be a happy moment for them. She couldn't help but feel the dark clouds still lingering over them.

"I know you have been through much in a short time, Eden. I also know there are things still hanging between us, things up to me to repair, but you need never fear confiding in me. I will be what you need me to be. I swear it."

He spoke softly, but with confidence. Eden felt his love through the bond.

She hugged him, kissing the sensitive skin under his earlobe. His length hardened fully, pulsating between them.

She pressed her lips against his ear and told him, "I'm so glad you came back in one piece. I needed you to come back to us, Viktor."

"I—wait, what do you mean, come back to *us*?"

When she did not respond, he pulled on her hair so he could look upon her face. Eden bit her lip. Her pulse accelerated, causing his incisors to ache.

"Well," she licked her lips, "it means there is now more than one person who needs you."

Viktor became still as a statue. He didn't react at all and Eden worried her lips. Nothing was coming through their bond. In fact, it felt almost numb. *With shock?*

"I think," she said as she grabbed his hand and brought it to her lower belly, "if we are very quiet, you can hear him. Though, perhaps, not under the water."

*Him*, she'd said. A son.

Viktor finally took a breath. His heart took off, racing wildly. He clutched Eden's hips and lifted her out of the pool. The heated water sluiced down her body, the rivulets dripping onto the surface of the water, echoing soft plunks.

Tilting his head, Viktor put his ear against Eden's abdomen. The muffled whoosh of a tiny heart greeted him. Like tiny horses galloping in the distance.

Heat crawled up his neck. His pressed lips quivered. For a second, he lost control of his emotions. Hope, excitement, and love mixed and tangled with a morbid measure of fear. The snarled ball of emotions worked its way through the bond before he could get a handle on it.

"Viktor," her hoarse voice croaked under the strain of his varied reactions.

Viktor allowed Eden's body to slide down his until they were nose to nose. His glassy eyes broke her wide open.

"It will be alright. You'll see," she comforted him.

His lips turned down. An errant tear was close to slipping free from the rim of his eye.

"You cannot know that," his hush voiced disputed.

"You're right. I cannot see the future. So, let us look at facts. No sievas had been joined in the past century. Then you found me."

She kissed him sweetly.

"I know it's been some weeks since we bonded, but Luka has since found his mate, as well."

Another kiss.

"Now I am with child. Theron said it used to be that the vampires did not produce young until the leader did. This might be the start of things to come."

Logically, Eden's words made sense. Viktor wanted to give in to her optimism, to trust her reasoning. He feared he was incapable of it, not with what was at stake.

Outside of his experience with Eden, he'd rarely felt much of anything. He didn't trust the barrage of contradicting sentiments his overactive mind was producing.

This pregnancy should be something in which they rejoiced. It could signify the end of their curse. His people's lives might change for the better.

In this moment, however, he cared not what others faced. He only cared what happened to his mate and the babe growing inside her body. For all the responsibility and sense of duty he'd always internalized, none of it mattered when it came to Eden.

One truth ate away at his joy. The Prajna had never had difficulty with conception. Carrying young to term and delivering healthy babes was the plague the curse had produced. If something happened to his child, or to his mate, he would not survive it.

"It is not the pregnancy itself that worries me, Eden. Holding onto it—to *him*—is ..." Viktor inhaled.

341

No, he'd not voice it and give it power. He straightened his spine and cuffed her neck, holding her attention.

"We will take every precaution. You will see the healer first thing in the morning. I will bring in midwives and you may choose two to keep here at the castle. You will rest. You will not exert yourself. You will definitely no longer ingest liquor. It can affect your reflexes and I won't have you vulnerable. You'll not eat or drink anything else the healer tells you to stay away from. You probably shouldn't port with anyone. I'll have to ask about that. We'll come up with a list and you will follow it. Understood?"

Eden's chest shook.

"I'm serious, Eden."

Her lips stretched, showing her teeth. "I can tell."

"Eden," he growled.

"Viktor, I am pregnant, not made of glass. I'll not be treated as though I'll break at any moment. Women have been doing this for thousands and thousands of years."

"I only care about one woman and one babe. I'll do what I have to in order to ensure they're both healthy and happy."

"And I love you for it," she sighed, brushing her mouth across his and planting featherlight kisses upon his sinful lips.

"Tell me you're okay with this. Tell me you'll try to be happy about it," she whispered against his skin.

Viktor's face softened. "Ah, *moj vestica*, nothing could make me happier. Do not mistake my concern to mean I do not want this. I want it very much."

342

Eden's arms and legs tightened around his frame. Her tongue invaded his mouth, searching, demanding. She groaned, rubbing her slick body against his.

Viktor held her head still and took over the kiss. He slowed it, needing more from his sieva than her lust. He pulled on their connection, his soul coaxing hers. Probing. Cocooning itself in the splendor of her untainted spirit.

He explored further, opening himself up to what Eden held so preciously inside her body. There, deep within the link he felt the tiniest of threads reaching for him.

Eden and the babe were already connected in a way only mothers could be with their children. Fathers had to forge bonds. Nikolai had never bothered, and both Viktor and Luka had suffered for it. Viktor would never be like his father. His child would never wonder if he was loved.

Viktor's soul linked to the babe's and he gasped. The absolute sensation of rightness, of unconditional love and acceptance locked into place. The three of them were now bonded, as a family should be.

He wanted to live inside those bonds. Nothing so pure had ever touched his life. Surrounded by Eden's essence, touched by his babe's fledgling lifeforce, his soul felt worthy in a way it never had before.

Eden was growing impatient. She wanted Viktor to make love to her, to alleviate her mounting need. She reached down and palmed his shaft, stroking it slowly.

Viktor's hand landed on hers, tenderly pulling it away.

"Why are you stopping me?" she complained.

"Eden, we cannot."

"What are you talking about?"

"We shouldn't do anything that could jeopardize this pregnancy."

Eden cocked her head. "You're serious."

"Yes."

"Intercourse will not harm our child."

"Not one live birth in decades, Eden. Not one. I'll not endanger him. Or her. I'm not sure I should feed from you, either. It's been so long since I've been around an impregnated female, I just don't know what is safe. If I harmed you or our young, it would destroy me."

The crack in his voice killed her lust. Viktor was beside himself, to the point he was refusing to bed her or take from her vein.

"Okay," she assured him, stroking his face with both palms. "It's okay."

She reached for the soap. "Let's wash today away. Tomorrow will be better. Yes?" she asked hopefully.

"Yes," he agreed. "Then we will sleep and you'll stay in bed until the healer has seen to you."

"Of course."

Eden lathered the soap, massaged his rigid muscles, and washed away the blood.

# Chapter 32

*One month later ...*

"How are you feeling, love?" Viktor asked, his warm breath puffing on the back of Eden's neck as his large hand snaked around to hold her stomach possessively.

"I feel wonderful," she answered lazily.

"You should. You've been napping for over four hours."

His large hand lightly swatted her behind and she laughed, not in the least insulted. She'd been napping daily. The midwife told her she would feel tired for much of the first half of the pregnancy.

When Eden had asked how long, in weeks, that would be, the midwife could only guess. A vampire's pregnancy was much shorter than an elemental's—only six months compared to ten.

She already had a small baby bump. Whenever Viktor was near, he was touching it or speaking to it, as though the babe within could understand him.

It had earned him a number of double takes from his people. Especially when he did it at court. No longer content to allow Eden to sit on the bench beside him, he'd started sitting her in his lap so he could keep one hand on her abdomen.

Viktor had offered her the throne. Not to sit on, but to rule upon, as his Queen. When Eden hesitated, he told her to think on it. He hadn't brought it up since.

Matehood in Prajna did not require matrimony to be official. They valued the soul-bond beyond any ceremony. But to be Queen, that would require they marry.

Eden had forgiven him for his transgression. She had no doubts over her decision to stay with him. Her hesitation lied with the people of Prajna. She wasn't sure how they would react to her.

Bianca would have been accepted because she was vampire. Viktor assured her no one would question it. Eden wasn't quite as certain.

For now, she was content to be with Viktor as his *sieva* and focus on the birth of their son. Or daughter. She secretly believed Viktor wanted a girl based on the little jolts coming through the bond when he used feminine pronouns when speaking about the babe.

"It's late, completely dark outside, *moj vestica*. Get up and get dressed. I want to take you someplace."

Eden stretched and rolled, waking up her lethargic muscles. "Very well."

Yawning, Eden got up and slipped on one of the high-waisted dresses Viktor had asked to be made for her. Her other clothing was too tight around the middle, especially the trousers.

Though, Viktor didn't like her wearing her riding pants anyway. He said they revealed too much of what belonged to him. She wore them for as long as she could just to tease him.

The day she couldn't button them, Viktor shredded them with his claws. She'd only laughed, knowing she could have more made after she gave birth.

"Where are my boots?" she asked.

"You won't need them."

Eden glanced at Viktor's bare feet. He'd rolled up the legs of his pants. They must be going to the beach.

Taking his extended hand, they ported away. Viktor had been most relieved when both the midwife and healer laughed at his question about whether or not porting would harm the babe. He'd been too relieved to even reprimand them for daring to laugh at their King.

They landed on soft sand. Viktor held onto Eden, waiting for her to be oriented. When she was steady enough to look around, she smiled.

Viktor had brought them to the lagoons. The sun was gone from the sky and night had risen. The emerald algae's glow danced along the ripples in the water.

"Walk with me," he said, sliding his palm down her arm to clasp her hand.

They strolled in silence, wading in the shallow pools along the shores. The wind was nothing but a warm breeze this night, driving out any chill Eden might have felt.

"I have been thinking, *mala vestica*."

"Should I be afraid?"

"Definitely," he chuckled, warming her insides.

"I find," his voice deepened. "I find myself experiencing jealousy for the first time in my long life."

"Whatever for?"

"Yuri and Mariana. When we are with them, I find myself envious."

"Oh?" she asked, her voice clipped.

Eden's hand flexed in his. Viktor did not allow her to slip away.

"Yes. He constantly refers to her as, *Wife*. She is his sieva, yet he brands her as his in another way. A sieva is fate. A wife, however, is a choice."

Viktor stopped and pulled Eden towards him, careful of her small belly. His hands fell to her hips.

"You were a surprise, Eden. A gift from Fate. I was beyond blessed to have found you. I never knew happiness until you were in my arms."

Eden lifted her palms to his chest, touched by the sincerity of his proclamation.

"You are also my choice. I *choose* you. I believe I am just as much your mate as you are mine. I know elementals do not think they have fated mates, and according to general history they do not. What I am saying, what I am trying to ask, is I want you to choose me. Choose me in the way of your people. Marry me, Eden.

You do not have to be coronated as Queen. I care nothing of titles. I only desire the right to call you *Wife*."

Viktor dropped to his knees. He kissed her stomach and lifted his eyes to hers.

"Let our child be born to parents who are bound in every way possible, in the ways of both their people. Choose me, Eden."

Drops of her tears fell onto his hands. He rose and rubbed them away from her cheeks with his thumbs.

"I choose you," she hiccupped, rising to her tiptoes to kiss him soundly.

All too soon, Viktor broke the kiss and slipped something on her finger. She held it up. Dark red facets of a large ruby twinkled in the dim lighting. It was set in a thick gold band. It reminded her of Viktor's throne.

"It was my mother's," he told her. "You honor me by wearing it."

"I love it. I love you, Viktor. I would choose you a million times over."

"Thank the Goddess," he said unto the sky, pulling Eden into his arms once more. "I was afraid I was going to have to resort to drastic measures."

"Torture?" she giggled.

"Worse."

"What could be worse than torturing your cherished mate?"

Viktor turned her around and pointed towards the beach. On the wet sand left behind by the low tide was a configuration of phosphorous algae. It looked like it was supposed to be the shape of a heart, but the sides were terribly uneven and the waves had shifted part of the top.

She laughed through her tears. The Heartless King was actually terribly romantic.

"She laughs. All that work and she laughs," he pouted.

Eden leaned back into her beloved and his arms enveloped her from behind.

"Are you happy, love?"

"I am so much more than happy, Viktor."

"Good. I have one more thing to show you."

Viktor ported them back to their chambers. Wordlessly, he went to the door of his feeding room and disengaged the lock.

Eden quirked an eyebrow with interest. Their recent lovemaking had been slow and sweet. He'd reluctantly given in after the midwife's reassurances intercourse was actually good for an expectant mother.

"I'm not sure I like what's going on inside your head, Sieva."

"Oh, I think you'd like it very much."

"Hold that thought."

Viktor opened the door and stepped aside.

"After you," he insisted, sweeping an arm towards the room.

Eden walked through the doorway and froze.

Gone. It was all gone. No restraints. No black towels. No strange furniture designed for carnal activities. There was no trace left of what this room had been.

In its place was a room fit for a king. Or, in this case, a little prince or princess. Viktor had built a nursery.

A large, plush, gold and tan rug covered the floor. The walls had been covered in tapestries of similar coloring depicting animals from the forests.

A sizeable crib was in the corner, the white bedding already in place. Not one, but two rocking chairs sat side by side next to the crib. On the other side was a changing table.

A small wardrobe stood against the wall nearest the outer door. Eden knew if she opened it, she would see it was filled with clothing and supplies.

The other side of the room was filled with wooden toys and expensive dolls. A giant rocking horse, hand-carved, sat in the corner. Viktor's family crest was stamped onto its side.

"When did you do this?" she asked.

"Do you like it?" he replied, his voice a tad unsteady.

"I love it!" she jumped into his arms and he readily caught her.

"I've told you before, you really shouldn't jump like that," he chastised.

Eden rolled her eyes and his irises flashed brightly.

"You thought of everything," she complemented, distracting his thoughts.

"I wasn't sure what a babe needed. I had to ask. Mariana helped."

"It's wonderful. Truly. And there's so much."

"Too much?"

"No, no, of course not. You really did think of everything."

"Well, we don't know the gender, so I had to think of everything a son or daughter might need or want."

"Should I worry you're going to spoil our child?"

"Probably."

Eden laughed and started urgently kissing him all over his face.

"Take me to bed," her breathy voice instructed in between kisses.

"Eden."

"*Now*," she demanded.

His eyes flashed again. Eden blinked and she was on her back on their bed. Viktor grabbed the front of her dress and ripped it open. He threw the material onto the floor.

"First you defy me," his deep voice hummed across her heated skin.

His head dipped and pulled her taut nipple into his mouth. They'd become overly sensitive and he loved making her writhe when he bit them.

"Then you attempt to tell me, the King of Prajna, what to do."

"Hurry, Viktor," she whined.

Viktor rolled her to her side and playfully spanked her bottom. "You're not in charge here, love."

Eden rolled her lips over her teeth to keep from arguing. As a reward, Viktor divested himself of his clothing expeditiously then crawled back onto the bed, lying down behind her.

His warm fingers glided across her ribs, trailing ever so slowly down her abdomen. Eden shuddered when Viktor reached his destination and began rubbing his palm over her sex.

He dipped his finger into the folds of her cleft, loving how aroused his little mate was for him. He withdrew his hand and hooked Eden's leg under the knee, spreading her wide. His blunt tip nudged at her opening.

"Put me inside you, love."

Eden panted, reaching down between her legs to grab his hardened flesh. She wiggled until she had him where she needed him.

Slowly, Viktor rolled his hips forward. Eden pushed back, trying to get more of him. She knew he wouldn't allow her to control the pace, but she was desperate to be filled.

"Does my mate like this?"

"Yes," she exhaled.

Viktor continued his slow movements, gliding in and out of her tight sheath. He kissed under her ear and she shivered, her core flexing.

He always felt he was out of control when he was inside his sieva. Fast or slow, Eden brought out his beast. He needed to own her, to possess her, to bring her to the height of pleasure. It was only fair since she had him constantly enraptured and practically wrapped around her little finger.

He licked down her neck and sucked on the sensitive skin close to her shoulder. Eden whimpered and rocked her hips frantically.

Viktor could not deny his pregnant sieva. He would wait until after the babe came to torture her body. He'd been considering restraints on their bed. The thought had him engorged inside her channel.

His incisors lengthened and he struck. Eden cried out as his bite launched her into immediate climax. Just as always, her clenching walls were too much for him and he spilled inside her.

Viktor withdrew and flipped Eden to her hands and knees before plunging back inside. He'd meant to go slow, to be gentle. Her shouts and cries for more destroyed his resolve.

For the first time since he'd found out she was pregnant, Viktor allowed himself to take her for hours on end. Only when Eden showed signs of overtiredness did he relent.

Finally confident they were both fully sated, Viktor pulled his mate into his body and held her, listening as her breathing slowed. Eventually, sleep took him, as well.

Visions of mismatched eyes and a slobbery, toothless grin claimed his slumber.

When he awoke at dawn, he allowed himself to embrace the hope he had long denied. The Heartless King grinned, for he had met his daughter in his dreams.

# Epilogue

"She's beautiful!" the midwife proclaimed, placing the newborn upon her mother's chest.

Viktor kissed his wife, then bent to nuzzle his daughter's cheek. Silky wisps of dark as night hair tickled his skin.

"She is perfect," he whispered with relief that both his mate and his youngling were alive and well.

Months of worry and endless visits with the midwife had started to get to them both. At some point, their child's heartbeat had become too fast, to the point it sounded like an echo inside her womb.

Now that the babe was here, the worry disappeared. Eden smiled and then suddenly lurched, bellowing in pain. Her fingernails dug into Viktor's hand.

"Take the child, Sire," the midwife commanded.

"What?"

"Pick up your daughter. Eden needs to push again."

Viktor's trembling hands reached for the tiny being. She fidgeted and stretched. He was careful with her, terrified he'd drop her or damage her in some way.

He brought her to his chest and bounced gently as he'd been told to do during what Eden called Father-School. For weeks, he'd watched and listened aptly as the midwives taught him how to care for an infant.

Eden moaned. "What ... it shouldn't be this painful again."

The midwife's pinched face glanced at Viktor, then back to Eden. She patted the new mother's belly, then pushed down.

Eden screamed and Viktor snarled ferociously.

"I swear I will remove your head, woman!"

"You might want to wait until the other one comes out."

Viktor blinked. "What did you say?"

"It seems there is another."

"Another what?" he snapped.

"Dragon," the woman snapped back.

"What?!" Eden shrieked.

"Babe, dear. There's another, and you need to push."

Eden concentrated, pushing and holding it for the count of ten. She did it once more and a screaming babe came into the world.

"It's a boy," the midwife announced, "Loud and angry. Like his father."

Eden sank with relief, watching the female clean off her son before placing him upon her chest. Her arms wrapped around him and she wept.

Nothing had been wrong with the heartbeat. The echo had been two heartbeats, so similar in their rhythm they were indistinguishable from one another.

"Sire, are you okay?" the midwife asked.

Viktor was wiping at his eyes. "I'm fine," his gruff voice reprimanded. "See to my wife and do not concern yourself with me."

"Come here, Husband," Eden beamed, despite the strained effects of her labor.

Viktor sat down next to her pillow. He bent and kissed Eden's lips, then nuzzled his son's pale brunette head, as he had done to his daughter.

"You've given me the greatest of any possible gift, *moj vestica*."

"A son?"

Viktor shook his head.

"Two offspring?" she teased, wanting to lighten his mood.

"No."

"What did I give you, love?" she asked, using the endearment he liked to use on her.

"My heart. You gave me back … my heart."

Viktor kissed Eden again, then nuzzled the babes once more. He remained leaning over his wife and children protectively, his body shaking with emotion.

The midwife finished cleaning up and left the new family to bond. She vowed she would never tell a soul of the King's sobs echoing off the walls of his chambers.

Kings of Prajna, after all, did not cry. That was an honor reserved for only the most loving of fathers. She was pleased he was a male worthy enough to fill both roles.

Smiling to herself, she whistled down the hall, feeling lighter than she had in a hundred years. The tide was turning and her services were sure to be needed once again.

# The End

## Note from the Author

Thank you so much for reading <u>The Vampire King's Mate</u>! Evelyn's story is next, in <u>The Demon King's Destiny</u>

This series is my first attempt at writing something where humor is not the star of the show. There are snippets, of course, but it's not my usual in-your-face nonsense. This is one of the reasons I released it under a different name.

If you're new to my work, the bulk of my publications are penned under the Cass Alexander moniker. It's the name I use when I'm feeling the funny—which has been every moment of my life until this series.

If you're interested in receiving notifications for new releases, or joining my team of ARC readers, or just seeing what sort of nonsense I put out into the universe, you can follow my blog:

**caworleyauthor.wordpress.com**

Lastly, if you enjoyed the book, please, please, please leave a review. Reviews are an author's lifeblood. Much obliged!

Made in United States
North Haven, CT
29 April 2023

35998296R00202